SURRENDER
YOUR
LOVE

...

J.C. REED

Cover art by Larissa Klein

Editing by Shannon Wolfman and JM Editing

ISBN: 1482747634
ISBN-13: 978-1482747638

1

I WAS SITTING at the bar, sipping on my second margarita. My knee-length pencil skirt brushed the empty stool next to mine, my fingers tapped on my thigh to the rhythm of the music coming from the invisible sound system. This wasn't the kind of establishment I usually frequented, but my boss had been adamant that I meet Mayfield in his preferred environment. And so I agreed, albeit with trepidation, at the outlook of entering an expensive gentlemen's club where beautiful girls breezed around in classy lingerie, and the two drink minimum rule had already cost me more than my weekly grocery shopping.

Judging from the countless twinkling lights and polished marble floors, the place oozed style and money. Even though it was still empty, I had no doubt it would fill up soon and earn the owner a fortune. A racy girl that looked like she belonged on the cover of FHM magazine climbed up a pole and dropped down into a split to 'warm up', as the DJ announced tonight's program to the few punters in tailored suits. I sighed with impatience, and sank deeper into my slouch on the luxurious bar stool overlooking the soft leather couches and mirrored walls near the entrance.

Mayfield was late. In fact, very late. I didn't appreciate lateness, and particularly not when I should've been home by now, unwinding with a glass of wine after a long day of sucking up to the big guys in real estate. The job was meant to be a filler until I could get my hands on a position with a company like Delaware & Ray, but as filler jobs go, they're a dead end. And two years later I was twenty three, stuck and overworked with no promotion in sight.

Maybe it was the way the guy walked—full of confidence and cockiness—but the moment I saw him entering the bar I knew he was the kind that would bring me nothing but trouble. So I buried my gaze in my drink, avoiding the stranger's curious look. The hairs on the nape of my neck prickled. I turned slowly, realizing he was standing behind me. His hot breath grazed the sensitive skin of my cheek as he leaned over my shoulder to whisper in my ear.

"You stick out like a sore thumb. I'm not sure whether

that's a good or a bad thing."

His voice was low and hoarse. Scorching.

Bedroom voice… the words echoed somewhere in the back of my mind.

My heart jumped into my mouth, which I attributed to the fact that I didn't like strangers leaning over me. And particularly not those with a deep, sexy rumble of a voice that had just a hint of a Southern accent. Fighting the urge to jump up from the bar stool and put some much needed distance between us, I straightened my back and turned to face him, ready to hit back with a biting remark.

Holy cow.

He was dazzlingly gorgeous. Forget gorgeous. He was beautiful. Utterly, totally, mind-blowingly stunning. On a scale from one to ten, he was a hundred.

For a few seconds I just stared at him as my abdomen twisted into knots and my pulse quickened. The guy was hot and, judging from his wicked grin, definitely not the kind of man you bring home to meet your parents. He was tall, at least a head taller than me. Maybe six feet two. His wet, dark hair was a tad too long and disheveled—like he had run his hands through it. His coat, now damp from the rain that had been cascading on downtown New York for the last three days, did nothing to hide his broad shoulders and muscular build, nor his insolent stance. In the dim light of the bar, his electric eyes shimmered like emeralds.

I had never seen eyes like his. Dark green. Smoldering. Ready to undress a woman with a single glance. Already I felt naked in spite of several layers of clothes. His gaze traveled down the front of my shirt appreciatively, and lingered on my legs for longer than was polite. My skin prickled from his gaze. I tucked a stray strand of curly hair behind my ear and moistened my suddenly dry lips. The effect he had on me was both unnerving and exciting. I crossed my arms over my chest and bit my lower lip hard to regain my speech. He regarded me with raised eyebrows and unconcealed amusement, as though he knew what a single glance from those eyes did to me. But it wasn't his obvious arrogance that made me instantly angry. It was the way his spread fingers lingered intimately on the small of my back as though they had caressed the spot before. As though they belonged there.

"Why would you say that? Because I'm not wearing a skimpy G-string and stilettos, and my boobs aren't half falling out of a leopard print bra?" I asked through gritted teeth, ignoring the delicious pull gathering somewhere in my abdomen.

"Jett Townsend." His lips twitched. "Mayfield couldn't make it, so you'll have to make do with me. But don't worry, you and I will get on just fine." The skin around his stunning eyes crinkled, and his mouth quirked up in a grin, flashing perfect dimples. Why did I get the feeling there was a double meaning to his words?

"Brooke Stewart," I said. My gaze lingered on his pale blue shirt and faded jeans with a stringy fringe that brushed his cowboy boots, and I couldn't help the scoff forming at the back of my throat.

"Wine?" I asked, ready to order.

"I'd rather have Sex on the Beach." He winked at me with a devilish grin. I figured his words could be interpreted in two ways, but judging from his flirtatious smile, I doubted he was talking about the cocktail. Heat began to pour through me at the unwelcome image of us having sex on sand and water. My skin tingled from the magnetic pull between us.

What the heck?

I peeled my gaze off him in the hope the instant attraction was nothing but a figment of my imagination.

"So, Brooke. Tell me all about yourself." He leaned forward, flashing me a drop dead gorgeous smile.

I inhaled a sharp breath, suddenly fuming. How dare he call me by my first name? And most importantly, how dare he look so darn sexy doing it?

"May I remind you this is a business meeting and not a date?"

He raised his brows. "Do you want a date?"

"What?" My cheeks caught fire, and my heart pumped just a little bit harder. "That's not what I meant. I—"

His eyes twinkled with humor. "Apparently, you like what you see, and so do I. So…" He shrugged and trailed off, leaving the rest to my imagination.

I hated hot guys, and particularly those who knew just how gorgeous they were. "Trust me, there's nothing I haven't seen before." My lie sounded ridiculous and he knew it. I could tell by the irritating, self-assured yet gorgeous grin he was sporting.

My temper flared.

This was supposed to be an initial attempt at finding out where our companies stood in terms of a potential partnership. The fact that Mayfield Properties would send someone who couldn't even dress to suit the occasion was laughable. Why would Mayfield want to be represented by someone who clearly lacked any knowledge of what is acceptable when dealing with a potential business partner? Or maybe Mayfield didn't value our cooperation, and this was his way of telling me to fuck off. Either way I wasn't pleased, and I had no intention of making a secret out of my displeasure. Mayfield was known to be a real son-of-a-bitch. He was also known to take no crap from anyone. If I wanted to make it in this cutthroat business world dominated by men, I had to mirror his tactics, or give up on a career which was already going nowhere.

"Look, I appreciate your coming, Mr. Townsend, but I'd rather speak with at least a regional vice president. Please tell Mr. Mayfield to call me once he's ready to reschedule. Good evening to you." Grabbing my purse and coat from the polished counter, I jumped down from the barstool and headed for the exit when strong fingers curled around my upper arm. I froze in my tracks.

"Don't forget your umbrella. We wouldn't want that pretty face to get soaked," Townsend whispered in my ear, sending another delicious tingle through my body. What was it with this man and whispering? Couldn't he just talk like normal people? I reached blindly around me and yanked my umbrella out of his hand. Without a look back I marched out of the bar, keeping my head high. Only when I reached the parking lot twenty feet from the bar's main entrance did I stop and finally let out a long breath.

The night air had cooled down. I shrugged into my coat and hurried to unlock the door to my Chevrolet. It was an old thing, but it had been a graduation gift from my stepdad, so I loved it. Even though it was a pain driving in the city, I preferred it to being stuck in a cab with a male driver I couldn't trust.

I jammed the car into first gear and pulled out of the parking lot. My gaze brushed over the stranger towering in the bar's doorway, watching me a moment before I drove past.

Did he follow me out? My heartbeat sped up but I didn't halt. If anything, I floored the accelerator and the car spluttered forward. The engine lets out a drawn-out protest, but I didn't care. Whatever Townsend's business was, I decided he was a creep, and I had no intention of ever seeing him again. I was definitely not the kind of woman who'd ever succumb to a hard body and dimples to die for.

I reached my tiny apartment in Brooklyn Heights in less than an hour and parked the car opposite from the five-story building that had been my home ever since graduating from college two years ago. The street was damp and deserted. The street lamp in front of the building cast a golden glow on the steel door, which led into a narrow hall with a lobby area. Minding the large rain puddles, I fished my keys out of my bag and let myself in, then rode the elevator up to the fifth floor.

My roommate and best friend, Sylvie, wasn't home. Ever since she landed the investment job of her dreams, she barely ever made it home before midnight. I had been taught to put one hundred and ten percent into everything I did, but Sylvie took working hard to a whole new level. She went so far as to sacrifice her hobbies, friendships, and health by doing unpaid overtime in an attempt to gain recognition for all the extra effort. Any attempts I ever initiated to make her realize just how unhealthy her stress level had become were futile so far, but I wasn't going to give up.

Dropping the umbrella into a brass holder and my

handbag and coat on the old coffee table in the hall, I kicked my shoes off and headed for the kitchen to pour myself a much-earned glass of wine. I was halfway through my second glass when the key turned in the lock and Sylvie's blonde head popped into my line of vision.

"What a surprise!" I sat up and pointed at my glass. "Want one?"

"You better have a bottle." She slumped onto the couch next to me and put her long legs up. I scanned from her striped skirt that rode just above her knee up to her face and damp, blonde hair. Something was different. Her mascara was smudged. The skin beneath her blue eyes was swollen and red as though she had been crying, which was impossible. Sylvie wasn't the crying kind. In all the years we had been best friends, I never once saw her shed a tear. She never looked anything less than perfect and happy.

I sat up, instantly feeling something was wrong. "What happened?"

"I got the boot."

"What?"

She took the glass out of my hands and drained it in one big gulp. "They kicked me out. Said something about not needing another intern. Blah blah." She rolled her eyes. "Whatever."

"Oh, crap." I shook my head in disbelief. "But you worked so hard."

"I know, right? But you know what? I am okay. C'est la vie. Time to move on." She jumped up, and a smile spread across her lips. "Let's get plastered."

I narrowed my gaze. There was something in the way she avoided looking at me that raised my suspicion. "Wait!" I grabbed her arm and pulled her back down on the sofa. "You're not telling me everything."

She rolled her eyes again.

"Spill it," I said.

She pressed her mouth into a tight line.

"Sylvie," I prompted.

"Fine. I slept with the boss."

My jaw dropped. "No."

She nodded. "I did. His personal assistant, who's best buddies with his wife, started to suspect. So the bastard got the jitters and decided to get rid of me."

"Is that even legal?"

Was it?

Sylvie shrugged. "Probably not, but it's a small world, and I need this reference if I ever want to land another banking job."

"The bastard," I mirrored her words. Sylvie was the brightest person I knew. She had graduated in the top of her class, and any firm would have been happy to have her. "You'll find something else in no time." I had no doubt about that.

She smirked. "Yeah, only next time remind me not to screw the boss, no matter how hot he is. You're so lucky you have Sean. At least he's not married and lying to you about not having slept in the same bed with the wife for the last two years. Talk about cliché."

My arms wrapped around Sylvie, and she leaned her head against my shoulder the way she always did when a relationship turned sour. They always did, whether we wanted it or not.

"Sean's not perfect, you know. And I don't want commitment," I said.

"At least he's honest. That's more than you can say about the majority of guys out there."

Call me a romantic, but I didn't agree with Sylvie on that one. Surely not all men were liars or commitment-phobes. I rolled my eyes as I thought of the guy everyone seemed to think was a catch. Sean—the boyfriend who wasn't ready to commit, and neither was I, for my own reasons. He was good-looking, successful, and the guy I had been hanging onto for almost a year even though I knew it was a dead end relationship that might be over any minute. If you'd call his 'let's hook up every now and then' a relationship, then that was about all we had: a sort of friends-with-benefits thing.

Less of a friend, more of a sex buddy.

We met when Sylvie left her handbag in a bar on a

drunken night out. Sean found it, and when he turned up at our doorstep she should have been the one to thank him for not stealing her money and tossing her ID card in the nearest dumpster. However, Sylvie had been puking in the bathroom for nearly an hour...so Sean met me instead. We hit it off instantly, and I really thought he might be long-term material. As it turned out, even planning a weekend break was too much commitment for him. I couldn't remember the last time we went on a romantic date. In fact, I couldn't remember ever planning any sort of event that didn't involve a drunken night out with our friends.

Right from the beginning, Sean had made it clear we weren't exclusive, and I was fine with that because he made me feel comfortable. Around him, I felt as though I could be myself. When we talked time seemed to fly, and we'd end up talking the night away. Okay, so I wasn't in toe-curling, belly-warming, butterfly-feeling love, but then again does that even exist outside of *Barbara Cartland's* novels?

"Anyway," Sylvie continued, jerking me out of my thoughts. "How was your meeting with that guy?"

"Mayfield," I said to refresh her memory.

"Mayfield," she repeated.

"Don't even get me started." I waved my hand, choosing to avoid this particular conversation. "He didn't turn up."

"It seems like we both need a drink." Sylvie jumped to

her feet again and pulled me up with her. I hesitated. She might be unemployed now, but I still had a job. While it might be fun to linger around New York's bars, sipping on margaritas at midnight, I didn't have Sylvie's platinum Visa card—courtesy of her dad—to pay my bills. I had to get up early in the morning and do my job.

"Come on, babes." Knowing it would make me laugh, she put on the fake British accent she picked up on one of her family vacations. "Let's forget this bloody day." My lips twitched. "We'll be back in a jiffy." Which, in Sylvie's personal dictionary, was the equivalent to a whole-night bender. But she was my best friend; she needed me. She would have done the same for me. Naturally my resolve never stood a chance.

Rolling my eyes, I shook my head and followed her out the door. The cool night air whipped my hair against my skin. Luckily our favorite drinking spot was just around the corner, so we didn't have to brave the cold for long before we settled into our usual booth, surrounded by Sylvie's countless admirers and a few shots of tequila with lime.

***

A penetrating ringing noise woke me up too soon. I groaned and covered my ears with my pillow, silently begging whoever was making such ungodly noise to shut it.

It took me a moment to realize it was my alarm clock. I rolled on my side and knocked it over in the process. A male voice let out an amused snort. I sat up, instantly awake. My gaze settled on the guy on the left side of my bed, and I felt the telltale heat of a major blush rushing to my face. He was propped up on one elbow, one arm tucked beneath his head; his chiseled chest with dark hair trailing down his flat abdomen was on full display. The sheet covering his modesty left nothing to the imagination. In fact, it only managed to stir an unwelcome pull between my legs. Not only was he strikingly good looking, he was also well endowed. A heady—yet dangerous combination—in a man. My tongue flicked over my suddenly dry lips as I pried my gaze away from the bulge that was evident beneath the thin sheet.

What was he doing in my bed? And why was he naked?

What do you think, stupid? It doesn't take a genius to figure it out. Just look at his smug grin.

I peered at his face. In the bright morning light falling through the window he looked younger than last night, but just as arrogant. His gorgeous lips curled into the most stunning smile I had ever seen. A panty-dropping smile, as Sylvie would have called it. I paled at the realization. Had I dropped my panties for him?

He regarded me with mild amusement in his smoldering eyes—the color of dark moss covered by a thin layer of opal mist. The way he looked at me, I felt as though he saw through my body and directly into my soul. No one had ever made me feel like that before. Then again, I had never met someone so electrically good-looking, but there's a first time for everything.

"Are you ready for Round Two?" His voice dripped with insinuation. I had heard that hoarse voice before, but where? My brain fought to make a connection through the alcohol infused haziness clouding my memory retrieval system. And then it dawned on me.

"You were at The Black Rose. I was supposed to meet with Mayfield, but he sent you instead."

His grin widened, revealing two strings of pearl white, even teeth.

Beautiful, strong teeth that nibbled on my neck and grazed the sensitive skin on my thighs.

Whoa, where did that come from? I shook my head lightly and tried to cling to the memory before my eyes, but it was gone already.

"Did we—" I gestured at his naked chest. My heart stopped beating for a moment as I waited for his assurance that it was all a misunderstanding, that I didn't bang a stranger, because one-night stands weren't my thing. Besides, I was in a relationship, albeit an open one, but cheating wasn't my thing either. I wasn't turning into Sylvie, was I? And I probably wasn't so stupid to have banged the guy.

Mystery Guy opened his mouth to say something, closed it again, and in that instant I knew.

I was cheap, not least because I couldn't even remember his name.

"Oh, God." I jumped out of bed, vaguely realizing I wasn't wearing anything, not even my panties—probably courtesy of his panty-dropping smile. Mortified, I pulled the sheet from him and covered my naked body, then scooped up what I assumed were his jeans from the pile of clothes scattering the floor and tossed them toward Mystery Guy. He caught them in midair but didn't hurry to put them on. Well, he obviously was comfortable with his private parts on full display. Good for him.

I cringed and hissed, "Get out."

He blinked and frowned, as though he wasn't used to this tone from anyone. Was that a hint of disappointment in his eyes? I shook my head at my confusing thoughts. Why would he feel that way when he didn't even know me? And then it was gone, and his blazing gaze turned to ice. My heart sank in my chest.

I turned my back on him and called over my shoulder, "You found your way in here, so I'm sure you can find your way out," as I sprinted out the door and headed for the safety of the kitchen, running right into Sylvie brewing our morning coffee.

"Is somebody doing the walk of shame?" Sylvie pointed at my burning cheeks.

I stared at her made-up face and perfect hair. Seriously, how could she look as though she just went through a beauty treatment at a spa after a long night of binge-drinking and barfing all over the small patch of lawn outside our building?

Sylvie held out her coffee mug. "Here, take it. You need it more than me."

"Thanks." I took a sip and burned my tongue in the process. The sharp pang of pain offered a welcome diversion from the question at hand. Why did I bring a guy home?

"Is he still here?" Sylvie whispered conspiratorially.

I almost spit out my next sip. "You know?"

She nodded. "You didn't exactly make a secret out of wanting to bed him."

What the hell did I do? Strip off and give him a lap dance? Sylvie made it sound like I acted all sex-starved. No wonder the guy was disappointed not getting a morning quickie.

"You're my best friend. You should have stopped me!" I was so mad at her, at myself, at Hot Shirtless Arrogant Guy for accepting my obviously drunken advances. But, even as I was seething, I knew he was the last to blame. What guy would say 'no' to a willing female with loose morals?

"I was drunk," Sylvie whispered, like that would explain everything.

Heavy footsteps thudded across the narrow corridor and stopped in the doorway. Holding my breath, I buried my gaze in my coffee and willed it to swallow me up so I wouldn't have to face the shame of my actions.

"Good morning, ladies," Mystery Guy said.

"Want a cup?" Sylvie strolled over and poured him some coffee, ignoring my venomous look.

What the heck?

Was he now staying for a cup of coffee? Didn't he get the memo?

"Cheers." He took a gulp and sighed slightly. Damn! Why did he sound so sexy doing normal stuff like *drinking*? My cheeks began to burn as my gaze trailed his strong chest, my mind conjuring images of him on top of me. Was this my brain's attempt at reminding me of what we did, or just a fantasy?

"How did you get such a hottie? I'm so jealous, and proud of you," Sylvie whispered, not the least bothered by the fact that my conquest could most certainly hear every word. Her gaze brushed him appreciatively, her X-ray gawk probably undressing him this very instant. While I usually didn't mind her leering, for some inexplicable reason it bothered me. Her lips curled into a lascivious smile, and she began to play with a golden strand of hair. I wouldn't have been surprised to see her glued to his leg, drooling all over him.

"Stop it." I nudged her in case she could no longer hear me in her lust-induced stupor.

She shrugged and took a step back but didn't stop her leering.

"Any plans for the day?" Mystery Guy asked. The kitchen remained silent until I realized he had been addressing me. I peered up all the way from the floor to his impossibly green gaze and instantly wished I hadn't. No one had eyes like that—green like sin, but never had sin seemed so tempting. I swallowed hard and beseeched my heart to slow down before it burst out of my chest. Was it an invitation to spend the day with him? Surely, it couldn't be. The guy got his one-night stand. Isn't that every man's dream: sex with no strings attached? So why would he be interested in seeing more of my panties…unless said panties were worthy of a second try?

My blood began to boil at the way he smirked at me: self-assured. So he enjoyed dinner and thought he might just stay for a top up. See what else my downtown store had to offer today. Well, good news: it was closed. He wasn't going to get any, even if my whole body screamed to go for it and see where that happy trail might lead me.

"I have plans. Very important ones." I straightened my

back and held his intense gaze, ready to stare him down. He cocked his brows. His eyes blazed with challenge and determination.

"Then cancel them," he said in that husky tone of his.

I suppressed a snort and crossed my arms over my chest. Seriously, who did he think he was? Maybe most women tripped over their own two feet to spend the day with him, but I wasn't one of them. "Not happening."

"Playing hard to get?" He flashed a sexy dimple. "You sure weren't last night."

My cheeks were on fire. I wished I could turn invisible and disappear from the face of the earth. Then I might just be able to work through the shame and humiliation burning through me. Maybe.

"Grab your stuff and get the hell out." I pointed at the door. He didn't move, so I clutched his upper arm and pushed hard. His bulging bicep strained under the thin material of his shirt, but he didn't budge from the spot.

I took a sharp breath and let it out slowly as I gathered my words. "Look, whatever happened last night, it won't happen again."

"Why not?" He laughed. "I thought you wanted...*more*."

A sharp pang of scorching mortification burned through me. Back there in my bedroom, while we were having fun, did I tell him that I wanted more?

Oh God.

My heart began to pound harder in my chest as he looked me up and down, enjoying every moment of what I would call the biggest humiliation in my life.

"Why not again?" he prompted.

I balled my hands into fists and cringed at the amused flicker in his gaze. "Because it was a mistake. We were supposed to have a business meeting, not hump each other," I hissed at him, stabbing my finger in his strong chest. His lack of any sort of reaction made my temper flare. "*You* were a drunken mistake, which I'd never repeat in my sober state, so you might as well leave now." For some inexplicable reason, I regretted my words the moment they came out, but there was no backing off. He was a devilishly sexy guy with a beautiful face and the body of a god, but I couldn't ignore the knowledge that as hot guys go, tempting a woman into bed is nothing but a game to them. A game to assert their hotness level. Judging from the lazy grin on his lips, I bet he couldn't agree with me more. So, no matter how strongly I felt attracted to him, the guy was a no-go for my own sake.

It's called self-respect.

Of which I didn't show a lot last night.

The guy was a player who would bring me nothing but trouble. I knew that the moment he entered The Black Rose, and my intuition had been spot on, as usual. Swallowing my pride, I walked past furiously, not quite able to ignore the flicker of amused interest in his eyes.

2

MYSTERY GUY DIDN'T follow me out of the kitchen. I felt a hint of remorse as I grabbed the first shirt and jeans I found in the closet and barricaded myself in the tiny bathroom cubicle to take a quick shower before heading for work. I inspected myself in the mirror. Dark circles rimmed my hazel eyes. My brown hair looked a mess, just like his disheveled mop had, only it didn't quite suit me as much as it did him. My skin looked pale, but it had a dewy glow that comes only from lots of sleep or post-coital hormones. No need to ask myself where it came from, because I sure as hell didn't have a good night's sleep, so the glow only managed to enrage me more.

Seriously, what had I been thinking—bringing a guy back home with me? And what had Sylvie been thinking, letting me make any sort of decision in my drunken stupor?

Now I was facing another dilemma. Did Sean, my so-called boyfriend who wouldn't quite DTR (define the relationship), expect me to tell him? Would he be honest with me about a possible conquest?

Furiously I rubbed shower gel into my skin and shampooed my hair. The hot water cleansed my body, but it didn't quite manage to wash away my shame. When I came out again, I had made a decision. Sean's promotion party was only a few days away, and I wouldn't spoil it. But I vowed to tell him right after the party, ask him for forgiveness, and do my best to work through our issues. I liked him and wanted to see where it might lead in the future, so I wouldn't let a one-night stand come between us. What happened last night was nothing but a bad decision made under the influence of booze and raging hormones. Mystery Guy would not mess with my life, head, or panties ever again.

Bracing myself for more heated glances from those penetrating green eyes, I took a deep breath and left the safety of my bathroom.

"He's gone," Sylvie said as soon as I entered the kitchen. She shot me a disapproving look, as though his leaving was my fault, and turned away to wash her coffee cup. I should have been relieved and yet, for some inexplicable reason, I sort of felt empty. Betrayed. Probably just another notch in his bedpost.

"Did he say anything?" My voice came out all squeaky. She looked at me from under thick, mascaraed lashes.

"He asked a few questions."

"Oh? Like what?" I brushed a trembling hand through my hair and moistened my lips. "Not that I care," I mumbled, in case Sylvie got the wrong idea.

She shrugged. "Since you don't care, it doesn't really matter. Shouldn't you be at work?"

I hated when she changed the subject like that. Or when she sided with a guy, which she often did, and in particular when said guy was good-looking. If I pressed the issue, she'd get instantly suspicious and think I might have fallen for Mystery Guy, which wasn't true because I didn't even know him and had no intention of ever seeing him again. Besides, what could he have possibly asked? Maybe he wanted to know who won last night's Lakers game. Or he had asked her for a favor like calling a taxi. Whatever it was, I didn't need to know. He belonged to a past I was ready to forget.

I heaved a silent sigh and grabbed my purse from where I must have tossed it on the floor last night. "See ya," I grumbled, heading out the door.

"Wait," Sylvie called, running after me. "When are you coming back home? I'm making dinner."

Which, in Sylvie's dictionary, was the equivalent of sifting through hundreds of takeaway menu pamphlets and ordering in. She was unemployed for less than a day, and already she sounded like a bored housewife. I needed to get rid of her, and pronto, before I decided I might just have to get a divorce—metaphorically speaking.

"Sorry, Sylvie. I'm at my mother's tonight." I couldn't help the feeling of complacency washing over me at her lost expression. Punishing anybody wasn't usually my style, but she should have just told me what Mystery Guy said before he left. It would have made me more inclined to invite her over to Mom's, even though their icy silence and disapproving looks made me want to run as fast as I could. Mom thought Sylvie was a pretentious bitch who was friends with me because I was a pushover. And Sylvie thought Mom was a bitch for not settling down with one guy for the sake of her only daughter. In other words, Sylvie thought Mom should have provided a stable home rather than move from town to town and man to man throughout my vulnerable adolescent years. While they both had a point, I preferred staying on neutral ground, and keeping out of their love/hate relationship, which is why I avoided throwing the two of them in the same room at the same time.

"Is she still with—" Sylvie snapped her fingers in thought. "What's his name? You know, the guy from last week."

"It was last month, and his name's Gregg," I said.

"Uh-huh. Not worth my brain cells remembering his name when he'll be old news by next week." She waved her hand as though she couldn't care less.

I hated to admit Sylvie was right. "He's old news already."

"No. Already?" She laughed. "What was wrong with him? Too nice? Too cute? Had a snoring problem?"

I shook my head signaling that I had no idea.

"There'll be a new one soon," Sylvie said. I raised my brows meaningfully. She laughed, getting my hint. "Already?"

I nodded. "Apparently I'm meeting him tonight."

"Can I come? Pretty please. You know how much I love to meet Tina's boyfriends. They're like squeezing your hand into a Halloween candy bag. You never know what you'll get." Her lips curled into a smile, and she cocked her head to the side the way she always did when she was about to start a major persuasion campaign.

"Hell, no." I blinked and took a step back. "You're not coming." She opened her mouth to protest so I cut her off. "Don't even pretend to like her, when you're at each other's throat all the time."

"That's not true...okay, maybe a little, but you know what I like even less? Being forgotten by my best friend on a Tuesday night. Come on, Brooke." She leaned in conspiratorially. "Do you have any idea what might happen if I spent a night all alone?" She paused for dramatic effect. "Someone could break in. Or I could get so bored that I might end up finishing all the booze and make out with our neighbor from number 4."

Gross. The guy from number 4 was a major creep who walked around in a bathrobe. Every time we stepped out of the building, he was in the hallway, as though he knew we'd be leaving.

"Oh, come on, Brooke. Pretty please, I don't want to be all alone on Tuesday the 13th."

I rolled my eyes. Sylvie loved melodrama and, in particular, if it helped her get what she wanted. Soon bargaining would follow, and if that didn't do the trick she'd revert to good old blackmail. She had followed the same patterns for the last twenty years, or ever since I refused to give her my lunch box in kindergarten. I wasn't going to stick around for that.

"I'll scratch your back if you scratch mine," she whispered. "You want to know what Jett said?"

"Who's Jett?" And that's when it dawned on me. Mystery Guy. He had introduced himself the evening we met, but the name was so unusual I didn't really catch it. I thought it was something like Jack, or Jake, or Jeremiah, and the strange pronunciation was the result of his Southern accent.

Even his name sounded sexy and forbidden. I couldn't

help but picture me moaning it while he kissed me all over my body. My face grew hot and hotter. Dammit. This was all Sylvie's fault. She knew more than I did. If she wasn't so openly ready to trade in her information, I wouldn't be literally panting at the sound of a guy's name.

"Jett...I mean, Sylvie, I don't have time for this."

Crap. I was under his spell. I needed to get him out of my system. And quick before I ended up making a complete fool out of myself. I clutched my handbag to my chest and walked out the door, ignoring Sylvie's incredulous gawking.

"Wait, Brooke! Don't leave me hanging," she shouted after me.

Throwing glances over my shoulder to make sure she wasn't following, I dashed for the parking spot around the block and jumped into my car, ready to head out for a day of hard work, or what was left of it now that it was almost lunchtime.

3

NEW YORK TRAFFIC was a nightmare. By the time I fought my way downtown I was already three hours late. Dammit. Not only was Jett—aka Mystery Guy— messing with my life, he was also ruining my career. My boss, James, wouldn't be pleased. In fact, as I reached the office and dropped into my swivel chair, my fingertips starting to type furiously on the keyboard to check emails and appointments for the day I could almost feel the hot waves of anger coming from James's office. Maybe he hadn't noticed my absence. Oh, who was I kidding? The guy knew *everything*. And, for a gay guy, he sure knew how to yell, which was what I was about to hear in three…

Two.

One.

"Brooke! Move your sweet ass over here this instant!"

The office dragon had spied me. Now I was in big trouble. With a deep sigh I sat up, smoothed over my pencil skirt, and headed for the inevitable with slow, measured steps. In my mind I could hear the scary pounds of a drum warning of imminent doom. Wendy, the receptionist, shot me a pitiful look. I smiled back and fought back the urge to pretend I had to leave again for a business meeting. I was a grown up and by no means scared of James.

"Close the door," James said as I entered his office. I did as he bid and settled into the chair opposite from his huge mahogany desk. My hands folded in my lap, I looked up to meet his angry gaze.

Even though he had to be at least ten years my senior, he didn't look a day older than thirty. His highlighted blond hair was brushed back from his smooth forehead. His skin had a golden glow which everyone attributed to weekly tanning sessions, and it stood in strong contrast to his crisp, white shirt and black suit. His piercing blue eyes focused on me, measuring me up and down. I wrapped my suit jacket tighter around me as though to protect myself from his inquisitive gaze. Why was he staring at me like that? Why wouldn't he just start his usual tirade, include a warning or two, and get it over and done with?

I was about to apologize for my lateness when a knock rapped at the door.

"Come in," James said, looking up from me to our new

intern, a twenty-something guy called Tim.

"Here are your papers, boss." Tim smiled shyly, which in turn had James's face lighting up like a Christmas candle. Tim had a great body with well-defined muscles and taut skin the color of melted chocolate, which made me believe he spent a lot of time at the fitness center.

"Thank you, darling. Better now than never." James's lips curved upwards as his eyes devoured Tim's perky ass.

"Those are the ones you requested last week. Sorry I'm behind schedule, but I was late today. Traffic." Tim shot me a conspiratorial look, as though I knew exactly what he was talking about, which I didn't. Tim had made it a habit of being late; I was always on time.

Apart from today.

"Don't worry about it." James waved his hand playfully. I wondered if he would be so kind to me? "Isn't there a saying 'save the best for last'? Catch you at lunch."

Tim flashed his white, even teeth before closing the door behind him.

"So." James sighed and turned to face me. I swallowed past the sudden lump in my throat as his easygoing expression turned a few shades darker.

No preferential treatment for you, Stewart.

"I'm sorry I was late," I said to break the uncomfortable silence. "There was some paperwork I needed to go through, and I thought I might as well do it from home."

Which wasn't a lie. I had been planning to go through paperwork last night when Sylvie persuaded me to join her at our usual joint and Mystery Guy came in between.

"Don't bullshit me. I know you're lying. But that's not why I called you in." He moistened his lips and his gaze scanned the door behind me, and then settled back on me. "What went down with Mayfield?"

"He didn't turn up." James's eyebrows shot up and he looked displeased. A sense of foreboding washed through me. Maybe Mystery Guy reported back to his boss, who complained to James, and now I was in bigger trouble than I thought. "Why are you asking?"

"Because I had a phone call this morning." James's frown intensified. Uh-huh. That wasn't good. I swallowed hard and imagined myself cleaning out my desk.

"Mayfield's offering you a job in his department," James said, eyeing me. "He wants you to start straight away."

My mouth dropped and I almost toppled off my chair. Holy cow. Being rude was all it took to land a job with a big firm? And that's when I remembered that I had been doing more than talking. All heat drained from my cheeks. I had banged Mystery Guy, who in turn persuaded his boss to hire me. I could only imagine his arguments.

She is very, *very* good. We need more people like her, people who are cooperative and forthcoming, and who take business to a whole new level.

Oh, God.

I had just slept my way up the corporate ladder.

Talk about cheap.

"Obviously, I said that you'd rather stay with us because you're very happy with your benefits package," James continued.

I bobbed my head to signal I was following. Actually, my benefits package wasn't that great. I wanted to point out I was still waiting for a promised pay rise six months ago, but I kept my mouth shut.

James grimaced, and my heart sank in my chest before he even opened his mouth to relay the bad news. "I'm sorry, Brooke, but I'll have to fire you. Mayfield said he'd cut off all our contracts if I didn't let you go." He brushed his hand through his hair, as though relieved it was over, adding, "It was great working with you though."

Holy mother of pearls!

That wasn't a good enough reason to fire me, was it? Somewhere at the back of my mind I realized I could sue his ass for...oh I don't know...but a lawyer sure as fuck could come up with something. James said Mayfield would cut off all our contracts. What kind of psycho would do that to hire one person? It's not like I got famous showing off my skills on *The Apprentice*. Nor I was like Sylvie, graduating in the top of my class. What the hell did Jett— no, I wouldn't even give him the courtesy of calling his name—Mr. Arrogant Guy, say about me?

My mind was spinning, and I could hear the blood rushing in my ears. I was not sure if I should be angry or happy or both?

It took me a moment to grasp the meaning of James's words. My heart began to drum in my ears and my cheeks burned. I had finally landed a job with a big firm. Granted, it wasn't Delaware & Ray, but a beginning. The big break I had been waiting for. So why was I hesitating? Why didn't it feel like sweet success?

Because you didn't earn it.

My subconscious reared her nasty head. I had slept with someone in a higher position than mine, but I didn't do it on purpose. I wasn't a ho, because that's a woman who deliberately sleeps with a guy for the sole purpose of gaining a personal advantage, financially or otherwise.

"I'll have to think about it," I said.

"No, Brooke, you won't. They're huge. They have connections. They deal with the big jobs. Without them we'd be long lost in the pond of small-time realtors." James hesitated. I sensed there was something he didn't tell me, but I didn't press the issue. Whatever he had going with Mayfield was none of my business. An array of emotions washed over James's face, and then his features relaxed and his face became an impassive mask. "Come on, you knew you wouldn't be working here forever. It's a great chance for you. Don't mess it up."

I took a deep breath and willed my trembling hands to stop shaking. Mayfield Realties was a huge firm with offices all around the States and Europe. While I didn't quite agree with their business practices, I couldn't argue James's case.

"You might want to hurry. They need you in their head office before the end of the day," James said, jolting me out of my guilty conscience. He turned away from me and grabbed his phone to signal the conversation was over.

"So that's it?" I stood and regarded him incredulously. Granted, this hadn't been my dream job, and I never expected to be getting all mushy about leaving, but I couldn't help the sudden melancholy. James had given me a job during the recession, when no one was willing to take a chance on an inexperienced college graduate. He had taught me a lot about the business, so I sort of expected more than a head nod and showing me the door.

"Don't forget us when you're making it big in the business, Chica," James whispered not looking up from his phone.

I smiled and walked around his desk to give him a hug, whispering in his ear, "Thank you for everything." Without looking back, I left James's office and said a tearful goodbye to Wendy, who was surprised to see I was fired, and even more surprised to see how happy I was. After lots of promises to keep in touch, I packed up the few belongings that cluttered my old desk: a few pictures of Mom with the two men that came closest to being a dad, and a cactus Sylvie got me the morning I landed the job. It was my lucky cactus.

"No man's left behind," I whispered as I placed the cactus on the front seat and secured it with the seatbelt, then programmed the GPS to take me to the Mayfield Realties main office opposite from Delaware & Ray.

4

MAYFIELD REALTIES WAS located on the sixtieth floor of *Trump Tower*. The elevator chimed, and I was spit out into a friendly and luminous space I instantly fell in love with. Thick burgundy rugs swallowed up the noise of my heels as I made my way toward the tall brunette typing on her computer at the glass reception area. She was immaculately dressed in a chocolate brown tight overall and seven-inch stilettos that made her already long legs look sky high. Her glossy lips diverted attention from her strict ponytail and gave her an ethereal flair. Peering up, she smiled and pointed to her right at the white leather chairs that blended in with the wall behind.

"Miss Stewart, please take a seat. Someone will be with you shortly. Would you like some refreshments? We have latte macchiato, espresso, Chai latte, or maybe bottled water? " Her voice was professional but had a sharp edge to it, as though she was used to giving commands. I mouthed a 'no thank you', wondering how she even knew my name. Then I remembered the receptionist downstairs who must have called up to announce my visit. Basically, I was playing in a whole new league here, so I had to up my game.

I sat down and ignored the glossy magazines stacked neatly on the polished coffee table. Keeping my poker face on, I looked around Mayfield's reception area as I waited for my new boss to greet me. Holy cow, I had never seen anything like it. Spacious was an understatement. The place was huge and classy in a minimalist kind of way. Mirrored glass reached from floor to ceiling and offered a bird's-eye view of the busy street below. Black and white art adorned the wall behind the reception area. Huge Bonsai trees in Chinese flower pots were arranged down the large corridor, which I assumed led to the big guys's offices. If I wanted to fit in I had to take Sylvie up on her offer and let her take me shopping. She had been nagging about my outdated wardrobe for ages, but until now I never felt a need to splurge money I didn't have on clothes.

I didn't realize the brunette was standing before me until she touched my shoulder with perfectly manicured fingers.

"Miss Stewart?" She handed me a thick manila envelope. "This is your work contract highlighting your pay package and benefits. Furthermore, you'll also find a plane ticket to

Italy, where you'll be assisting Mr. Mayfield in the Lucazzone acquisition, and information on what will be expected of you as Mr. Mayfield's senior assistant. The plane will board tomorrow night. You can take the rest of today off to pack your bags, and find a pet minder for the next two weeks in case you have a pet." She trailed off and smiled again. "If your passport's expired, please report to us immediately and we'll take care of it." She paused, waiting for my answer.

"My passport's great. It's never been so valid." I cringed inwardly at my odd choice of words, which did make me sound a bit dumb.

"Great." Miss Brunette Receptionist beamed. "Congratulations on your new job and have a nice trip."

My jaw dropped as my brain finally registered the meaning of her words. "Wait, did you say I'm going to Italy?" She nodded. "Tomorrow?" She nodded again.

"Don't miss your flight. Mr. Mayfield is expecting your arrival."

I nodded, dumbfounded, my thoughts still twirling around the words *senior assistant*. But I was a realtor. I had assisted James with the odd project, but he had never taken me to Italy, and he sure as hell didn't expect me to deal with an acquisition. I swallowed hard and stood. I couldn't speak Italian. Maybe I should have clarified with James what this job entailed, to see if I could keep up with the big guys, instead of assuming I'd get a few weeks of training.

"If you have any questions or would like to discuss your contract, Rita Young from Human Resources will be happy to assist you," the brunette said. "Once you're happy with the terms, please make sure to sign the contract and post it back to us before you leave. I'm sorry, but work's calling. It was lovely meeting you." She turned to walk away when I grabbed her upper arm to stop her.

"Wait. I'm a little confused. You said I'd be assisting Mr. Mayfield, but I haven't even met him. So, who hired me?" I don't know where the question came from when there were at least a dozen more important ones I could have asked. Such as, for example, did I get medical insurance or did I get a company phone? Or, most importantly, how much I would get paid?

"That I don't know. Since Ms. Young has been keen that the contract's to your liking, I can only assume you've been headhunted. Now, if you'll excuse me." She batted her lashes impatiently. Slowly it dawned on me: the woman was busy and I had taken up enough of her time.

"Thanks."

The thick manila envelope was heavy in my hand as I made my way downstairs, past the gathering of business people waiting for the elevators in the main reception hall. Only as I reached the confined space of my car did I dare let an idiotic grin fall into place. Seriously, I couldn't stop grinning because I, Brooke Stewart, had been headhunted. It was a huge word. An important word. And it happened to *me*. And I, Brooke Stewart, would go to Italy. I was about to take my very first trip to Europe.

I fished my phone out of my purse and considered whom to call first. Mom was my first option, but then again wasn't my boyfriend supposed to know first? He deserved to be put first, particularly after I cheated on him. I ignored my guilty conscience as I speed-dialed Sean's number. He answered on the second ring.

"Sean McDermott." I could hear the usual cafeteria background noise: students talking and laughing, trays shifting, and cutlery clinking. He was probably having his lunch break.

"Guess what?" I didn't wait for his reply. "I just got a job with Mayfield Realties."

The line remained silent. I held my breath as I waited for Sean's reaction, which came a second too late. "Wow, that's awesome. Let's celebrate tonight. I could pop over." He sounded strained, which wasn't the reaction I expected. Maybe he had other issues on his mind and was trying hard to be happy for me.

"Yeah, that's not all. I'm going to Italy. There's some big acquisition, and I'm supposed to assist Mayfield."

A pause again, then, "That's great. We'll celebrate next weekend."

"Yeah, about that. My flight's tomorrow and I'll be back in two weeks."

"Then we'll catch up when you get back."

Did I detect a hint of irritation in his voice? I frowned and moistened my lips. "Are you okay, honey?"

"Yeah, I'm good." He didn't sound good at all. We remained silent for a second or two. Sean resumed the conversation first. "Actually, no. Can we talk? There's something I need to tell you."

Why didn't I like the sound of that? My hands grew clammy, and my heart began to pound like a sledgehammer "Sure." I tried to infuse a cheeriness I didn't feel into my voice. "Our usual place? I can be there in half an hour."

"Okay." He hung up.

"Bye," I whispered, even though he couldn't hear me. My heart pounded so hard I thought my ribcage might explode. Maybe Sean saw me and Mystery Guy. Maybe he somehow found out about last night before I got a chance to tell him, and he cared after all. This was my chance to be honest and set things straight before I headed off to Italy. I didn't want to part with something this major standing between us.

***

Twenty minutes later, I took my seat at our usual table

overlooking the east side of NY University campus and ordered a large latte, a chicken panini, and fries on the side. The café was almost empty at this time of day, which I attributed to lunch break being over and everyone stuck in class. Sean arrived a few minutes later. I had a few seconds to regard him before he spied me and strolled over. He was a few inches shorter than Mystery Guy, with dark-blond locks that tended to curl behind his ears, and hazel eyes to die for. If his blue shirt and black slacks didn't scream PhD student and teaching assistant, then his rimmed glasses did. He looked a bit like a book nerd, which couldn't be further from the truth. Coming from a family of academics, Sean was pushed into following an academic career, but his dream had always been becoming a pro racer. He had the physical strength, talent, and experience, but not the will to pull it through against his family's wishes.

"Hey, you." I raised on my toes to kiss him on the lips. He smiled and brushed his lips fleetly against mine. The feeling that something was amiss intensified. "Want something?" I asked. My hunger dissipating, I pointed at my still warm Panini. Whatever he had to say, I decided I wouldn't like it.

"I just ate," Sean said, and took a seat opposite from me. I didn't fail to notice how much distance he put between us. He folded his hands on the table and gazed up. His expression remained dead serious as he regarded me.

His typically warm hazel eyes exuded none of the love I usually saw in them. Holy cow. I had never seen him this cold and calculated. It could only mean one thing. I might not have much experience with relationships, but I could see the telltale signs. My heart sank in my chest.

"You wanted to talk," I prompted him to get it over with.

"Yeah." He ran a hand through his locks, bidding for time.

"Just say it." In spite of the turmoil going on inside, my voice seemed surprisingly calm and composed.

"Okay." His eyes settled on my lips for a second, as though he was about to kiss me. And then his gaze moved down to his folded hands. He couldn't even look me in the eyes. "I can't do this anymore."

"Do what? Go to work? Study for a PhD? Live in New York? You'll have to be more specific, Sean." Hysteria bubbled up somewhere at the back of my throat. I swallowed hard to get rid of it.

"Us." His eyes settled on me, and in that instant I had my answer. The last grain of warmth seeped out of his expression. Maybe he was scared that I might make a scene, shout, ask questions, beg him to want me. "We can't do *us* anymore."

He was breaking up. Call it intuition, but I had known it since the strange phone call; I just didn't want to acknowledge it straight away. Strangely the realization didn't hurt as much as I thought it would. I didn't want to ask, and yet I had to know. "Is there someone else?"

"No."

My gaze searched his expression for a clue that he was lying, but found none. I took a deep breath and let it out slowly.

"What then?" I asked.

He sighed and shook his head slightly. The passion I was used to seeing in his eyes returned, but this time it had nothing to do with me. "Do you ever get the feeling there's more to life than what you have and what you do? I mean, I wake up, go to work, come home, do the same things over and over again. I don't want to waste my life with this shit. I need more."

I nodded even though his rambling made no sense whatsoever. The guy was twenty-five. How could he possibly have a midlife crisis? Black dots clouded my vision. I rubbed my eyes to get rid of the throbbing sensation gathering behind them.

"So you're going for the racing thing," I said.

"A while back I got a sponsoring offer from a French auto manufacturer," Sean said, unaware of what his words did to me. "I'm flying over to sign the deal. It's done. I can't back off."

"I didn't ask you to," I said softly.

His hand wrapped around mine, and he looked straight into my eyes. "You know you're amazing, and under different circumstances I would have never let you go. But this is what I'm supposed to do. I can't focus on both my career and this relationship. You deserve better than that."

"Your calling, I get it." You can still follow your calling while remaining in a relationship with the one you once claimed to love, I felt like shouting. And yet I remained composed, ignoring the sharp stab piercing my chest. Since Sean was breaking up anyway, now was the time to tell him about my cheating, but for some reason I remained quiet. Maybe it was selfish for me to want to part ways in good light, even if that light was nothing but a sham.

He gave my hand a light squeeze. "I want us to stay friends."

I nodded. The pain in my chest grew stronger.

"So, you got a new job. Tell me about it," Sean said, suddenly changing the topic. I smiled bitterly and waved my hand.

"Compared to yours it's nothing special really."

He smiled, not pressing the issue. His eyes sparkled again, and in that instant I felt a strong urge to get up and leave him behind. I had been wrong to think what Sean and I had was special. He wasn't 'the one'. He couldn't be. 'The one' would never leave me behind.

"I've got to get packing," I whispered, jumping from my

seat. A forced smile played on my lips.

"Sure. Want me to—"

I held up my hand to interrupt whatever half-hearted offer he was about to make. "No, I'm fine. And congrats on finding a sponsor. It must have taken you weeks, if not months of hard work." Hard work he failed to tell me about.

He straightened to kiss me on the cheek. I somehow managed to dodge him, grabbed my bag, muttered a 'see you around' and ran for the door, eager to get away from him as fast as I could. I didn't hate him, but I also didn't feel the way I knew I should have felt.

Once I reached my car and I dared take a deep breath of cold New York air, my heartbeat slowed down, and my hands stopped trembling. I drove home more carefully than usual. My cell rang once, and then beeped a few times with incoming messages. I looked at the caller ID and switched it off. I couldn't blame Sean for following his dreams, when I was about to do the same. But I sure as hell couldn't bear listening to him talking about it the way he did—with that sparkle in his eyes that told me he had found a passion greater than our relationship. My insides felt numb, but my brain was surprisingly lucid. So this was it. A year with Sean wasted, gone in the blink of an eye. The pain might come later. Right now I felt stupid for ever believing we had a future together. This job couldn't come at a better time, and

I was determined to get over Sean by focusing my whole energy on it.

Sylvie wasn't in, for which I was grateful. I didn't feel like company and even less like bitching about Sean, which was the only way Sylvie knew how to get over a breakup. I locked myself in my bedroom and texted Mom, telling her I couldn't make it tonight because of my new job, and promised to call her as soon as I landed in Italy. For a minute I considered texting Sylvie in case she didn't make it home before I left for the airport. It wasn't unusual for her to find some guy and then spend the next forty-eight hours shacked up with him, oblivious of the world outside their bedroom. Eventually I decided to wait until ten p.m. in case she found her way back home after all.

I made myself a cup of hot chocolate and settled on my bed to flick through my contract. So far it looked better than expected. Great perks like health insurance, a brand new smartphone with two lines, one being mine and one belonging to Mr. Mayfield, and even a bonds package. A ten per cent pay raise once I got through the initial trial period of three months, company traveling with all expenses paid, and even a Christmas bonus. I liked what I saw and signed it right away, then spent an hour flicking through my wardrobe to choose what to take with me. I had clothes, lots of them, but I didn't feel they looked like something a senior assistant would wear. Living in New York wasn't cheap. After nine months of unemployment right before I landed my job—previous job, I reminded myself—my credit cards were maxed out, and I was still repaying my debt, so getting out there to buy new stuff was out of the question.

In the end, I borrowed Sylvie's navy *Jil Sander* suit, and from the same collection a tailored, long-sleeved dress that ended just above the knee. They were the least expensive clothes in Sylvie's stuffed-to-the-brim wardrobe, so I knew she wouldn't mind me borrowing them. She usually preferred a riskier style anyway, think short and sheer, so she'd probably not even notice them being gone.

I was still flicking through Sylvie's wardrobe when her key turned in the lock, and she walked in a few moments later.

"Are you ransacking my stuff?" She lifted the navy suit I had decided on earlier and smirked. "You could have picked something less—"

"Boring?" I prompted.

"I was about to say *matronly*, but boring will do." She tossed the suit aside and sat down on the bed, tucking her naked legs beneath her. Her skirt was so short I could see her frilly *Victoria's Secret* panties.

"I hope you don't mind."

"Actually, you're doing me a favor." She shot the suit a dirty look like it was about to steal her purse.

"I got kicked out of the department," I said, ready to share my big news.

"What? Was it that prick, James?" She inched closer and wrapped her left arm around my shoulder. "I'm so sorry, Brooke." I could tell by her excited expression that she wasn't. "But seeing the bright side: now we're two unemployed chicks with the margarita world at our feet."

I smirked.

"See, I don't get it. Why do you always have to be so *conventional?*" She emphasized the word like it was a bad thing. "You don't slack off at work. You don't sleep around for the sake of it. You're just—" She waved her hand in the air, looking for the right word.

"Dull?" I prompted, smiling.

"Responsible."

My smile turned bitter as I looked away. She had asked me the same question many times during our friendship. I always avoided giving her an answer because I knew she wouldn't understand. No one would. The world didn't like to hear about that part of my life. Luckily Sylvie knew me well enough not to press the issue.

"Let's have another drink," Sylvie said. "Knowing you it'll be a brief stint, so I say we make the best of it."

I hated to shatter her alcohol-fueled dreams, but someone had to do it. I owed it to mankind. "I wasn't sacked. James signed the company over to Mayfield

Realties, and Mayfield promoted me to senior assistant. I'm leaving for Italy tomorrow."

"Hell, no." Sylvie's jaw dropped. For a moment she looked disappointed, until she realized as my best friend she was supposed to be happy for me. "Yay! Well done, you." She didn't mean one single half-hearted word of it. Her expression was as enthusiastic as a salmon about to be fished out of the water.

"Save it. Gee, you're pathetic." I rolled my eyes and snorted. "You'd rather have me home with you, picking up guys and getting to bed when others wake up for work."

She laughed that tinkling laughter of hers that only managed to confirm my suspicion. "A promotion is almost as good as running around in PJs all day long. This calls for a celebration. *Vixen's* in half an hour?"

"It's four p.m."

"You're right. It's getting kind of late. Let's make it ten minutes."

I stared after her open-mouthed as she grabbed a handful of stuff from her wardrobe and headed for the bathroom to change.

5

TO CALL SYLVIE'S patch of fabric a skirt was an offense to whoever invented the skirt. It was nothing more than an over-sized belt and barely covered her modesty, let alone provide any protection from the cold and damp New York air. I tried my best to persuade her to wear something else, something with more length, but she wouldn't have it. So I clamped my mouth shut and let her dress in the clothes—or lack thereof—of her choice.

She downed a glass of red wine before we even left the apartment, then another as soon as we hit *Vixen's*. By the time our usual clique arrived a few hours later, we were both intoxicated and having a good time slagging off Sylvie's ex. I didn't see the mop of dark hair and green eyes until Sylvie pointed, slurring, "Isn't that your guy?"

"What?"

"You know, your *plan cul.* Bed candy. Fuck buddy." She collapsed in a fit of laughter.

Oh, gosh.

If it was him I could only hope he couldn't lip-read. My vision blurred as I turned my head. I narrowed my eyes to focus, but the only things I caught were broad shoulders and a strong back heading straight for the door.

I rolled my eyes. "You're so drunk you'd mistake Bruce Willis for a girl."

"Who?"

She seemed genuinely confused, so I mumbled, "Never mind" as I waved my hand and signaled the bartender to get us another round of shots. That sparked instant recognition.

"You're the best girlfriend in the world," Sylvie slurred, and placed a wet smooch on my cheek.

I forced another shot down my throat, then another. The room began to spin until it looked like a giant merry-go-round of laughing people, clinking glasses, and ear splitting music. Something about a job and a new boss briefly popped up at the back of my mind, but it all got lost in the alcohol-induced sense of freedom that was beginning to wash over me. I felt as though I had no care in the world, and I intended to keep it that way until strong arms wrapped around me, and I was tucked into something warm and fluffy. I opened my eyes to peer into the most electrifying green gaze reflecting a dark puddle of annoyance.

"You have the most gorgeous eyes. I could stare into them forever," I mumbled giggling.

And then I passed out.

6

I WASN'T A wallflower when it came to partying and having a good time, but I didn't usually have more than two glasses. So two nights in a row drinking my head off with Sylvie hadn't been a wise decision. I opened my eyes groggily and blinked against the bright sun spilling through the window.

Good grief.

My head felt as though someone was pounding it with a sledgehammer and my tongue was stuck to the back of my throat. At least I didn't feel sick. I sat up and placed my naked feet on the rug in front of my bed, testing the ground. It felt a bit shaky but otherwise okay. I walked to the kitchen for a glass of water when I remembered the green eyes from last night.

Did I have sex with him again? Or had I been imagining

him? No idea what might be worse.

"Sylvie?" My voice sounded so hoarse it made me cringe. I called out louder but got no answer. She was probably still sleeping off her hangover. I padded through each room, looking for a sign that I brought a man home, but found none. Eventually I knocked on Sylvie's door and entered. Either she left early, which couldn't be since she would have left me a note, or she never accompanied me home. The stack of clothes she had tossed on the bed while rummaging for something to wear last night persuaded me to go with Option B.

So the guy had been just a figment of my imagination. I couldn't help the sudden disappointment grabbing me.

Why did I even care whether I ever saw this guy again? Sean had just split up with me, and I had barely wasted a minute obsessing over it. Yet Jett and I had talked for all of five minutes, and I was all but planning out our future together.

Because no one's ever made you feel this way. Sexy. Confident. Wanted.

I groaned at the thought, even though I knew it was true. He wasn't just hot; he had something about him that turned my insides all mushy and made me want to do stuff. To him. With him.

Get your head out of the gutter, Stewart.

I made myself a cup of coffee, grabbed a piece of dry

toast, and sat down at the kitchen table overlooking the busy street below. But it wasn't old ladies and moms holding onto their kids that I saw.

My mind could only focus on one thing: smoldering eyes and a hard body leaning over me. I sighed and let my imagination roam freely where it wanted to go.

***

Late afternoon, Sylvie was still not back, probably busy hooking up with last night's conquest. In case she worried or needed me, I left a note on the kitchen table with my new number and the promise to call her as soon as I arrived in Italy. Half an hour later a cab pulled up in front of the building, and I drove to the airport with the setting sun behind me.

Once at JFK and waiting in the boarding area, I switched on my smartphone. The plan was to transfer my old cell's contact list, excluding Sean's number, to my company phone. Instead, I was instantly awarded with a long list of redirected calls and text messages. I knew nothing about my new boss, so I figured flicking through his messages would help me paint a picture before I met him in less than nine hours. I took a sip of my water and almost choked on it. He sounded businesslike and curt. While I understood that smileys and kisses were to be avoided in business correspondence, Mr. Mayfield also seemed to harbor a great aversion to saying 'please' and 'thank you'. I frowned as I made a mental list of his favorite words: *great, okay, fine, yes, no way, done*. His longest sentence was: *If you need to talk, my assistant will be happy to assist you.*

I sighed and rubbed my still throbbing forehead. James hadn't been the greatest boss in the world, but he didn't seem allergic to talking. I certainly liked engaging in dialogue every now and then, so my new job might turn a bit challenging, and not in a good way.

I was about to switch off the smartphone when an IM from Sylvie came through. Glancing at the clock to make sure I wasn't late, I opened the conversation and quickly skimmed through to the bottom. There was a brief mention of a letter and some guy with a strange and (according to Sylvie) extremely sexy accent calling to talk to me. I was listed in the public phone directory and was used to the usual financial and insurance companies soliciting me, so the information didn't bother me. Maybe the fact that I had other things on my mind further contributed to my lack of interest. Switching off the smartphone, I headed for the gate to board the plane, wondering for the umpteenth time why a headhunter would headhunt *me* to work for someone like Mayfield. Judging from his brisk tone and my fondness of human conversation, we sure weren't a match made in business heaven.

7

THE PLANE LANDED at Malpensa airport nine painful hours later, which was the longest period I had ever spent on a plane. I knew I didn't look my best. My head reeled, my eyes burned from a lack of sleep, and my thighs ached for a jog, but at that moment, I couldn't be more excited. Milan's ancient buildings and twinkling city lights were waiting just outside the sliding doors. I was ready to explore each and every part of this wonderful city on my days off, of which I hoped I would have plenty.

Smiling, I gathered my unruly hair in a high ponytail and pinched my cheeks to look more presentable, then picked up my luggage from the carousel and made my way through customs. The arrivals area was filled with waiting families and taxi drivers. I spied a cardboard plaque the size of a notebook with my name written on it and walked over, expecting my new boss to be waiting for me. The middle-aged guy greeted me in broken English, and I knew it couldn't possibly be Mayfield.

"Seniorita Stewart, I'm your driver. May I take your luggage?" He didn't wait for my answer. He grabbed my suitcase and heaved it up in a fluent motion, then carried it to the parked SUV, dodging the dissipating crowds and taxi drivers vying for tourists's attention. I hurried after him, concentrating hard to keep up with his chitter-chatter as he went on to tell me about the weather, the country, sightseeing opportunities, and who knows what else.

Night had descended, but the airport was brightly illuminated, allowing a breathtaking sneak peak at the mountain scenery I had seen outlined through the plane's window. I smiled and nodded politely as he opened the door for me, and I jumped onto the back seat of the car. He paused in his conversation for all of five seconds, or as long as it took him to pull out of the parking lot. As we headed up the highway he resumed his chat.

"You had a nice trip but very long?" I nodded, and he laughed. "But now it's over and you'll have a beautiful vacation." I didn't want to point out that I wasn't on vacation, so I just nodded again. The driver continued his half-English, half-Italian monologue through the drive to Bellagio. By the time he pulled over thirty minutes later, my head was reeling, and not from the fresh air and stunning backdrop I had glimpsed outside the window. I jumped out on shaky feet, my hand clutching the car's door for support, as I gawked at the hotel in front of me.

The architecture was definitely neo-classical, reminding me of Ancient Greek and Rome with its little columns, capitals, and beautiful sculptural bas-reliefs that my fingers itched to touch. It was big but not oversized, about five stories high with a beautiful illuminated fountain spewing up water onto two embracing angels from which a thick, red carpet was stretched out to the heavy glass door. As I entered my home for the next two weeks, my breath caught in my throat.

Holy cow.

The reception hall, though not big, was absolutely stunning. Glass candelabra dangled from the high ceiling, illuminating the polished ivory marble floor below and accentuating the flower reliefs adorning the ivory-colored walls. But what impressed me most were the two Corinthian columns behind the reception desk.

Silvio passed my luggage to a uniformed bellboy and instructed him to bring it straight up to my room, while I waited at the reception desk to check in.

The receptionist smiled. She was a woman in her thirties with glowing olive skin and glossy hair to die for.

"Welcome, Miss Stewart," she said in heavily accented English. "You've been booked on the upper floor. This is your key." She held up a white piece of plastic the size of a credit card. "The restaurant's open from seven to midnight. Room service is available around the clock. If you have any questions, I'll be happy to answer them. Let me show you the way."

I shook my head and returned her generous smile. "That won't be necessary. I think I'll be fine." Architecture had always been my thing, only I never had the chance or money to visit a place this grand. I didn't want to have to make small talk when I'd rather gawk at every single detail without anyone watching over my shoulder.

"But I insist. The elevators are over here." She pointed behind her at the narrow corridor leading past the columns and around a corner. I followed her upstairs while listening to her recommending Italy's must-see sights and excursions. And then she let me into my room and closed the door as she left, wishing me a pleasant stay.

I tossed the swipe card on the nearby coffee table realizing I hadn't thought of tipping her, the bellboy, or the driver. "Oh, crap," I muttered. Was it too late to run downstairs and do it now? Should I wait until the morning? I had never stayed in anything remotely expensive, so my knowledge of proper tipping etiquette was rather limited.

"Are you okay?" The male voice coming from my right startled me. I shrieked and jumped a step back, dropping my handbag in the process. My head turned in the intruder's direction, and my mouth opened to let out an earsplitting sound, but what came out resembled more a surprised grumble that slowly turned into a sensation of anger pounding against my skull.

"Are you following me?" I was so angry I almost choked on my words.

"I could ask you the same question, since I was here first." Mystery Guy cocked a brow and moved closer until he stood mere inches from my face. From this distance, or lack thereof, I could take in each and every detail of his face. His luscious lips were slightly curved in the most arrogant smile I had ever seen. Almost hidden by his day-old stubble were two tiny indentations in his cheeks, which I knew could turn into full-blown dimples. Dimples were my weakness. My fingers itched to reach up and touch them, touch his skin, feel his stubble to see whether it was as deliciously scratchy as it looked. His beautiful green eyes shimmered. His lips parted slightly, and I knew he could either sense my naughty thoughts or had some of his own. Maybe he remembered something I didn't about our night together. My cheeks were on fire.

Swallowing hard, I looked down his delicious body and instantly regretted it. His shirt stretched over broad shoulders, leaving no doubt that the guy worked out. A lot. A dark patch of curly hair peeked from beneath his undone top button. It was the same color as his happy trail I had glimpsed when he didn't bother to cover up in my bed.

In my bed.

God, I liked the sound of that. My cheeks flushed again as I cringed inwardly at my thoughts. What was wrong with me? The guy had trouble written all over him, and yet I behaved like a pubescent teen in heat, unable to control my own hormones. I had to find my wits, or what was left of them, before the guy's ego grew bigger than the Eiffel Tower.

"What are you doing here?" I asked bending down to pick up my handbag from the floor. His gaze followed my ass and stayed glued to it a bit too long. I hurried to straighten up but not fast enough. A low, appreciative growl escaped his throat.

"Looking at my favorite spot. Need help with that?" He pointed in the direction of my heavy suitcase, but his gaze remained glued to my ass. My clothes seemed to evaporate into thin air. I fought the urge to shrug into my coat and keep it on for the rest of our unsolicited conversation.

"I'll be just fine, thanks." Irritated, I turned to face him, which in turn forced his gaze away from my ass and back to my face. A glint of disappointment appeared in his expression, as though, unlike my ass, my face wasn't quite worth his time. I crossed my arms over my chest and regarded him coolly. "What was your excuse again for breaking into my room?"

"I'm staying here."

I smirked. "Unless Mayfield invited you over for the ride, and he's a stingy SOB, I don't think that's the case."

He laughed. His voice sounded like satin silk caressing my skin, velvety soft yet luxurious. I shuddered lightly.

He's bad news, Stewart, I reminded myself.

"I'll try not to be offended this time, but for future reference, my employees don't usually talk to me like that." His lips remained curled into that gorgeous, lopsided smile, which made it hard to focus on anything else. It took me a few seconds to realize the meaning of his words. We were in a different country at the same time. I was supposed to meet my new boss, whom I had just called a stingy SOB, and Mystery Guy felt offended.

"You're Mayfield, aren't you?" My voice came low and hoarse. He nodded slowly, staring at me. "But you said your name was Jett Townsend."

He nodded again. "Townsend was my mother's name. I like to use it when I meet potential employees. It makes the whole recruitment process easier and, let's say, refreshing."

All heat drained from my face. *Holy shit.* I hadn't even started my new job and already I was insulting my new boss...right after sleeping with him. I was worse than Sylvie. "So you're—"

My speech eluded me.

"Jett Mayfield, the stingy SOB who just hired you." He

held out his palm. I didn't want to touch him but what choice did I have? I placed my hand into his and flinched at how deliciously warm and manly his touch felt. His calloused palm scratched my skin, sending an electric jolt into my lower body. I wondered how it would feel to have Jett Mayfield's hands stroking the inside of my thighs.

Get a grip, Stewart. After this stunt you're lucky if you still have a job. Let's keep it at that.

"I'm so sorry," I said pulling my hand away and jumping a step back to put some much needed distance between us. "I didn't know who you were. Usually, I'm way more professional. I take my job very seriously and know my place."

"I hope you do because I have great plans with you."

My breath hitched in my throat. Why did I keep hearing double meanings in his words?

"Ready to see your room?" Jett grabbed my suitcase and set off through what looked like a living room, toward three doors. I hurried to keep up with him. He opened one of them and moved aside to let me through. "This is it. If you need anything I'll be next door." He pointed at the closed door. "I'll leave you to unpack. Work starts at eight sharp. I like my employees to be punctual so don't be late."

The guy was sleeping next door. With only a few inches of wall between us. I wondered whether he slept naked. He sure had been in my bed. The picture of a naked Jett

Mayfield looking all self-assured and *not bothered* flashed before my eyes. My cheeks began to burn.

Not again.

Talk about being doomed.

He smirked as though he could sense my thoughts. My temper flared. What sort of sleeping arrangement was that? Was it even legal? I opened my mouth to protest when he pressed his index finger against my lips, silencing me instantly.

"I like to keep my personal assistants at my beck and call. I hope you don't have a problem with that." His gaze bore into me, challenging me to show just how much his proximity blew off any sense of self-control. Did I have a problem with that? You bet, and yet I shook my head no. He was just a man, for crying out loud. I could deal with his kind. Besides, I had a million other questions that needed addressing. Like why he employed me and brought me in on such an important job at the last minute, when it'd take me ages to get acquainted with all the details.

"Eight a.m. it is." My voice came lower than expected and a little bit hoarse, but at least I managed to speak.

"Sleep well, Miss Stewart. I'll make sure to make this stay worth remembering." He smiled and my heart dropped into my panties. A big neon light flashed before my eyes:

BIG MISTAKE, BIG MISTAKE!

I had to get the heck away from him, and yet my feet

remained glued to the spot as I watched him stroll into the living room. His narrow waist accentuated the broad shoulders and sculpted upper arms that were clearly visible beneath his thin shirt. My gaze moved down to his long legs and strong thighs—thighs I imagined parting and settling between my legs.

I groaned, irritated with myself, and slammed the door a tad too hard.

8

WHEN MY ALARM went off, I could have screamed. I had been right in the throes of a fantastic dream during which I was holding on tight to a hard muscular back while being devoured by soft luscious lips. I glanced down at my wet naked skin and the crumpled silk sheet between my thighs. One more second and my nerve endings would have exploded like stardust. Instead, I was left panting and frustrated with a delicious ache in my lower body.

It was official. Jett Townsend was haunting my dreams. As my pulse settled down again, I got up and straightened the sheets as best as I could. What the hotel staff thought of me should have been the least of my worries, but for some reason it mattered because I cared about my job and reputation. Deep in my heart I knew having sex on a business trip was nothing but a meaningless fling. If

Mayfield propositioned, and if for some stupid reason I wouldn't be able to resist his sexy charm, the whole hotel would know I had succumbed to the temptation and surrendered to his lust. I didn't want anyone to think Mayfield scored with the arguably professional assistant on the first day. It didn't feel right.

But isn't that exactly what happened back home?

Pushing the irritating yet accurate thought to the back of my mind, I implored my brain to become obsessed with something or someone else...and failed. I hadn't heard a sound since last night when Jett had left me standing in front of my door, which led me to believe that he was either very quiet or didn't spend the night in his room. Call me opinionated, but I was ready to bet on the latter. He was the bad boy type all right. The type my mother warned me about. The type you have a good time with, then forget about as you go home to live your boring life, while he moves on to the next skirt ready to give him the time of day.

Only this bad boy wouldn't be so easy to forget because we worked together. I had only two options: either get rid of him or find a way to ease those hormones that followed me even in my dreams. Quitting my job wasn't an option so Number Two it was. If only I knew how to stop turning into a drooling teen every time I so much as heard his voice.

Maybe it won't be so bad in the light of day.

Guys tend to be hot when you're under the influence of either horniness or beer goggles. I was neither, so Mayfield was powerless. Besides, he couldn't possibly be as good-looking as I remembered. If my horniness wouldn't stop anytime soon, I was sure seeing his flaws in broad daylight would do the trick.

After a brief shower I dressed in Sylvie's navy suit, pinned my hair up in a strict bun, and nervously perched on the sofa to await Mayfield's arrival. Last night's questions popped back into my mind, and I made a mental note to get answers straight away. First I'd find out why he employed me, and then we'd establish a work routine and what he expected of me. As a professional, nothing could faze me. Absolutely nothing. Not even his lean, muscular body with rock-hard six-pack abs, strong shoulders, and a wide chest. And surely not his stunning green eyes, full lips, and beautiful face.

He was off limits. Forbidden to touch or drool over.

Everyone but him. Got it, Stewart?

I breathed in and out as I steadied myself, centering my resolve in the knowledge that I had it all under control. I thought I was doing great...until my weak body betrayed me.

My heart began to thump a little harder. As I took deep breaths to calm my nerves, the door opened and in he walked... six foot two of toned muscles. I knew I was blushing, but I couldn't stop. Just like I couldn't stop my knees giving way beneath me. Thank goodness I was sitting, otherwise I might have landed flat on my ass. Staring at him, I ran my tongue along my suddenly parched lips to moisten them. He looked so darn sexy, dressed in a tailored business suit and a crisp white shirt; the upper button was undone, revealing that delicious patch of skin I had started to look out for. His thick dark hair was shiny, but unruly, and looked as though he'd just stepped out of the shower and didn't bother brushing it. I wanted to run my fingers through it. Without thinking I sniffed, and a sassy non-invasive cologne intermingled with a more masculine shower gel shot my reserve to pieces. It instantly turned me on, making me want to—

Dammit.

It wasn't just my body that betrayed me. My mind wouldn't stop conjuring images of Jett and me, together, doing naughty stuff. I bit my lower lip hard as I fought the urge to jump on his lap and bury my fingers in his hair and draw us onto the couch with him on top of me. His weight would pin me to the spot and—

"You okay? You look a bit flustered." Jett Mayfield sat down opposite me and inched forward, lower arms resting on his thighs, as though to inspect me. An amused glint played in his devilish green eyes. The guy was a piece of sin.

If he were the devil holding a contract, this would be the moment I might just give in to temptation and sign over my soul.

What was it with my inability to focus around this guy?

I leaned back to put a few more inches between us. "I'm just surprised you scrub up so nicely in a suit."

He raised a brow. "Was that a compliment, Ms. Stewart?" It was, but the guy's inflated ego was already so big I doubted he would fit it through Manhattan. I wasn't going to contribute to mankind's doom by letting it grow to even bigger proportions.

"Not really. After what you were sporting at that club, even a lumberjack shirt thrown over a spandex bodysuit would be a vast improvement." My brain only realized what I'd just said after the words left my mouth. Not only was I incapable of keeping my body heat under control, my potty mouth also couldn't stop insulting him. I swallowed hard and peered at him. An apology rushed to my lips.

"Spandex bodysuits, huh?" His eyes twinkled. "If that's what turns you on—I'm all for giving it a try."

My breath hitched. "I'm sorry, Mr. Mayfield. I don't know what came over me."

He raised his hand to stop me. "We can discuss today's schedule over breakfast. And please call me Jett. We'll have to work together around the clock, so we might as well drop the formalities and start getting to know each other better in every sense." There was that double meaning thing he kept doing. Or was it all in my head?

Stop putting words in his mouth, Stewart.

"Great. I'm Brooke." I smiled and followed him out the door to the restaurant downstairs, aware of the jealous glances from every single female we passed. As Jett began to talk about my job and what he expected of me in a no-nonsense voice I assumed was his business tone, I relaxed a little and even managed to swallow down a few bites of the best butter croissant I ever had.

It was just a job. He was just some (I admit way beyond the usual standard) good-looking guy lucky enough to inherit the hotness gene. I could deal with him.

I stared at the urns overflowing with blossoming flowers lining the sidewalk outside our window and inhaled the clean, morning air wafting in through the open door. Bellagio was so beautiful and serene; I felt I could deal with anything...until Jett smiled that lopsided smile of his that screamed trouble. I frowned. Why was his gaze lingering on me longer than was acceptable? His gaze dipped slowly from my eyes to my lips and then to my shirt—or what I hoped was my shirt rather than my breasts—before shifting back to meet my eyes. My heart skipped a beat.

"Do you like your room?"

I nodded, not quite understanding the sudden change in topic. "It's beautiful."

"I want you to pack your bags." He stood and held out his hand to help me up. I ignored it.

"Why? Where am I going?"

"No need to waste company money on a hotel when I own a property on Lake Como. It's very private. Very secluded. I'm sure you'll like it even more than this place." He signed the bill on the table and tossed the pen on top of it, then turned to me. Danger shimmered in his eyes, and for a moment he reminded me of an eagle closing in on his prey. I felt like butter melting under his sexy gaze full of dark and sinful and forbidden promises.

"You have half an hour. Can you do that?" Jett asked, breaking our eye contact.

"You could have told me last night," I said, trying to keep my voice strong. All I could think of was Jett and I, alone in a secluded place with no one to bother us. No one to ask questions. No one to watch what we were doing. Why did the outlook seem so erotic?

"I could have told you." His gaze bore into mine again and a flicker of amusement played on his lips. "But I didn't." My mouth went dry as I tried to read his enigmatic expression. An inner voice told me he wasn't as unpredictable as he pretended to be. It was just a game. But there was something about him that kept me on edge, wanting—waiting for his next move, reaction, word— anything that might give away what was going through that damn mind of his. Either he liked to keep his employees on their toes or this was nothing but an experiment to test my patience, devotion, and consequently my aptness for the job.

I raised my chin a notch and stared him down. He could test all he wanted. I was born to do this job, and nothing he said or did could break my reserve.

He peered at his watch, signaling I was wasting his time.

"I'll be back in twenty." I hurried past, my heart thumping in my throat. Private and secluded were two adjectives I'd rather avoid with Jett Mayfield around, and yet here I was—running to do as he bid instead of protesting and insisting I stay behind, even if it meant paying for my room out of my own pocket.

Could you have afforded it?

I smirked. Not likely.

As I passed a mirror in the hall, I noticed how incredibly ridiculous I looked with that grin on my face.

There's nothing to be so excited about, Steward. It's just a job. A job for which you get paid.

For some reason I couldn't shake off the feeling spending time with Jett came at a price, and sooner or later I'd have to decide whether it was worth it.

***

Jett's reluctance to engage in business conversation rather than focus on the road ahead was understandable, given that we were stuck in his convertible Ferrari driving down the narrowest, most winding, cobbled paths I had ever seen. I would have literally soiled my pants sitting in the driver's seat and was thankful for the fact that driving didn't seem to be part of my job duties.

During the half hour drive, he kept our conversation businesslike and mostly focused on my duties as his personal assistant. Upon my asking, he mentioned our job here was a deal running in the millions, but he remained tight-lipped on the details. He gave me a short verbal list of important names to remember and an even longer list of names he didn't want to be bothered with. His deep, smooth voice kept conjuring the wrong pictures in my head, so I remained mostly quiet, as I tried to focus on his instructions.

It was late morning when he finally took a sharp turn and parked the car, then held the door open. I stepped out gingerly, minding my step on the gravel stones.

"What do you think?" Jett asked.

Inhaling the air thick with the smell of trees, water, and sunshine, I spun in a slow circle as I tried to take in the picturesque scenery stretching out in front of us. To me professional meant not wearing my emotions on my sleeve. But how could I keep my cool with mountaintops covered in sparkling snow surrounding a shimmering Lake Como as a backdrop, green ivy climbing up the sides of the balcony, and blossoming flowers at my feet?

"I love it," I whispered because no other words could convey how I felt. My answer seemed to please him because he smiled. As he held the door open so I could enter, I thought I caught a glint of lust in his dazzling green eyes.

"After you," Jett said, still staring at me.

I nodded, unable to bring out a simple 'thank you' under the spell of his gaze.

What Jett had called 'his place' was in reality a three-level villa situated on a raised, secluded spot overlooking the lake and beach below. As I moved from one immaculate room to the next, I could smell the sultry scent of lavender, roses, and other fragrances you'd normally only find in expensive Eau de Toilette. Eventually, we stopped on the patio overlooking Lake Como.

"This is my favorite view in the world," Jett whispered in my ear. I turned my head to look up at him, expecting him to gaze at the scenery ahead, and was surprised to find his eyes focused on me. His heated gaze penetrated the cotton material of my suit and sent shivers down my spine. I froze to the spot as everything else faded to nothing. His lips were slightly parted. His tongue left a shimmering wet trail where it flicked over his lips. I stared at that moisture, wondering what it would taste like. What his skin would smell like.

I noticed how quiet we had become. How his gaze seemed to remain glued to me. How his fingers lingered on the small of my back. A few moments later, he leaned forward until his hot breath caressed the corner of my mouth. We were so close. Inches away. My gaze focused on his lips, pleading with them to kiss me. A moment passed, then another. My breath hitched in my throat with anticipation.

"You smell great," Jett whispered, his deep voice turning my knees to melted cream. The smell of his body and the feel of his breath on my skin sent a shudder through my body, rocking me to the core. I longed to touch him, and yet I didn't give in to the strong urge.

And then he pulled away. I exhaled the breath I didn't know I had been holding.

"Let me show you the office," Jett said. His voice was back to its nonchalant self, and his expression was casual, friendly, but distant. How could he be so unaffected when I was boiling with want inside? Maybe he wasn't as attracted to me as I was to him. The thought hurt, particularly since no other man had made me feel this way. I couldn't figure him out, which scared the hell out of me because I had no idea how to react to it.

He grabbed my hand and pulled me into the living room, completely unaware of the electrical current piercing my skin where his fingers briefly touched me. As I followed a step behind, I barely managed to avoid stumbling over the white leather sofas set up in front of a huge fireplace. I had to get over this ridiculous attraction to him before I made a fool of myself. And I would start right away by focusing on other things, like the interior design.

The floors reminded me of light ivory with only a splash of color in the form of thick rugs, and marble urns filled with stunning flower bouquets. The large abstract painting in various shades of red hanging over the fireplace looked familiar. Similar paintings, only smaller in size, hung in the hall.

"This is it," Jett said opening a door. Careful not to touch him, I walked past him into the bright but small office with two desks set up opposite from each other. On top of one laid a laptop, a phone, pen, a notebook, and nothing else.

"I hope you don't mind spending so much time with me," Jett said. "I promise to be good, and I won't be too hard on you." His tone oozed amusement as he added, "Unless you want me to."

My cheeks burned. I turned away so he wouldn't catch my panic. Being in the same secluded house was bad enough, but we'd be basically sitting in each other's lap. How could I turn off the steady stream of hot emotions washing over me every single time he so much as smiled at me? How could I possibly work with him obstructing my view and keeping my mind occupied all day long?

9

I NEVER THOUGHT I'd get to miss my old boss, James, but an hour into my new job and already I felt like calling him and asking for a return to my realtor position with Sunrise Properties. Not that it was on offer, but a girl could at least give it a try. James was a snarky bitch most of the time, however he was also a friend and a sucker for tears and drama. He had cried his way through *The Notebook,* and I figured I could find a good enough excuse (think a relative's last wish) so he'd take me back.

And risk Mayfield backing out of their deal to buy James's company? Fat chance.

If James liked anything more than drama, it was money. And Mayfield's offer would persuade anyone to reconsider employee contracts and friendships.

"Don't be a wimp," I mumbled to myself as I neared

Jett's bedroom door with a certain trepidation. It's not every day that you're being summoned to your boss's bedroom to assist him with 'choosing clothes'. Technically, yes, that was mentioned as part of the job description, but I figured I'd get to advise him in the safety of a department store with lots of other people around. No one mentioned I'd be locked up with him in a stunning Italian mansion, surrounded by romantic views of mountains and lakes that basically invited you to let down your guard and enjoy a fling.

And I had no doubt Jett was up for a fling all right. I could read it in his heated gaze whenever he so much as glanced in my direction.

What did he see that other men didn't? I had no idea, and if he wasn't my boss I might have asked. But as things stood, this attraction was unwelcome, and I'd be damned if I'd admit it to him by blatantly talking about it. No matter how much his undressing looks invited me to get closer to him, he was my boss and I wasn't going to sleep with him. Again.

Jett's bedroom was situated on the first floor, mine was on the second. Thank God for that. The few steps and extra ceiling between us provided a bit of protection, albeit a weak one. I had no doubt he'd be professional about the whole situation and wouldn't impose on me without my explicit permission. The sad thing was that I sure as hell would give it to him if only he proposed. Which he wouldn't, of course.

I knocked on the door gently. When he didn't answer, I knocked once more, this time a bit louder.

"Come in," he called. His voice was low and slightly choked as though he was in the middle of a workout.

"Am I interrupting? I don't mind coming back later," I said, hesitantly pushing my head through the open door and scanning the room. It was about the same size as mine and looked almost identical, but with stark masculine furniture, cherry hardwood floor, wide bay windows, a cream ceiling, and spotlights. A wide king-sized bed with a thick, cream spread and two rows of cream cushions was set up in the middle. The padded chair, night tables, and a mirrored chest were all a few shades lighter than the floor and built a beautiful contrast to the white walls.

By the balcony door was a computer desk. The notebook sitting atop it was still running. When Jett didn't answer I entered the bedroom but left the door ajar. Ignoring the notebook's screen and email inbox, I headed for the mirrored chest. And that's when my gaze fell upon the walk-in closet to my left. Holy cow, it was huge, and by that I mean it would have served as a whole apartment in New York. No wonder the guy was out of breath searching through what looked like the whole floor of a department store.

"How can a man have so much stuff?" I mumbled, scanning rows over rows of shirts and slacks and expensive shoes. He'd made a fortune selling them on *eBay*.

"In my position you can't be seen wearing the same suit day in, day out," Jett said. My gaze snapped sharply in his direction, and I almost choked on my breath.

Apart from his navy CK pants, which were so snug they left nothing to the imagination, he was naked. I knew I was staring at his naked chest like an idiot, and yet I couldn't force myself to peel my gaze off his glorious body.

He was all bronze skin and defined muscles. I bit my lip as my gaze wandered down his sculpted chest to the three rows of hard muscles on his abdomen—muscles my nails itched to graze and bury themselves in. My gaze followed his happy trail to the narrow hips. His underwear hung so low I could see just a hint of neatly trimmed hair and then a well-defined bulge—and a big one at that. Heat traveled through my abdomen and pooled between my legs. My pulse picked up speed, and a rush of excitement washed over me. I had never stared at a man like this. Then again I had never met such a fine specimen. Did I want to pull off his pants and see whether the real deal was as hot as the one conjured by my imagination?

Hell, yeah.

Would I do it?

Hell, no. Or at least I hoped not.

"Like what you see?" Jett asked, a little hoarse.

His voice jerked me back to reality. I was furious, as much at his cockiness as at my own reaction to the mere sight of hard muscles and taut skin. I bit my lip so hard it hurt, and finally managed to avert my gaze. "I think you asked the same question a while back, and I told you my answer back then."

"Yeah, but your answer was a lie, and we both know it."

"Was it?" It was a feeble attempt at hiding the fact that he was right. The question was meant to shake his oversized ego, maybe even leave a tiny dent in it, but it only managed to summon a crooked smile to his lips.

Dammit.

I loved those lips.

He inched closer until he stood mere inches away and his breath almost caressed my face. We were so close I could smell his manly scent—a mixture of shower gel and deodorant and *him*.

It was intoxicating. I wanted to bathe in his scent and to spread it all around me. To have it inside me.

"Was it, Brooke?" he whispered.

My breath hitched in my throat. I loved it when he said my name like that. It evoked all sorts of emotions in my lower abdomen and between my legs. I swallowed hard, probably too loud, but I didn't care. All I wanted was—

"What do you want?" I asked so low I had no idea

whether he had heard me.

"What do you think?" His heated gaze scorched the front of my top. The tip of his tongue flicked over his lips, leaving a shimmering, wet trail behind. I was standing behind the closed door, my heart beating wildly as he flashed a meaningful smile, leaving no room for interpretation as to what exactly he wanted.

"You can't have it."

He cocked a brow in wry amusement. "Why not?"

"Because it's not available."

"You're seeing someone?" His tone became frosty but he didn't pull back from me. "Even if you are, I'm not afraid of competition. I'll make you forget him in a heartbeat."

I smiled at his cockiness. Boy, was he confident. One day I'd recover my own feistiness and verbally punch a hole in that unhealthy confidence of his...just not this minute because right now I couldn't think straight.

"Want me to make you forget him, Brooke?" Jett whispered, leaning closer. I barely had time to breathe before his lips lowered onto mine. He kissed me with such ferocity I felt I had never been wanted so much in my life. His tongue swirled in and out of my mouth in the sweetest and most delicious dance, and I melted into his embrace. My fingers clutched at his arms as my head began to spin and my legs threatened to give way beneath me. He pushed his hips into my abdomen and I groaned into his mouth. Beneath his expensive underwear he was hard. If only a mere kiss from me did this to him, I wondered what my touch could achieve. Slowly I reached up and ran my fingers through his dark hair and down his strong chest, touching every inch of soft skin. His chest hair was dense but soft, manly. I laced my fingers in it and pulled gently until his hips rocked into my belly, rubbing gently. My groan was swallowed up by his exploring mouth.

One minute we were kissing, the next it was over with absolutely no transition. His arms dropped me so quickly I lost my balance and almost landed flat on my ass. My eyes fluttered open and I looked up at Jett's cool expression.

"What's wrong?" I croaked confused, my mind fighting its way back to reality. Telltale dampness had gathered in my panties. I crossed my legs and pressed my thighs together to hide the shameful result of my lust.

Jett's lips were still moist from our heated kiss, and his eyes shimmered with need. Apart from that, he seemed unnaturally collected, unfazed by what happened between us.

Well done, Brooke, one day in the job and already you're trying to jump the boss's bones.

I hadn't started it, but I sure did nothing to stop it.

Flames of shame burned my cheeks and wandered down my neck. I moistened my lips and looked away. "I'm sorry.

I—"

"Don't be," Jett cut me off.

I shook my head. "It's all my fault. I probably gave you the wrong impression, which wasn't my intention. My boyfriend and I just broke up and I—"

Jett's thumb moved beneath my chin and he pressed gently, forcing me to face him. His expression was dark, menacing even, and his face was a mask of controlled irritation. Whatever I did or said didn't seem to please him, so I clamped my mouth shut before I managed to humiliate myself even more.

"We need to sort this out before it gets out of control," he said matter-of-factly. He made it sound like what happened between us was nothing but an inconvenience that needed immediate dealing with.

"Don't worry, it won't happen again."

"It will, Brooke. The moment I met you, I knew you wanted me as much as I wanted you. Don't even pretend it's not true." His gaze settled on my open lips. For a moment I thought he'd kiss me again…until he let go and turned his back on me. "Wait for me in the living room. I'll be with you shortly." His tone was hard and left no room for discussion. I regarded his strong back and shoulders. His muscles were tense beneath his smooth, taut skin. A tiny drop of sweat rolled down his spine and gathered at the waistband of his pants. Whatever issues he had, he wasn't as unperturbed as I thought.

"Yes, sir," I said with a smile as I walked out of his bedroom holding my head high, quite pleased with myself. Whatever strange reaction Jett Mayfield could evoke in me with nothing but a handshake, he wasn't immune to me either. The realization excited me. It made the trouble I knew I was getting myself into almost worth it.

10

"SO," JETT SAID, pushing a sheet of paper across the couch table toward me. He was fully dressed now in black slacks and a pale blue shirt that emphasized his broad shoulders. Unfortunately, his fully clothed status did nothing to diminish his sex appeal.

I narrowed my gaze as I tried to scan the paper without looking too obvious. He pressed his palm on top of it, obscuring my vision. "It's sort of a CSACA."

I peered up at him. "A what?"

"I don't fuck my staff, Brooke. I know better than that." He drew a sharp breath and held it for a moment before he let it out slowly and shook his head, as though irritated with whatever he was about to say. "And yet here I am, almost taking you on that bedroom floor. Apparently there's something about you that makes me want to rip off your clothes, and I know you feel the same way about me. If we're to work together, we need to sort this out once and for all."

Boy, was I cheap. What gave me away? My wet panties, or the labored breathing every time he so much as gazed at me? I heaved a silent sigh. Had my attraction to him been so obvious? And more importantly, was I really so delusional to think I could hide it?

Yeah, I was.

"I'm not really sure where this is going," I said more to myself than to him.

"By agreeing to an arrangement, there'll never be a misunderstanding as to what's happening between us and where we're standing." His gaze plunged into me with an intensity that frightened me. I just stared at him, lost in his eyes. The guy was not only stunning, he also seemed to know what he was talking about. You can't keep your head screwed on while lusting after the boss. And we both needed a clear head if we wanted to get this job done.

"I agree. What sort of arrangement do you propose? Working in different rooms? Communicating via email and text messages?"

"Not quite, Brooke." His lips curled into a wicked smile. "Since we're adults and this goes way beyond the usual sexual attraction, it's about time we gave each other what we so desperately crave."

My jaw dropped and my cheeks flamed up. Was it the kind of proposition I thought it was? He couldn't be serious, and yet I knew from his no-nonsense expression that he was. "Pardon me?" He must have noticed my shocked expression because he remained silent for a moment, giving me time to process his words. I released a hissing breath I didn't know I had been holding. While my brain was still protesting, my abdomen did tiny somersaults at the prospect of getting down and dirty with the guy. What would be the harm in following Sylvie's advice and giving in to my own needs for once? I was single and had nothing to lose.

Apart from your job and heart.

No, my heart wouldn't be in it. Just sex. And lots of it, or as much as it'd take to get bored and move on.

"Why did you hire me?" The question burning in my mind for the last forty-eight hours finally snaked its way out of my throat.

"It's not what you're thinking, Brooke," Jett said calmly. "James wants out of the business. For weeks he and I had been talking about signing Sunrise Properties over to our company. The contract we drafted included a clause that I take a look at what James called the 'brightest star' in the real estate business. He arranged a meeting at The Black Rose so we could discuss a position best suited to your qualifications and goals."

I leaned back, surprised. My boss went behind my back and got me an unofficial interview to not only help me keep my job, but get a promotion. I felt a strong and overwhelming gratitude toward him and made a mental note to send him a thank-you gift basket as soon as possible.

"He asked me to talk about the company's portfolio and pitch ideas for a future collaboration." It only now occurred to me just how unlikely and far-fetched it all sounded. Mayfield Properties was huge, with the kind of contracts James could only dream about. No company owner would send an employee to meet with a Fortune 100 company director and risk messing up the chance of a lifetime.

Jett nodded. "Only I arrived late, which made you angry, and you stormed out on me." He smiled at whatever memory crossed his mind. Actually, that wasn't the whole truth. I stormed out on him because he was irresistibly sexy and touched me in a way that made me feel all sorts of emotions I didn't want to feel.

I interlaced my fingers in my lap, mortified. Yep, I had behaved like a real bitch in front of my future employer. Why he still took me on board was beyond me. Oh wait, we sort of had sex after that; so there was my answer.

"Did you employ me because we spent the night together?" I blurted out.

Amusement glittered in his eyes, but he shook his head

slowly. "No, I hired you because you were brutally honest, just like now. You weren't prepared to suck up and take crap from anyone. That trait's hard to find. Besides, you came highly recommended. Sunrise Properties might not play in the big league, but James managed to survive years of recession and sell out big, which can only mean one thing: he knows how to pick his employees."

I bit my lip as I thought back to my former job. Not only had James decided to sell the company, he also made sure his employees wouldn't face unemployment. I made a mental note to send him a big fat thank-you card, together with a huge bottle of his favorite champagne. I figured I owed him that much.

"Thank you for listening to him." Let's face it, there was nothing on my resume that could possibly impress Jett Mayfield. That he took a chance on me based on my boss's recommendation showed me that maybe Jett wasn't the cold-hearted business shark I made him out to be. His company was overly successful and didn't have the best reputation in the States, but his employees—or what I had seen of them so far—seemed to like working for him. I flashed him a hesitant smile. His beautiful lips curled into the most stunning grin I had ever seen. My chest tightened, and a warm feeling rushed through me.

He leaned forward and brushed his thumb against my lower lip as he whispered, "I hired you for your attitude, and so far I'm pretty happy with my decision. But I'm not sure I can work with you until I've fucked this attraction out of my system."

I swallowed the lump in my throat. Seeing him with his shirt off, dressed only in his underwear, I wasn't so sure I could work with him until he had been inside of me. Every part of me wanted and demanded him, requested that his mouth kiss me and his fingers touch my body to ease the throbbing need inside of me.

I peered into his heated green eyes. The passion I saw in them burned through me like a wildfire. Holy shit, he meant every word of it, which scared the crap out of me because I knew he wanted me just as much as I wanted him. Somewhere at the back of my mind it occurred to me every lawyer would have a feast filing for sexual harassment. But, hell, he could harass me all he wanted.

Get a grip, Stewart. Switch your mind on for a change.

Every rulebook argues against getting involved with a coworker, and particularly against enjoying a fling with the boss because it tends to backfire. I thought back to Sylvie and how she got herself unemployed. What would keep Jett from firing me once we were done?

"So you're telling me you'll sack me unless I have sex with you."

He cringed, hesitating. "That wasn't what I meant, Brooke. I wouldn't sack you, but we both would have a hard time doing our job."

I cleared my throat to get rid of my fear of making a wrong decision. For some reason I believed he wouldn't sack me, but there were a million other reasons why getting involved wasn't advisable. What if he was married? I wasn't a home wrecker. "I'm not sure sex is such a good idea."

His brows shot up. "Why not?"

"Because—" I brushed my hair out of my face as I considered my words. In the end I decided to be frank. "You could be married."

"I'm not."

"Oh." My heart did a somersault. I could barely keep myself from smiling like an idiot.

"No girlfriend either," Jett whispered, staring at me with those green, sinful eyes that made me want to peel off his clothes to see what sin tasted like. "Look, Brooke. After we work this out of our system, we'll both be able to focus on the goals of this company without any distractions."

He made it sound like a business plan, clear and straightforward. It wasn't the most romantic agreement, but it was the most reasonable move given the circumstances.

"So, what are you saying?" I said, my voice hoarse. "Just sex? No feelings involved? No expectations?"

"No strings attached." Staring at me, he reached out his hand. "You can end it any time. No hard feelings when it's over. I suggest you first take a look at the details. If everything's to your liking, sign it."

"You won't sack me once it's over?"

He shook his head and pointed to the paper. "You have my promise. Everything's specified in there, including that your job's secure."

I hesitated, thinking back to Sylvie's advise to start taking risks and finally have some fun. Jett wanted me, I wanted him. No harm in having a little fun on the side.

His glorious lips curled up into a wicked grin, turning him from hot to downright perfect like a sex god, and in that instant I made up my mind.

"Okay." With a deep breath, I placed my hand into his and let his warm fingers caress my skin. My heart fluttered all the way down from my chest into parts I never knew could pulsate like this. It was beyond unsettling and…hot.

"Great. Why don't you take the rest of the afternoon off to look through the CSACA? I doubt we'd get much work done anyway." A soft smile lit up his eyes as he leaned forward and placed a gentle kiss on my cheek, then turned away and left for his office, leaving me alone to face an array of emotions.

What are you doing?

My stomach was in nervous knots as I raced down the stairs to my office and closed the door behind me. Pressing my back against the cold wall, I peered at the neat stack of folders on my desk. I should be doing my job, but all I could think of was Jett and the many ways I would love to get intimate with him. A no strings arrangement might just be what we both needed, what would make us both happy in more than one way.

11

I HAD NEVER heard of or seen a Consensual Sexual Acts and Confidentiality Agreement (CSACA) in my life, but a quick *Google* search told me they were pretty standard in the business and celebrity world. Apparently people didn't like the outside world to know what they were doing behind closed doors, and I couldn't blame them. When the media's following your every move, who'd want a bitter ex spilling the beans about your kinky sexual fantasies?

Compared to the information I gathered on Google, the two-page CSACA in my hand looked pretty standard. Sitting on my bed with my laptop balanced on my thighs, I skimmed the text briefly as I compared the points.

CONSENSUAL SEXUAL ACTS AND
CONFIDENTIALITY AGREEMENT

We, Mr. Jett Mayfield and Miss Brooke Stewart, from henceforth known as Parties, hereby declare under penalty of perjury that we are over 18 years old and enter into this contract fully aware of its nature and undertake to abide by its conditions. The Parties wish to summarize their understandings in this agreement as follows:

1. Both parties declare that this agreement is of their own free will and that neither they nor anyone mentally, physically or emotionally close to them has been threatened with bodily or mental harm.

2. Both parties agree not to disclose any information considered confidential, including the whole or any portion of this agreement and any details related to the sexual activities, to any Party not associated with this agreement without the express written consent of the other party.

3. Both Parties agree to keep the nature of this relationship monogamous. If one Party gets romantically or physically involved with a Party outside of this agreement, the contract is to be terminated with immediate effect.

4. It is the duty of both Parties to inform the other Party of any suspected or known sexually transmitted diseases and infections prior to commencing this agreement.

5. Both parties are forbidden from using mood altering substances including but not limited to medication, drugs, and sexual mood enhancers prior and during sexual congress without explicit agreement by the other Party.

6. Both Parties are forbidden from using any recording devices before, during, and after acquaintance and subsequent sexual congress, without express written consent and agreement by the other Party.

7. Both Parties agree not to seek financial gain, notoriety or advancement in career in any form as a result of this relationship.

This Contract constitutes the entire Agreement between the parties. No modification or Amendment to this Agreement shall be effective until set forth in writing, executed by the parties and attached as an amendment hereto. Breach of Contract or a failure by one party to uphold their part of the deal will result in immediate termination. In the case of breach of any sections by either Party the offended Party may seek all remedies available at law or in equity. This section shall survive termination of this agreement and remain in effect for a period of 1 year from termination of this Agreement.

By signing below, I/we acknowledge that I/we have received, read, and understood the terms and conditions outlined, and agree to abide by the above.

Slowly, I scanned the rest of the contract until I found the clause stating I couldn't be fired from my job as long as I abided by the rules and did my job as stated in my work contract. I placed the paper on the bed and shut down my laptop. My mind raced a million miles an hour, circling around one single thought: sex. Hot sizzling, steamy, mind blowing sex. And all the great things that came with it: touching his skin, kissing his lips, wrapping my legs around his hips, and taking it all.

Jett made no secret of the fact he wanted nothing but a sexual relationship. Since my relationship with Sean had just ended and I wasn't the kind to jump head on into dating, Jett's proposition didn't offend me. In fact, the idea of no emotional involvement seemed quite intriguing. Men had meaningless sex all the time and they seemed happier for it. They didn't have their hearts broken and their plans for the future shattered. Lots of women were content with just the carnal side of a relationship. For once, I wanted a piece of that carefree living, of having my needs fulfilled without any sort of emotional involvement. It was just a bit of safe fun and nothing else. No harm in giving it a try because I knew right from the beginning what I was getting myself into.

I chewed my lip as I kept going back and forth between my arguments. Jett was my boss, meaning there was a bit of a conflict there. Could I accept him as my superior during working hours and get down and dirty with him at night? The thought sent a delicious shiver down my spine. It was a challenge that was hard to resist.

Get your mind out of the gutter, Stewart.

Sylvie's relationship with her boss turned sour, but this was different. First, Jett wasn't married. Second, we had a contract, so there would never be any sort of confusion. And last, Sylvie had assumed she was having a romantic relationship and that Ryan loved her. Jett and I had nothing but a sexual arrangement that was tailored to our needs and suited the both of us.

The pro points began to dominate, or maybe it was the way I subconsciously wanted to progress. Somehow I knew I'd accept Jett's offer before I admitted it to myself.

The screen of my smartphone lit up with a text message from Sylvie. I skimmed its contents about an important looking letter that had arrived on the day of my departure. Deciding it wasn't important, I made a mental note to call her later. My stomach grumbled, and I realized not only had

I wasted my afternoon obsessing over a decision that had been made the moment Jett entered The Black Rose, but I had also skipped lunch.

Night was slowly falling, and a million stars dotted the black skyline. The air had noticeably cooled down, making me shiver in my thin shirt and skirt. I changed into a pair of blue jeans and a red snugly pullover, and made my way downstairs to find something to eat.

***

The scent of pasta, fresh pesto, and seafood hit my nostrils the moment I descended the stairs and turned right, following the narrow hall to the kitchen. Was Jett cooking? Hardly likely. I had yet to meet a man who could do more than warm up macaroni and cheese. He probably had a chef at his beck and call, and good for him. And me, because I was famished.

Through the open door I heard the clanking sound of pots and pans being hazardously moved around. Whoever was cooking had a hard time not breaking anything in the process. I gently knocked on the door, then pushed it open and froze to the spot as I took in the picture before me. Jett, dressed in blue jeans and a white tee, was standing in the middle of a cream-colored state of the art kitchen that looked like it cost more than I had made at Sunrise

Properties in a year. The place was a mess—with dirty pots piling up in the sink, dishes, chopping boards, kitchen utensils, and flour littering the work surfaces.

"Hey." He barely looked up as he dove his fingers into a pot of hot water and fished out a thin green Fettuccine band and popped it into his mouth. I stared at him as he chewed slowly, his brows furrowed as though he couldn't decide whether the pasta was boiled to perfection or needed another minute. In the end he nodded, satisfied, and emptied the pot into a stainless steel colander.

"Need help?" I inched forward, then stopped in mid-stride, my breath catching in my throat as he turned to me with a dazzling smile that made me want to throw myself into his arms and beg him to do whatever he wanted to do to me. Moistening my lips, I took a step back but didn't avert my gaze. His feet were bare; his blue jeans hung low on his hips. His hair was damp from the heat, and the muscles of his torso were clearly visible beneath the white snug cotton of his tee. But what drew my immediate attention was the tattoo covering his upper left arm. I hadn't noticed it the morning I woke up with him in my room, maybe because his left side had been turned away from me and there were so many other things that had captured my attention, like his barely covered modesty.

I inched closer to peer at it, but didn't dare touch him. The solid black curves ended in points and interlocked in a complex pattern that looked like your usual tribal tattoo, only there was something about it that seemed odd. Right in the middle of it, the swirls combined to resemble a face surrounded by tiny leaves. For some reason it seemed strange that Jett had a tattoo. Judging from his business reputation and the fact that he had no problem signing a sex contract, I figured him as your usual I-don't-love-just-fuck type, but the tattoo made it seem as though he had a past people didn't know about. I wondered whether his confidence was the result of once being a bad boy. Maybe his assertiveness wasn't just cockiness. Maybe he dared take what he wanted because his past had taught him he could.

"Brooke?"

Jett's voice jolted me out of my thoughts. I peered up into his deep eyes the color of green marble, only now realizing he had been speaking to me.

"Sorry, what?"

"I asked whether you liked seafood."

"Seafood's great, thanks."

Something shimmered in his gaze. He regarded me in silence for a moment, his expression indecipherable. And then his mysterious mood shifted, and a lazy smile lit up his face. "I gave the chef the evening off."

"Why?" I leaned against the counter and watched him decorate the plates by pouring a thin layer of cream sauce onto the white china and then drawing thin, concentric circles with a teaspoon.

"Why not?" He shrugged, as though no further explanation was necessary. "We're in Italy."

"Ah." I nodded. "It smells amazing."

Jett finished his concoction while I decked the table and steered the conversation toward the history of the house, which was the safest topic I could think of. Eventually Jett ordered me to sit down as he opened a bottle of white wine and poured two glasses, handing me one.

"Here's to a new business venture." Jett raised his glass to mine, and we chinked.

"And to a new job." I took a sip. Although I couldn't usually tell the difference between one wine brand and the other, even my inconsequential taste buds picked up a hint of gooseberry and apple. "This is good." I took a generous sip and forced myself to put down the glass before I ended up drunk and generous, like the last time I mixed alcohol with Jett.

"It's a *Fumé Blanc*," Jett said. "My favorite with fish. Dive right in."

He gestured at the plate before me. I plunged my fork into the fish trimmings, tiny shrimps, scallops, and clams atop a pasta nest, and rolled a few bands with the help of my spoon, then pushed them into my mouth, chewing slowly. The aroma of fresh pesto spreading over my tongue almost made me moan with pleasure.

"It's delicious," I said, licking my lips.

Jett's eyes wandered to my mouth and his gaze turned a shade darker. Self-consciously, I wiped my fingers across my lips, and then put my fork down, my appetite slowly dissipating at the lust in his eyes.

"Do you have any idea how hungry I am, Brooke?" he said so low I had difficulties hearing him. He wasn't talking about the food and we both knew it. I swallowed hard and took a gulp of wine to moisten my dry mouth. It didn't help.

"I—"

Holy cow, the guy knew how to turn up the heat. My whole body was on fire, and he hadn't even touched me yet. Well, not physically. His eyes were doing all the work. I should be playing hard to get. But for once in my life I didn't want to. I was in a different country, stuck in a beautiful villa with a bottle of wine and a hot guy who knew how to make a woman feel special. Sylvie always said a bit of danger never hurt anyone. Well, why not have it all? Life's too short and I had nothing to lose anyway.

Jett's gaze moved down my neck to my chest, then back up again, lingering on my mouth.

"More wine?" he asked hoarsely. At my nod, he stood to refill our glasses. His fingers touched my hand, sending delicious electric impulses down my spine. I gasped and bit my lip to stifle the sudden need pooling between my legs.

In one swift motion Jett captured my face in his hands and pressed his mouth against mine. His lips melted into mine, and then his tongue slipped inside my mouth, pushing, probing, circling my tongue in a slow and erotic dance. Fire spread through my body and gathered in my abdomen, waiting to erupt like a volcano. I pressed my thighs together to intensify the aching sensation that could take me over the edge.

"Brooke," Jett moaned into my mouth. The tone of his deep voice with the slightest hint of a sexy Southern accent vibrated inside of me, tugging at the right cords. His palm moved to my neck as our tongues entangled one more time before he let go. Leaving us both breathing heavy, he returned to his seat, his eyes fogged over with lust.

Don't stop.

If there wasn't a table between us, I would have clung to him, begging him to finish what he started. But there was the table. And reality.

Thank goodness for reality.

It kicked in pretty hard and fast. Drawing a long breath, I folded my shaky hands in my lap and gazed up at him. His burning eyes were shaded by long lashes that brushed his tan skin as he closed them for a second.

"We should eat. Dinner's getting cold." As though to demonstrate his point, he retrieved his fork. I watched him take a bite, and then wash it all down with half a glass of wine. "Aren't you eating?" he asked, not looking at me. His voice seemed slightly detached, as though he didn't know how to deal with the situation, which was strange coming from someone who had presented me with a no strings sex agreement.

I wasn't hungry, at least not for food, and yet I nodded. It was rude to leave the food untouched when he had made the effort to prepare it.

Taking a bite I forced myself to chew slowly. "Where did you learn to cook like this?"

"You mean where did I learn to prepare more than the contents of a can?" He looked up with a strange glint in his eyes. "Let's just say I wasn't always who I am now."

"You weren't always rich?" The question slipped past my lips before I could hold it back. Luckily, my directness didn't seem to irritate him.

"No, I wasn't."

Thinking he'd elaborate I waited a few seconds, but he remained silent. His reticence didn't come as a surprise. There were only two types of guys: the ones who talked about their childhood to get sympathy and cheat their way into a woman's panties, and the ones who bottled up because talking about the past, be it good or bad, required them to open up more than they wanted. While Jett didn't look uncomfortable, he definitely belonged in the second category.

I thought back to everything I knew about Mayfield Realties. The company had been a major player in the real estate market for over fifty years, with a profit margin of several hundred million. Jett's family had been rich long before he was even born, so his statement made no sense to me. But I knew enough about men not to press the issue. For one, it wasn't really my place as Jett's employee. And then there was also the fact that most men find questions prying. We hadn't yet reached that particular level of intimacy that sanctions curiosity.

"Did you take a look at the contract?" Jett asked.

Oh, boy.

Heat immediately rushed to my cheeks. I put my fork down and drained my wine glass. He hurried to refill it. "As a matter of fact, I did."

"And what do you think?" His voice was nonchalant and his expression non-descript. If he felt the least bit embarrassed talking about a sex contract, he showed no signs of it.

Damn him and his overinflated confidence. I bet he got at least a dozen women to sign contracts like this. The thought sent a bolt of jealousy straight to my heart, which should have made me reconsider my decision. Yet it didn't. I wanted this just as badly as he did, maybe even more.

"It looks well-drafted. You put much thought into it." I gritted my teeth at my own words. Yep, he put much thought into it the first time around with the first woman he wanted. Now it had probably become nothing but standard procedure.

"Actually, my lawyers did all the work." He crossed his arms over his chest and leaned back in his chair with a devilish grin. "Will you sign?"

I laughed. No pressure there. "I don't usually sleep with my boss."

"I know. James is gay."

"That's not what—"

"Brooke," he cut me off. "I'll have to be honest. When I first saw you, I felt an instant attraction. I told you I wanted you and still do, more than ever.... but I can't make mistakes. Not in my position."

He was rich and successful, and that's what rich and successful people do to protect themselves. "No need to explain." I moistened my lips nervously, unable to peel my gaze off him as he continued.

"You can't deny the attraction. And," he paused briefly, as though to prepare his words, "I think we're fooling ourselves in thinking we'll be able to get over it. There's no way this constant sexual tension won't make working together hard, if not impossible."

His eyes searched mine as his fingers slid over the table to caress my cheek. "I want to get to know you. You can stop any time; get out any time you want. I just don't want things to be awkward between us just because we have those needs."

He was right. Once more, I was reminded of the fact that desire would probably render us unable to work together. I was a grown woman with needs, living in a sexually liberated world. Guys do it all the time, so why not women too? Where's the equality in that? Sylvie liked to mention the same argument whenever she engaged in sexual activity outside of a relationship.

I was all for equality. I just had values. Was that so wrong? Maybe it was time to push my old-fashioned values aside.

Jett stood and pulled me up, wrapping his arms around my waist. We were so close his hot breath lingered an inch away from my mouth, singing my skin. "What are you afraid of?" he whispered.

You. This.

The fact that I had never felt this much lust for anyone in my entire life. Sure I got horny like everyone else, but the want currently consuming me wasn't natural. It was sinful, naughty, *scary*.

"Let me show you what real sex is like," Jett whispered, tucking a stray strand of hair behind my ear. "Let me make you come like you've never come before."

Oh, god.

I opened my mouth to speak and in my head there was

this long list of points that needed negotiation. My imaginary speech was elaborate and articulate, yet the only word that made it out was a simple and choked, "Yes."

12

I DON'T KNOW how I made it through the 'talk' without fainting from sheer mortification and growing arousal, as Jett started negotiating the things he wanted to do to me and some of which he expected in return. The expectations were pretty sketchy because, to put it in his own words, he left them to my imagination which, to be honest, was already running wild. I had never met someone who could talk about sex so openly and in such a controlled yet sexy manner. Maybe it was his deep, rumbling voice, or the details he seemed so happy to discuss, but by the time we finished the 'talk' I was so turned on, I couldn't wait to get started.

In the end I picked up the contract on my way back from the restroom, and we talked some more until we decided to give it a two-month trial run, see how it went, and take it from there. By the time we had eaten our dessert, a delicious tiramisu Jett said was bought at a pannetteria, we had also finished the wine bottle and had drunk our way through half of the second. The kitchen was spinning, the cabinets had become a big white blur, and my glass seemed to be constantly empty while his never seemed to empty at all.

"I think I'm drunk." I giggled as I tried to stand and miserably failed, falling back into my chair. How much time had passed? It seemed as though we had been talking for hours.

Jett smiled, though I couldn't really tell with all the spinning. It might have just as well been a smirk. "You're not much of a drinker, huh?"

I tried to shake my head, signaling that I wasn't indeed, but the motion didn't bode well with my stomach.

"I think I'm going to be sick," I said, shame burning through me. I didn't mean to drink the whole bottle. It must have been my nerves.

Seriously, Steward, how can you get that drunk in front of your boss...twice?

Maybe it was that seafood. It was a bit salty and made me thirsty, but that I wouldn't tell him. He was the first man who cooked for me. He deserved my respect and praise.

"Let's get you some fresh air," Jett said. His arms

traveled around my waist to steady me as he guided me through the hall and out onto the balcony.

The night sky was pitch black with a million stars sparkling like tiny diamonds. He sat onto a recliner and pulled me onto his lap. My ass settled against his crotch and I instantly froze. The drunken bubble around me lifted, maybe from the cold air that rustled the leaves and stirred the water shimmering in the moonlight. Or maybe it was his hot and heavy breath on my neck that made me realize this was it. We had signed the contract and now he wanted to seal it.

Jett's hand moved up my abdomen but instead of the fondling I expected, he wrapped his arms around me and pulled me back against his chest until his heat seeped into my clothes, warming me up.

"Feeling better?" he whispered.

I nodded.

"Then relax."

His words were a sharp command, which I didn't dare ignore. Taking a mouthful of fresh air, I ordered my muscles to relax and my mind to clear.

"When I fuck you I want you to remember each and every kiss, every moan, every scream, every sensation about the way I feel inside of you," Jett whispered. His arms tightened around me as he moved his crotch against my jeans. The coarse material rubbed through my wet panties against my swollen folds, making me ache with desire. My heartbeat accelerated and the tender buds of my breasts tightened.

Leaning into him, I trailed my fingertips up his shirt and brushed my lips against his. His mouth tasted of wine and *him*. The cloud in my head lifted as my pulse spiked with desire.

"Obviously you're intoxicated, Brooke, and I'm not going to risk you not remembering half of what we'd be doing," Jett continued. "I'm not going to take you tonight. You're safe...for now."

His deep, dark voice sent a pulsating sensation between my legs, and in that instant I regretted drinking so much.

13

"THE LUCAZZONE FILES," Jett said, tossing a thick blue file on top of my desk. The sound travelled all the way from my ears into my brain, causing a few neuron fibers to fire up pain in the process.

And dammit, did he have to shout like that? Or look so damn yummy when all I wanted was to roll into a ball to die?

I shot him a desperate glance. "I'll have a look at it." As soon as I can keep my eyes open without flinching from the glaring light flooding in through the high bay window.

"I need you to familiarize yourself with it, but don't take too long." Jett's brows burrowed into the sexiest frown I had ever seen. "The owner's health is deteriorating. We want his estate before—" He trailed off, leaving the rest to my imagination.

I knew what he was about to say.

Before the old man kicked the bucket.

"Have you made an offer yet?"

"Only about twenty in the past ten years." Jett's expression darkened. I sensed a hint of the wrong kind of determination and couldn't shake off the feeling Mayfield Realties's reputation was well earned. The Lucazzone estate was their latest acquisition-to-be, and I was about to be dragged into Mayfield's strange work ethics, which apparently included not giving up on a project even if that meant trying to change the opinion of an old man who clearly didn't want to sell.

"Ten years, huh?" I bit my lip, forcing myself to keep my mouth shut, and managed to do so for all of three seconds. "Maybe he loves that house and doesn't want to part with it." My gaze traveled up to meet Jett's gaze tentatively. He measured me up and down, probably considering whether to tell me off for expressing my opinion when I was a mere employee.

Eventually he just sighed and inched closer. His fingers clutched my chin and forced my head up as his dark eyes descended into my soul. "Look, Brooke, I appreciate your input, but this isn't Sunrise Properties, and I don't really have a choice. The board members want that estate, and I'm the one who has to make it happen. It's either getting the old man to sign, or be kicked out of my own company."

His lips trailed down the left side of my face to my ear. "You smell good," he whispered, his hot breath grazing my skin.

An involuntary shiver of pleasure traveled all the way down into my panties. I held my breath, but a low moan escaped my throat nonetheless, betraying my unsolicited state of arousal. Jett peeled his lips off my earlobe and put a few inches between us, grinning. "I have to make some calls. Catch you later?"

Holy mother of hell, he had noticed. What gave me away this time?

"Yeah, sure," I grumbled, and looked away—mortified.

"You know I'd help you out if I weren't too busy. You could ask me to stay and I might be able to squeeze you into my tight schedule." Jett trailed a finger down the nape of my neck, circling the spot where the tip of my ponytail touched my naked skin. His touch was so tender, yet sensual, it sent another jolt through me.

I wanted him. Badly. But right now I also wanted him to go away so I could gather some self-control to do my work and stop being so unbelievably horny. This whole thing, whatever it was that just made me feel so attracted to him, had to be reined in because it was taking up all space in my head.

"I'll get the file back to you ASAP." My tone ended up harsher than intended. His finger flinched away from me and he put a few inches between us. I ignored the sudden urge to reach for his hand and tell him that I didn't mean to be so abrupt.

"I'll be upstairs in my private office. Second door to the right." He barely looked at me as he turned around and left, closing the door behind him.

I breathed out, relieved, and yet not quite able to feel at ease. I doubted I'd ever feel relaxed with Jett in the same room, or with him in the same house. The guy was a mystery. One moment he picked up a drunken woman from a bar and ended up naked in her bed; the next he claimed he didn't take advantage of women under the influence of alcohol. For some reason I had believed him last night when we were sitting outside on the balcony, right before he helped me get into bed, barely touching me in the process. Either he was inventing and changing his own rules as we moved along, or he was playing some sordid game pursuing the incentive of—

What incentive would that be, Brooke?

I had signed the contract and was willing to sleep with him. What else could he possibly want?

Groaning, I shook my head at my own thoughts. It had always been like this. Whenever a guy I liked showed the slightest bit of interest in me, I couldn't take it at face value, and my brain concocted some morbid story about everything else he might want from me: attention, getting over an ex, easily available sex. Never just me. I thought they couldn't possibly want me for who I was. In the end I always ran, and ended up with someone like Sean, an emotionally unavailable narcissist who'd dump everything and anyone as soon as he saw a benefit elsewhere.

At least Jett was honest and didn't pretend to have feelings that weren't there. What was wrong with me? Why couldn't I stop looking behind a guy's intentions and just enjoy his attention? Was it because I still couldn't trust a guy after all that happened in the past?

Opening the Lucazzone file, I gulped down a glass of water to get rid of the dry sensation in my mouth, and focused on the task at hand. Alessandro Lucazzone, the current owner, was one of the most well-known and respected men in the area. He inherited the Lucazzone estate, including hundreds of miles of vineyards, forests, and fields, from his father who in turn inherited it from his father, and so forth. The estate had been handed down from generation to generation for centuries, withstanding revolutions and recessions. The Lucazzone family hadn't always been rich. A few times they lost most of their money in bad investments and gambling, but they always bounced back from their financial hardships, usually by marrying a rich spouse. Alessandro Lucazzone had managed to keep the estate in order and the vineyards thriving through World War II with the help of his wife's money. He and

Maria had no children, and when she died of cancer he never remarried. At ninety-seven the old man was dying, leaving no apparent heirs behind. According to Jett's research, the estate would fall into the hands of local charities, and I couldn't help but feel they deserved the money. They could certainly put the grounds to better use than Mayfield Properties. Besides, it felt wrong to tamper with the possibly last wish of an old man who seemed to believe in a good cause.

Taking a sip of my lukewarm coffee, I almost choked on it as I flicked the next page, finally realizing why my boss would be so interested in a remote estate in Italy where the price of acquisition and upkeep made no sense in terms of profit. My fingers slowly traced the jagged contours on the map. The west side was situated around a private lake about the size of Lake Geneva, with mountain views surrounded by untouched nature. Combine that with the sunny Mediterranean weather, a clean beach, and lots of privacy— and you had prime real estate ready to cater to the rich and famous.

I pulled out the architectural plan and shook my head in disbelief. Mayfield Properties was planning to build ten homes: each a five-room, three-bath, mansion-like holiday home, with ground to ceiling glass windows overlooking the shoreline and mountains in the distance. Each property would boast a large tiled hallway, a lounge, dining room, study, several bedrooms with walk-in closets, and bright open-plan kitchen and living areas. They would have a private garage, a swimming pool, a security system worthy of the White House, and a level of privacy ensured by high gates to protect the owners from prying eyes. Basically, they were about to rebuild the Hollywood Hills amidst the Italian countryside. Another oasis for the rich and famous. Given that the Italian government wasn't known for their cooperation, it was an ambitious project. However, a multi-million dollar corporation like Mayfield Properties always finds a way. No doubt about that.

I tossed the sheet aside, disgusted with the company's plans to destroy parts of the Italian countryside. Disgusted I had to help them make it happen. This was the reason why I had been more or less happy working for James. He wasn't hell-bent on finding and annihilating the last spots of untouched nature on Earth to build a few houses for people who already owned more than they needed. I wasn't your usual environmentalist, but I prided myself on recycling my garbage and not supporting the chopping down of trees and the asphalting of mountain paths by greedy corporations. And Mayfield Properties was one of them.

It was a matter of integrity vs. going against my boss's wishes and possibly losing my job in the process. If I consented and helped Mayfield acquire the Lucazonne estate, I was no better than all those money-hungry, designer suit-wearing corporations I always despised because of their work ethics. If I refused to do my job, Mayfield had no reason to keep me employed, meaning I might face unemployment within the week. What could I possibly say to prospective interviewers as to why I lost the job within a few days of commencing it?

The decision was out of my hands, but even though I knew I didn't really have much choice, I wasn't less disgusted with myself. Mayfield Properties was just a stepping stone, I reminded myself, and soon I could boast enough experience to get a job with Delaware & Ray. Taking a deep breath, I stood and smoothed over my skirt, vowing to stay true to my convictions as much as possible given the circumstances, while still doing my job.

14

HAVING LIVED IN New York for the last five years, I was no longer used to silence. Even when you were alone on a weekday afternoon, living on the sixth floor with the windows shut, some sort of sound inevitably found its way to you—like boots thumping up the stairs, a car horn beeping in the distance, or the fridge-freezer combo buzzing in the kitchen slash living room slash office. But that was the danger of living in an overcrowded, overpriced metropolis. While I loved New York with its stunning skyline and busy nightlife, I was more than happy to get away from it for a while and enjoy the solitude of the Italian countryside. So, naturally, the sudden blaring sound of my cell made my heart jerk in my chest.

I peered from the caller ID to the closed door, making sure Jett wasn't around, and pressed the respond button.

"Hey, you're harder to reach than the president. How's my favorite chief secretary?" Sylvie shouted with a slight slur. Earsplitting music, voices, and laughter echoed in the background. Judging from the noise, she was in a club, and it wasn't the kind you frequent to play bingo. I swear I could almost smell the booze on her breath and the cigarette smoke clinging to her expensive clothes—clothes she'd end up taking to the dry cleaner's and forget about them.

"Personal assistant," I mumbled, harboring no doubt that in her current state, she'd forget it the moment she hung up. I peered at the time symbol on my MacBook. It was a few minutes past ten here, minus a seven hour time difference. "Sylvie, why the hell are you calling me from a bar at three a.m.? You're obviously drunk, and I'm at the office, *working*, during which I'm sure you know you're not supposed to have private conversations."

"You never called."

It was true. With the stunning scenery outside and Jett around, I forgot to call her. Or my mother. Even Sean was history, which was great. I was moving on.

"I'm so sorry, Sylvie. I meant to, but there was lots to do. But you could have waited until tomorrow."

A pause, then, "I was lonely." Her voice raised a notch, making her statement sound like a question.

The throb in my head intensified, but Sylvie was my best

friend and she obviously needed me. My fingers began to massage my temples as I mentally prepared for a long talk. "What happened?"

"Nothing."

"Sylvie, I know your bizarre mood swings and behaviors better than the back of my hand, and right now you're lying. So, spill before I take the next flight up there, bind you to a chair, and torture you into confessing." I didn't mean it literally. It was our inside joke since college when Sylvie ended up drunk on my couch, bawling her eyes out, and wouldn't tell me what was wrong with her.

"Shit. You know me so well, I hate you renting space in my head." She let out a long sigh that turned into a whine. "I'm such a fuck up." Not really, but I didn't interrupt her lest she got sidetracked. She hardly ever talked about her problems, and when she did she barely elaborated on the real issues bothering her.

"Ryan offered me my job back," Sylvie said.

"Ryan—as in the a-hole boss who shagged you, and then broke up with you the moment he feared his wife had found out?"

"Uh-huh. That one." Sylvie didn't fall into a tirade of expletives, which could only mean one thing.

I shook my head, forgetting she couldn't see me. "No, Sylvie, you didn't listen to that idiot, did you? You might be my best friend and I love you to bits, but you're a moron."

She let out another long sigh. "I know."

"What were you thinking?"

"He sent over flowers and I thought he was serious about it, so I caved in and listened to his crap. You know I lose my head around guys and make the worst decisions ever. None of this would have happened if only you were here." Now it was all my fault. I rolled my eyes. "You're so lucky your boss plays for the other team," Sylvie continued.

My former boss, I mentally corrected her. The current one was far from it. This was my cue to assure her I was the even bigger fuck up but a.) the contract clearly stated I wasn't supposed to tell anyone about my arrangement with Mayfield, and b.) I seriously doubted Sylvie would be shocked. In fact, she'd probably cheer me on and expect a sex tape after I was done with Mayfield.

"So, what exactly happened?" I asked. "Because if you believed one word that lying, cheating bastard told you, I swear I'm cancelling our friendship this instant."

"I told him to stick it where the sun don't shine." She hesitated, adding something that sounded suspiciously like, "After."

"After what?"

"After I told him that I'd rather be celibate than sleep with him ever again. I think you're rubbing off on me." Her voice trembled slightly. Had she been crying?

So why the tears? Unless they were tears of joy, in which

case I made a mental note to drag Sylvie to the nearest bar for a round of celebratory drinks the moment I arrived back home.

"That's about when he said he was only looking for a quick shag and didn't mean a word he said. And then he dumped me, for good," Sylvie said.

Ouch. "The bastard." For once he seemed to have told the truth. Probably the only truth any woman would ever get from him. Okay, Sylvie was an easy lay, but did he have to be so hurtfully candid about it? You don't screw with a woman, her mind or otherwise, and then admit you were only using her just when she was about to develop a morsel of self-respect by backing out of your one-way, self-beneficial deal.

"It's okay. I'm over him," Sylvie said, sniffing. She wasn't. "He's already off my mind." He wasn't.

"You're beautiful, clever, young, everything he'll never be." I talked slowly and paused for effect so she'd understand just how much I meant each and every word. "Sylvie, you're amazing and deserve someone as amazing as you. Don't settle for less."

"You think so?"

I nodded. "Yeah, I do, from the bottom of my heart." Her huge smile almost shined down the phone line. "Now go to bed. I bet you're three sheets to the wind."

"I'm what?" She laughed, ignoring my jab at her

drunken state. "How's that job working out for you?"

"Good." I had completely forgotten that I was at work and not supposed to have personal conversations. I rolled in my swivel chair to peer at the door, almost expecting Jett to be standing there, eyeing me with a frown and demanding that I peel off my suit so he could spank my backside for taking the liberty to go against my work contract. The naughty thought sent an instant smile to my face. I had never been into spanking, but it sort of sounded hot—imagining him doing the deed. I opened my mouth to tell Sylvie all about the Italian countryside, but she'd already lost interest.

"Did you find out who sent the letter?" she asked.

Frowning, I tried to remember what the hell she was talking about. And then it dawned on me. The letter on the coffee table.

Freaking hell, it completely slipped my mind.

"Just open it."

"Don't think so," Sylvie said slowly. "It looks suspicious. It could be a bomb or something, and I still need my hands."

Sweetie, if it was a bomb, your hands would be the last thing to worry about.

"Okay…I'll check it out when I get back home, then."

We talked for another minute or two, mostly about her being bored to death without me. She emphasized how much she missed her best drinking buddy, by which she couldn't possibly mean me. I hardly ever managed to have more than a margarita before I was ready to hit the bed...facedown, while Sylvie partied the night away.

And then we said our goodbyes and I hung up, feeling strangely out of place in this huge-yet-beautiful house with this strange-yet-gorgeous guy. While Sylvie's stories didn't usually get to me, the Ryan episode somehow touched me because I knew Sylvie had fallen for him hard. I could never allow myself to feel the same way for Jett.

I finished my water, and then got another cup of coffee before heading for Jett's private office.

15

THE LUCAZZONE ESTATE started from just beyond Jett's huge property. I couldn't help but think that even though Jett had the most stunning scenery I had ever seen, he didn't buy his holiday home because of its view. I figured being close to the old man to follow his every move might just be the reason why he vacationed here in the first place. It was the way the big league played. They watched their market and competitors but, most importantly, they kept a hawk eye on the properties they wanted until the owners were ready to sell, and they all were eventually.

Sitting in the passenger seat of his Ferrari with the roof down and a warm breeze caressing my skin, I bit my lip hard so I wouldn't ask the question that burned a hole in my brain. Jett's motives weren't really my business, and yet I had to know. It was two days since we signed the contract and Jett hadn't made any sort of attempt to touch me. He continued to remain a mystery. I figured finding out why he bought his mansion might reveal more about his personality.

"When did you buy your house?" Moistening my lips, I focused my gaze onto the winding road so he wouldn't pick up on just how much I hoped to find out more about the real man behind his cool façade.

"A while back."

A vague answer, of course. I expected nothing less from him. Why did he have to be so equivocal about everything?

I nodded slowly. "What drew you to Italy, or this part of the country in particular?"

"The weather?" He shot me a sideways glance, and for a moment the bright sun reflected in his stunning eyes, making them shimmer in a million green facets. Dressed in blue jeans and a snug short-sleeved shirt, and with the wind blowing through his disheveled hair, he looked more magnificent than ever. His left hand was resting on the steering wheel and the right on the armrest, inches away from mine. I fought the urge to run my fingertips over the defined muscles.

"Could you possibly be more vague?" I asked.

He laughed that deep, brief laughter of his that always made my stomach flutter a little bit. "We used to vacation here a lot when I was a child. I wanted to preserve the memory by buying my own house here. Unfortunately, I don't come as often as I'd like to."

No hidden motives then. Just a rich man returning to the one place he adored as a child. I folded my hands in my lap and started to play with the hem of my shirt, not quite buying into it.

"So it wasn't because of Alessandro Lucazzone," I remarked dryly.

His head snapped in my direction, and for a moment our eyes connected. There was something in his gaze—a hint of determination, maybe even fear, I couldn't really tell—and then it disappeared and his gorgeous lips curled up into a lazy smile.

"I can see why you would think that, but I assure you it wasn't the case. We only recognized the estate's potential a few years ago. It was during my first year in college." He hesitated, as though considering whether to reveal more. I waited for him to continue, and when he didn't I wondered whether there was more to this freshman year story than he let on.

We drove in silence for a minute or two. It was a late Wednesday morning. Apart from the odd passing car, the street remained mostly deserted. Jett maneuvered expertly, barely slowing down at the sharper bends, which led me to believe he knew the way well. Either that, or he was the most reckless driver I had ever seen. Several times my heart jumped in my throat, and I clutched the armrest for support as he kept cutting corners, taking us dangerously close to the steep mountain wall rising to my right.

"You okay?" Jett asked, laughing.

"You drive like a maniac," I said through clenched teeth.

"That's not the only thing I do like a maniac, Brooke." His hand moved away from the steering wheel and settled on my thigh.

Heat flushed my cheeks. I was mortified, but not from shame or shyness. Frowning, I lifted his hand off my thigh and placed it back on the steering wheel, noticing how warm and calloused his palm was. Those bumps didn't come from sitting around in an office.

"Just keep a tight grip on that, will you?" I said dryly. "While I think Italy's beautiful, I'm not keen on having my brain splattered all over this place."

"You're the careful kind then?" His question sounded more like a statement.

I shrugged. "Not more careful than most people out there but definitely more careful than you."

The car slowed down a little but not enough. I heaved a big sigh and slumped deeper into the leather seats.

"You're not living a life in the fast lane?" Jett shot me a questioning glance. I sensed a deeper meaning in his words.

"Are you?"

His lips quirked up at the corners. "As you can see, I like

it fast and dangerous. I'll gladly teach you a thing or two about those two things, Ms. Stewart."

Whoa, when did the conversation take this particular turn? My cheeks flamed up, and I turned my head away from him so he wouldn't catch just how much his words affected me. Oh, I wanted him to teach me all right. If only he'd make his threat real. Or was that a promise?

The car slowed down and we came to an abrupt stop. I wet my lips nervously, unsure what followed next.

"Why are we stopping?"

He turned to face me. Dimples formed in his cheeks as his gaze lingered on me a tad too long, caressing my face, my breasts, my body. What the heck was he doing? And why couldn't I think with him so close?

"What?" I dared not take a breath under his electric eyes. His gaze narrowed on my lips and stayed glued to them. My blood rushed faster at the thought of him kissing me and making out in the middle of nowhere.

He leaned forward, tenderly grazing my leg, then my neck. And then his hand moved to the glove department to retrieve a pair of shades.

"Put them on," he said gently. "The sun's strong and we wouldn't want you to get a headache."

They were just words, but his gentle tone conveyed so much more. Warmth. Caring. I didn't know what to do or say. I didn't know how to protect my heart from the sudden array of emotions filling it.

"Thank you," I said eventually, slightly choked. "What about you?"

"I'll be okay." He hit the accelerator hard. "Faster's always better, but you have to mind those curves. They're wicked. They can kill a man in a heartbeat." He flashed me a grin as the car picked up in speed again, and for a moment I could swear he had been looking at my chest.

Our eyes connected in the mirror and I realized he had probably caught everything: the way my fingers seemed to want to rip a hole in my top's hem, the way my eyes kept darting toward him, eager to soak up his every move, the way my knees pressed together tightly so the scent of dampness coming from my panties wouldn't give away how much I wanted him to touch me there.

"Blushing suits you. I should make you blush more often," Jett said hoarsely.

Swallowing hard, I put on the shades to hide at least part of my burning face, even though it probably was useless. I had never been good at pretending, and it sure had gotten worse around him. I knew I should say something— anything—but my words remained trapped at the back of my throat.

"This is it," he said, taking a sharp right onto bumpy terrain. The lane was narrow with a ditch on both sides, and barely any space for oncoming traffic. The trees with rich crowns of leaves gathered into a thick canopy that filtered the warm rays of sun.

I removed Jett's shades and craned my neck to figure out where the path might be taking us. I thought for a moment, and then the penny dropped.

"This is Lucazzone's estate, isn't it?" I asked.

"Yep."

For some reason, I expected it to be majestic with a cobblestone path, trimmed hedges, maybe even a glasshouse, and hunting grounds—and definitely lots of flowers. This looked more like the forested backyard of a haunted and neglected mansion. It wasn't less beautiful, just not what I expected.

"What was your highest offer?" I asked Jett.

"Twenty million." He didn't even blink saying the number. I almost choked on my breath.

"US dollars?"

"Euro."

"Oh." That was big bucks for a bit of land and a few walls. I blinked rapidly as my brain began to do the math. Twenty million Euros divided by ten mansions equaled two million each. Given the skyrocketing lawyer costs and the paperwork involved, the labor costs to cut down the forest, prepare the building ground, and actually build the holiday homes, Mayfield Properties would have to invest another twenty million. So the actual asking price would have to be four million to break even, and even more to make a profit.

Blazing hell, who in their right mind would actually pay that?

The street widened as we reached a crossroad. Jett took another sharp right and parked the car a few feet from a sign written in Italian. I didn't understand the words, but the red outstretched palm didn't need much interpretation. This was private property and we weren't supposed to be here.

I peered at Jett who opened the door and exited, then walked around the car to help me out.

"Thanks," I whispered, grabbing his hand. The moment our fingers connected, an electric jolt ran through me. I gazed up into his moss-green eyes to catch his reaction but, like before, he didn't seem to feel it. "What are we doing here? Do we have an appointment?" It was a stupid question. No one with an appointment would park the car on a country lane and sneak up on the owner.

"I want you to see this place so you feel its magic," Jett said matter-of-factly.

"It's called trespassing."

"Lucazzone doesn't mind."

"How would you know that?" Crossing my arm over my chest, I stared at him. He flat out ignored the invitation to elaborate.

"Come on, Ms. Righteous. You're not being paid for

standing around and asking questions." He winked and turned his back on me. What other choice did I have than to follow?

***

It was so hot I felt as though my clothes were about to melt—and it wasn't just because of the heat. I let Jett guide me beyond the path, through the trees and the thick bushes. Even though Jett led the way, pushing thick branches out of the way so I could step through unscathed, for once I was happy to have opted for flats rather than my usual kitten heels. Not least because my gaze kept wandering to Jett's back and the defined muscles rippling beneath his thin shirt. Beads of sweat gathered at the nape of his dark hair, making my mouth water at the thought of making him sweat on top of me. His slacks strained with every step, emphasizing the hard muscles in his thighs. I felt like a teenager in lust who couldn't stop daydreaming about the hot football captain.

Eventually, we reached the highest point of the incline. Just beyond the trees and dense bushes stretched out a vast valley. Looking farther, I could make out the beautiful shoreline of a lake. The blue water caught the rays of the sun and shimmered in a million facets. Beyond it, on the other side of the lake, a Mediterranean-style house raised against the picturesque backdrop of a mountain, amidst yet more trees and bushes. In front of the house was what looked like a broad path leading to the lake's shore. To reach it, anyone would have to cross the lake. I scanned the area, looking for any sign of a boat, but saw none.

"Is that the Lucazzone mansion?"

"Villa," Jett corrected. "It's not that big."

"But where's the street?"

"There is none. The Lucazzone family has always been keen on privacy, so they built the house on a secluded spot and never bothered to make it accessible," Jett said.

The word 'secluded' didn't even do it justice. How did these people go grocery shopping? Did they even have electricity or Internet?

"Do they grow their own crops?"

Jett's lips twitched. "They might have a few centuries ago, but currently they have discovered the benefits of the local grocery store's home delivery service. Do you see that large oak?" He pointed beyond the lake to a thick tree with low hanging branches. I nodded and squinted to get a better glimpse, but couldn't make out more than contours in the blinding rays of the sun. "There's a boat hidden from view. It's been there for years, and once a month the old man would row the boat over the lake, meet with the waiting grocery store owner, stock up on supplies, and then return to the villa. As kids, my brother and I would be hiding up here, waiting for the old man in his black cape-like coat to appear. Usually it was in the semi-darkness of dawn. The way the boat broke through the morning mist clinging to the water surface made it look like a scene from a gothic vampire movie. For a while, my brother and I were convinced the old man was a vampire."

His eyes focused on a point beyond the horizon, and I knew he wasn't seeing the serene display of nature before our eyes, but the sweet memories of a childhood that would always live on in his mind and heart. I found myself smiling with him, seeing the past through his words, and for a moment I felt as though I was there with him, seeing the old man through the fanciful eyes of an innocent boy.

"You must have loved it up here," I said, gently squeezing his arm. His stunning eyes turned to me and a bright smile lit up his face, sending a jolt through my heart.

"We did. That was right before—" His expression darkened, wiping the gorgeous smile off his lips. Something had happened. Instead of sharing it with me, he was bottling up again. It wasn't surprising given that we barely knew each other, but I couldn't help the sudden disappointment washing over me. As strange as it sounded, I wanted to know everything about him and his life.

"Come on." Jett gripped my hand a bit rougher than before and guided me expertly down the slippery slope toward the shoreline. The flat soles of my ballerinas slipped in the soft earth, but I didn't argue in the hope he might still decide to resume our conversation and divulge what he wanted to say.

Eventually, we reached the shore and stopped a few feet from the water. Jett pulled me down next to him onto the soft ground and propped his arm behind my back, the material of his shirt almost brushing my skin. His dark hair swayed in the light breeze. I closed my eyes and leaned back on my palms, my face soaking up the sun. We sat in silence for a moment or two. I only opened my eyes when I felt his gaze on me.

Jett's eyes were hooded, filled with something dark and dangerous. His beautiful lips glistened as though he had moistened them quite recently and the moisture hadn't dried yet. I imagined the tip of his tongue brushing over them, then over every inch of my skin, meeting with mine in a tangled embrace. Would he find me intimidating if I just kissed him? Did our agreement involve only him getting close to me whenever he felt like it, or could I initiate sexual contact as well, maybe even during working hours? Such as now?

Damn sex contracts and their blurred lines! I had never played this game, so I had yet to figure out the fine print. Smiling shyly, I ignored the sudden need in the pit of my stomach that was slowly but steadily venturing down south.

"It must be pretty lonely over there," I said in a feeble attempt to conceal my nervousness.

"Probably, but I can also see the benefits of keeping away from civilization's stress and hassles, and having one's kids grow up in the serenity of nature." Jett fell silent again, his gaze never leaving mine. The air charged with tension. I bit my lip and broke eye contact, only to redirect my gaze to him a moment later.

He was sitting so close I could barely breathe. And while his proximity didn't feel uncomfortable, it was almost too much to bear.

"Tell me about your life," Jett said eventually.

I laughed. "What?" It was such a strange request. Men weren't usually interested in my life, past, thoughts, and so forth.

Jett grinned that lopsided smile of his that made my heart skip a beat. "We didn't go through the usual interviewing process, so it's about time to catch up."

"Well, we didn't really go through the traditional hiring process either."

He shrugged and his grin intensified. "You have a point. I could fire and re-hire you, if it bothers you so much. Or—" he turned onto one side, propping up on one elbow "—you could just answer my question." It wasn't an invitation but a demand.

I moistened my lips as I tried to push through years of memories in the hope I might find something that didn't give away too much, yet still enough to satisfy his curiosity.

"My dad died when I was a teen. I grew up with my mother who tried her best to fulfill the role of both. After finishing high school, I came to New York to study, and ended up working in real estate." Those were the boring parts of my life; the harmless ones barely scratching the surface. Usually, they sufficed in sending a guy into a disinterested staring stupor, meaning they never bothered to ask further questions. I searched Jett's gaze for any signs of disinterest, but what I found was an attentiveness that scared me. He seemed to really listen to me. While there was nothing wrong with it, the fact that this guy who hired me would be interested in me and in my life showed me he cared for me in some way. And that scared me even more.

"You always wanted to work in real estate?" His question seemed polite and harmless enough.

"I like houses. What about you?"

He smiled but didn't take the bait to change the object of focus. "It's a strange career choice for a college graduate. Either you were pushed into it knowing you could make big bucks once you built your portfolio. Or you had a serious interest in buildings and the market. Which one is it?" My throat dried up. The guy knew what he was talking about. I wondered whether it was one of his usual interview questions, or whether he pulled it out of his repertoire for someone like me.

"You don't have to answer if you're not comfortable,"

Jett continued slowly.

"It's pretty simple. I felt it was the right step." I shrugged because that was all there really was to it. Working in real estate was the right step—at that time.

Jett's eyes glittered with amusement, and I got the feeling my explanation pleased him. "You joined the business out of interest, then."

I groaned inwardly. He wasn't about to change the topic any time soon. I forced myself not to pull a face. "Yep."

"Did you know a lot about houses? Were you fascinated by them, by the people living inside?"

He knew something was off.

I don't know why, but the thought hit me the moment he regarded me coolly—his eyes clouded as though to hide his thoughts and emotions. My heart thumped hard against my rib cage, threatening to burst out of my chest. My palms turned clammy, and a thin rivulet of sweat trickled down my spine.

Stay calm, Stewart.

I knew answering his question would lead to more questions, until there were no secrets left. I had never told anyone, and I sure wasn't ready to share the dark sides of my past with Jett. My throat constricted with fear. I buried my fingers into the soft grass and ripped it out, barely acknowledging that the action was revealing more about me than a thousand words.

I wasn't ready to tell him the whole truth, so he had to make do with the little I could give him.

"We moved a few times." I cleared my throat, forcing the tremor away. "I've always liked the notion of having a stable family home. I figured by selling beautiful houses to people I might be helping them find stability in their lives. It was a stupid dream. About a week into the job, I realized the whole business was all about money."

His long fingers tucked a stray strand of hair behind my ear. The movement was so natural, it felt as though he had done it—*touched me*—a hundred times before. "You still like your job though."

I nodded and smiled. "I do."

"Because you want to change the world," he whispered as he moved closer, cupping my face with his hand and forcing me to look at him. "It wasn't a stupid dream. You won't be able to change the world, Brooke. But your example might just change the people entering your life."

His index finger traced the contours of my face, leaving a tingling sensation behind. The air was thick with the scent of wood and grass, but I all I could focus on was *Jett*. He was sitting so closely, I could smell his manly scent and take in every detail of his face and body. The barely visible laughter lines beneath his stunning eyes, the faded scar on his chin, the hard muscles of his arms. Those were all things that made him real. Beautiful. Perfect. I wanted to ask him about them so his memories would be mine.

"Hey, did you ever play football in high school?" I asked cheekily and slightly out of breath as my gaze swept over his broad shoulders.

"What?" He shot me a questioning glance. And then a deep chuckle rumbled in his throat as he probably caught on to my subtle implication. "As a matter of fact, I did. I'm glad you noticed it."

I rolled my eyes at the sudden onset of heat in my cheeks.

Well done—inflating his oversized ego even more, Stewart.

"I bet you were the book nerd who hung out with the whizz kids," Jett said.

"What makes you think I wasn't the cheerleading type?" My brows shot up. He was spot on, but that didn't please me. For some reason I wanted him to think me hot and desirable. I wanted him to think he might have competition.

"Nah, you weren't that boring." His arms moved around my waist to pull me closer as his green, heated gaze descended into my eyes and heart, infiltrating me to the core. The way he was looking at me, I felt everything that mattered fade away. The only thing that existed was the moment we shared.

Jett's lips lowered onto mine, almost brushing them, but not quite. "You were clever and stunning, yet you didn't know it."

"How do you know?" I breathed.

"It's not hard to guess. Girls like you keep boys at arm's length. I think quite a few of the boys tried, but none succeeded because you didn't realize just how gorgeous you were."

The guy certainly had a way with words. I blinked rapidly, intoxicated by the scent of his skin. He smelled of expensive aftershave and something else. Something manly. Something—

Him.

My lips parted, begging him to stop torturing me by being so close. Begging him to kiss me.

And he did, ever so gently. Like tiny butterflies brushing my skin with their soft wings. I groaned inwardly at the sheer torture. God, I wanted him so badly it hurt.

"Some guys might be into cheerleaders and flaunted beauty. I've always liked a challenge, and you were the kind of girl I wanted but couldn't have," he whispered.

He flicked his tongue over my bottom lip a moment before his mouth conquered mine in a long and heated kiss. He circled my tongue, sucking it deep into his mouth, as his hands roved over my body. I shuddered in his embrace, and my head fell back as I moaned with the storm rising within my abdomen. His hand tugged at my shirt, jerking it out of my slacks in one quick motion. The soft pressure of his calloused fingers undoing buttons set me on fire with the promise of what they might do to me.

What the hell was I doing?

This place wasn't secluded. Anyone standing above us or on the other side of the lake could see us. I should walk away, not let him have me in a public place where everyone could see us. I wasn't an exhibitionist, and doing it on a patch of grass with god-knows-what crawling up my skin wasn't my thing either. But my physical needs were getting stronger, screaming for release. What would it be like to sleep with someone I really wanted?

In an unexpected moment of lucidity, I poked a finger in his chest and tried to push him away, but my attempt was a feeble one.

"Not here," I mumbled.

"Why not? No one's here," Jett whispered, not backing off. The pressure of his mouth on mine intensified. His fingers skimmed downward from my neck to the sheer material of my now exposed bra, circling the pink bud I'd dreamed he'd caress ever since meeting him. I arched my back against his rough hand, closing the space between us, vaguely aware that if he continued his delicious torture I'd be lost.

"I want to know what you taste like," he whispered, fingers fidgeting with the bra clasp.

"Let me—"

With a flick of my hand, I undid my bra and rolled it

down my arms onto the green grass.

My pale breasts spilled free into his open waiting palms.

"You're beautiful," Jett said hoarsely, his eyes glued to my chest. As though to prove his point, he let out an appreciative moan and went about flicking his tongue across one hard nipple, then the other, sucking and licking in equal measures. He was sending me up in flames in a whirlwind of passion I never knew existed. Lowering myself onto the grass, my arms moved around the nape of his neck, pulling him on top of me in the hope he wouldn't stop. But Jett didn't need persuading.

His tongue swirled a few more times, then sucked so hard a short ripple of pain rushed through me, followed by a cascade of pleasure that travelled right into my sex. And then he stopped.

"No," I whispered, my gaze begging him to continue.

From under half-closed eyes I watched him place butterfly kisses down my abdomen, his hand already fumbling with the zip of my slacks.

He hadn't changed his mind. He was about to move on to the next step. Somewhere inside my brain, I could hear that tiny but annoying voice asking me what the hell this was, but for once I didn't want to listen to reason. I wasn't sure whether to be mortified that he was about to fully undress me in public, or excited at the outlook of more hot mouth action.

It was too late for second thoughts anyway. Before I knew it, the slacks were off and Jett slipped a hand between my parted legs, tugging my panties to the side.

Bloody hell.

I was already damp for him, waiting to be touched.

"Don't stop," I said.

"I wasn't going to."

Peeling off his jeans, he rubbed his shaft against my swollen clit until I lifted my hips to invite him in. My breathing came in short rasps. He opened my legs wide and moved two fingers over my clit, then slid them into my soft flesh. A deep thunder rippled through me, nearly pushing me over the edge, and then, as though sensing it, he pulled out.

"Not yet," he murmured, almost scolding.

"No! Don't stop." I sat up on my elbow and our eyes connected. He looked sexy as hell with his dishevelled hair and that naughty smile. My clit twitched at the sight of his tongue flicking over his lips.

"When I'm done with you you'll be panting my name, begging for release," Jett whispered.

Not likely, but I didn't want to shatter his illusion. Other men had never been able to get that particular response from me. Jett might be hot as hell with a body to drool over and a kiss to melt the Arctic, but in the end I doubted his dick could perform miracles.

He pushed me down onto the grass and lowered his face between my thighs, cupping my ass as he soaked up my female scent, making me blush. Raising his gaze to meet mine, he let his tongue swirl between my folds, focusing on the tiny nub at the top. A tremble began to form somewhere deep inside me and spread through my whole body, gathering in my vagina. I moaned and arched my back, bringing my hips closer to his magic mouth. If he didn't enter me soon I'd embarrass myself by begging him to take me on the spot.

"Jett." My voice dripped with want. He laughed briefly and continued his torture, swirling and licking. Quivering, I let out a broken moan and clawed at his shoulders. "I need you inside." My voice sounded hoarse with demand, matching the deep, approving rumble in his throat.

"Not yet, baby."

Holy mother of pearls, he was so good.

I pushed my fingers through his hair, not quite able to decide whether to force him up or pin him down. I moaned louder as he trailed the tip of his tongue through my sensitive slit, devouring every drop of moisture.

"Please," I rocked my hips against him.

His tongue continued to torture me, again and again, moving up to my clit, licking around it, causing a strangled scream of pleasure to form somewhere at the back of my throat.

"You want me inside?" Jett said, suddenly sitting up. I whimpered as the soft breeze hit my sex, cooling down the heated sensation left by his mouth. I nodded, and a wicked grin flashed on his face. Slowly he pushed a finger into me, followed by another, his gaze never leaving me as he pulled his fingers out again. The next time he entered me deeper and faster, thrusting in and out. I moaned as he repeated the process moving gradually deeper and faster until his fingers were all the way in, stretching me, teasing me, torturing me.

"Oh god." My back arched. My hips lifted to meet his fingers, begging him for more. This wasn't going according to plan. He wasn't supposed to make me feel so much pleasure, and yet the even thrusts of his fingers pushed me past anything I ever experienced before.

"A little bit more," Jett whispered. His eyes remained glued to me as he dipped back down. Keeping his fingers impaled in me, his tongue flicked over my clit once, twice, sending the world before my eyes into a spinning carousel. Heat pooled between my legs, and a deep moan escaped my throat—then another—while my heart began to race. I bucked against him, driving his fingers deeper into me. More heat seared me, driving me insane. My vision blurred into darkness as my body tensed.

"Let me see you come," Jett ordered. His deep, sexy voice was the last caress I needed. My clit began to pound with a steady hard throb that turned into all-consuming heat. With a stifled cry, my hips jerked against him, and I came against Jett's hot mouth. The world dissipated and I exploded in a million sensations that washed over me at once.

16

I BIT MY lip hard as I peered at Jett's relaxed features from the corners of my eyes. We didn't sleep together on the shore of Lucazzone's estate. For some reason he just adjusted my panties back in place and sat up, turning away from me as though to give me enough privacy to regain my composure. My hands shot up his strong back, massaging his lean muscles in the process, hopefully signaling just how much I wanted to go all the way.

"Don't," Jett said, holding me off with a simple request. My hands jerked away, as though seared, and somehow his words burned more than fire. No man I ever slept with had behaved like this. If they went down, they would demand that I return the favor. Why didn't Jett? Why wouldn't he finish what we started right there and then?

I couldn't stop the sudden onset of feeling inadequate

making me doubt myself. Had I done something wrong? Maybe it was the way I reacted to his touch that put him off sleeping with me.

Even though I didn't want to, my sex kept twitching at the sight of him. It wasn't natural and certainly not something I ever experienced before. This dark, sultry, earth-shattering lust had to stop. I couldn't deal with hot waves of wanting that made being around him—without touching him—unbearable. He was so close and yet so far. The attraction was palpable, and yet I didn't feel confident enough to act on it. I was in this zone in which things were not black and white, but a blurred in-between shade where nothing made sense.

Jett didn't say a word as I shrugged back into my clothes and followed him up the path and back to his parked car. We kept silent as he helped me into the passenger side and loped around to the driver's seat, put the car in gear, and drove all the way home.

His home, I reminded myself, the beautiful house on the lake and the pretend normalcy of a work relationship that wasn't. Ignoring the sting in my eyes, I peered out the window at the blurred countryside, no longer minding Jett's dangerous driving. It seemed like an eternity passed before we finally reached his house. The moment the tires screeched to a halt, I jumped out of the car and only stopped as I reached the front door, my back turned to Jett as I waited for him to catch up.

He unlocked the door and let me enter first, then closed it behind us. Avoiding his gaze I hesitated, unsure what to say. In the end, all I managed was a feeble, "Thanks."

His brows shot up, and a glint of irritation appeared in his eyes. "For what? The ride? My highly appreciated company?" A nerve twitched on his right temple.

He was angry and I had no idea why. My mouth clamped shut. What the hell was wrong with him? How could he change from sensual and passionate to cold and calculated in the blink of an eye?

"Or do you mean for going down on you?" He inched dangerously close. His fingers gripped my chin and forced my face up. His height intimidated me. Peering up his towering body into blazing eyes, I felt tiny and powerless against his caginess. Only he knew what went on inside his mind, and he certainly made no attempt to share it with me.

"Thank you for what, Brooke?" His arm wrapped around my waist and turned me around, pushing me against the wall, his thigh parting my legs in the process. His palms moved up the front of my shirt as his teeth grated my earlobe.

"The contract—I wanted to reciprocate," I whispered. "You didn't let me." I don't know why it was such a big deal, but for some reason it was. He had made me feel an intense pleasure I had never felt before, and I wanted to see whether I could make him feel the same way.

I wanted to be as special to him as he was to me. I wanted him to surrender to me. To what I could give him.

And where would that take you, Stewart?

Probably nowhere.

"Ah, the contract. You think it's about giving and taking in equal measures." He sighed impatiently. His hot breath on my neck made me shudder. "I play by my own rules, Brooke. As they say: sometimes it's all about you, and sometimes it's all about me."

I nodded slowly, wondering where he was going with this. His thumb brushed my cheek a moment before he moved away from me.

"Go take a shower and meet me in my office. I need you to prepare some paperwork for me."

What the hell?

He was playing mind games or how else could I explain his constant changes? My breath came in ragged heaps as I hurried past him and up the stairs to my room, eager to escape him, if only for a brief time.

***

The shower cleared my head a little. Unfortunately, it didn't clear my confusion about Jett. I kept telling myself that I only knew him for a couple days, which wasn't nearly enough to find out how a man ticked. My mother had taught me men were complex, but once you got to their core they weren't that different from us. Based on my brief encounter with Jett, I begged to differ. In the end he was my boss and not some random guy I dated, I reminded myself. So I didn't need to understand. All that mattered was doing my job well.

Figuring I had wasted enough time, I tied my long brown hair in a high ponytail, put on clean underwear, a new shirt and slacks, and headed for Jett's office, not knowing what to expect next.

I found him sitting at his desk, engrossed in a mostly monosyllabic phone conversation with the prevalent words being 'no', 'crap', and 'uh-huh'. He motioned for me to sit down on the padded chair opposite him and turned back to the notes in front of him, the frown on his forehead deepening. God, being serious suited him. I discarded the sudden memory flashes of his sexy mouth between my legs, and forced my mind back to reality. He didn't even bother to look at me as he resumed his conversation. I sat there for a minute or two, trying hard not to tune in, but Jett's anger was so palpable, it made focusing on anything else impossible.

"Next time, don't let anyone string us along. Either they sign or they don't. Have I made myself clear?" Jett said a moment before he slammed down the phone.

Bloody hell, he sure knew how to end a conversation. I definitely hoped I'd never have him on the other end of the line.

"Everything okay?" I asked hesitantly.

"Another fucked-up deal," Jett replied, massaging his temples. "I swear, at times I'm thinking I might just have to do everything myself if I want this company to stay afloat. It's hard finding reliable people." Looking up he smiled, and I knew he was about to change the subject, as though he'd already said too much.

"I need you to go through my correspondence and cancel any meetings, physical or otherwise, I might have this week," Jett said. "Then clear my schedule."

"Sure." I frowned but knew better than to ask questions.

"Good." He pushed a thick file across the desk. "I trust you're accustomed with the Lucazzone estate by now?"

The telltale heat of a blush rushed to my cheeks. Oh, I was accustomed with the Lucazzone estate all right, though not the way I'd initially thought. Jett's lips curved into his panty-dropping grin.

"I thought so. Anyway, I want you to take care of it. Look through each and every note, find a loophole and then get us the estate."

"But—" I almost choked on my breath. This was a multi-million dollar deal.

Jett pushed back his chair and walked around the desk.

Stopping in front of me, he sank into a crouch so I could feel his hot breath on my skin. "James said you were the best. Was he lying?"

God, he was beautiful. His eyes...his face...his lips. I leaned back, as if the little distance could protect me from his magnetism, and shook my head. "No. But this is huge and I—" Didn't have the experience, I wanted to add when Jett cut me off.

"I believe in you," he said slowly. "Don't disappoint me."

Jett Mayfield was huge and he believed in my skills. For a moment I just stared at him, unable to utter the two words I desperately wanted to communicate.

Thank you.

The air charged between us. My gaze lowered to his open lips, so close to mine, and moisture gathered between my legs, soaking the sheer material of my panties. Clearing his throat, Jett stood and returned to his seat, but not fast enough to hide his own shallow breath and the lust in his eyes. He wasn't as unaffected as he pretended to be. A sense of pride and victory grabbed hold of my heart. I crossed my arms over my chest, amused.

"Lunch should be waiting for you in the kitchen," he said coolly, avoiding my gaze. "I'll be in Malpesa for the rest of the day."

"Why?" The word slipped out before I could stop

myself. His gaze shot up, brows raised.

"Meeting with a client."

"There's nothing on your schedule."

He leaned back in his chair and regarded me for a few seconds. "Not everything's noted in my schedule, Brooke. Like our little stroll this morning. Do you think the Lucazzone household had an enjoyable view?" A devilish grin lit up his face, sending me into yet another blushing frenzy.

"What? You said—" I stumbled over my words, not able to finish the sentence.

"No. I said no one is living *there*...literally, on the shoreline. I didn't say no one is living *inside* the house." His grin widened. My cheeks caught fire from yet another wave of sheer mortification.

Dammit, the ball was in his court again.

I had just lost another battle.

"Do you think anyone saw us?" I whispered.

He shrugged. "Does it matter?"

It did because I wasn't the kind who had sex in a public place where everyone could gawk at me.

"Relax, Brooke," Jett said softly. "The house's been standing empty for months." His finger brushed my flaming cheek. "But you liked the danger of being caught, didn't you?"

I nodded even though it wasn't just the chance of being

caught that had made my blood boil.

"Good, because there are so many other things I plan to do with you," he whispered in that deep, sexy voice layered with intrigue.

My breath hitched. Oh, I definitely couldn't wait.

The phone rang, interrupting our moment. Jett groaned and turned to check the caller ID.

"Fuck!" Letting go of me, he grabbed the phone and pressed his hand against the microphone. His dusky eyes were on me, leaving no doubt his words were meant for my ears only. "I want you so badly but, unfortunately, work's calling." His mouth moved to mine in a quick but heated kiss, and then he was back in his no-nonsense work mojo.

"Mayfield," he said into his phone. His voice was hard and determined, showing none of the passion I could sure as hell still feel rushing through my veins.

Straightening my back, I mustered all my poise and forced myself to walk out of the room slowly, minding each step so I wouldn't trip over my own two feet.

17

AS JETT HAD announced, lunch was waiting for me in the kitchen. I lifted the lid off the serving plate and inhaled the aroma of some Italian pasta and meat dish I had never tried before. It smelled deliciously of herbs and fresh tomatoes. My stomach rumbled in response, reminding me that it was already well past lunchtime, and I hadn't eaten since last night. With the Lucazzone file still clutched to my chest, I grabbed my plate and sat down at the expensive mahogany table overlooking the lake. From up here, I had a grand view over the entire east side. Unlike the day we arrived, the lake seemed to have attracted visitors. I couldn't see as far as the shore, but I could make out the colorful flagpoles of two private boats sailing at a leisurely speed. According to Jett, most of the lake was privately owned, which led me to believe the owners had decided to fly over for a quick spring trip.

Popping a spoonful of delicious pasta into my mouth, I wondered what it must be like to be as rich as these people, and not have to worry about paying the bills or putting food on the table. Even when my mother lost my father and had to make end's meet by taking a minimum wage job stocking shelves in a local supermarket, I never felt like I lacked anything. But being with Jett in a villa that probably cost more than I'd make in a lifetime, I couldn't help but feel out of place.

I worked for him but wasn't part of his world. And I harbored no false hope that I'd ever be.

You don't want him, Stewart. So get those 'what ifs' out of your damn system.

"Damn straight," I mumbled, opening the Lucazzone file. To my surprise, it wasn't the same one Jett had left on my desk this morning. I finished my lunch quickly so I could engross myself in Mayfield's strange work ethic. By the time I leaned back in my chair, I couldn't help but admire his dedication.

Jett Mayfield knew what he wanted, and he wasn't afraid to take it, no matter how dirty he had to play.

***

The private detective had been following the Lucazzone

family for ten years, sifting through family trees, tragedies, secret bank accounts, and visitors with hidden motives. As it turned out, throughout generations the Lucazzone men had played away, taking their pleasure wherever and from whomever they could get it. Alessandro Lucazzone was no different, except that he played for the other team. He had wed his rich wife because he needed her money, which explained why he never fathered an heir. At some point, one of his lovers moved in, and they began to flaunt their romance until his wife put a stop to it by threatening to divorce him.

I wondered why she never carried out her threat. Any woman in her right mind would, and yet Henrietta Lucazzone stayed with Alessandro until she drew her last breath, her body destroyed by a mysterious disease she contracted while vacationing in India. Maybe it was her Catholic upbringing that made her value her vows more than her freedom or a life with someone who truly loved her. Or maybe Alessandro had an iron grip on her, forcing her into obedience. He was well known for his charm and good looks, and it was said that he could even persuade a cobra to hold back her venom at the sight of him.

Obviously, I didn't believe a word they said. The stories dated back to his youth, when the effects of WWI had made people poor and trusting of the high society that offered a free daily meal and gifted their children clothes to wear. Maybe it was the reason why Henrietta thought Alessandro Lucazzone got away with murder.

According to Jett's file, it was the first Sunday in December 1953. Henrietta Lucazzone had just returned from yet another shopping spree, of which she was so fond, only to find her husband in bed with another man. While this had happened before, this time the lover next to Alessandro was dead. His torso had been slit open from the throat all the way down to his abdomen. According to her diary, Henrietta never called the police and the body was later found buried in the woods, naked, the torso torn open.

No one ever asked questions, no one pointed fingers. Around the time the body was found, Alessandro gave money away to charity, and he was praised for his generosity. The man was identified as a former soldier in WWII, hooked on the bottle and in desperate need of cash to finance his next drink. Mayfield's private detective only stumbled upon Lucazzone's secret when he wasn't granted a visit entrance to Lucazzone's home, and he stumbled upon Henrietta's diary in the chapel behind the gardens, hidden beneath the kneeling pad facing the altar.

Although the diary was never sent to the police, the fact that a body was found inside the villa should have been proof enough that someone in the Lucazzone house was a murderer. And yet, the family's good reputation and wealth protected whoever committed the crime. In his correspondence with the detective, Mayfield had claimed the man was old and sick. If he was indeed the murderer, any justice would reach him after his death. I wondered why Jett wouldn't just hand the diary to the local authorities. If Alessandro was found guilty, the Italian government would auction the estate and sell it to the highest bidder, in which case I doubted anyone would make an offer in excess of twenty million. It would have been so easy, and yet Jett seemed to want to take the hard road for reasons unfathomable to me.

Closing the file, I placed my empty plate in the dishwasher and headed upstairs for the privacy of my office. Without Jett, the house seemed unusually quiet. As I booted up my MacBook from sleeping mode, I found myself easing slowly into work mode. I looked through the file from front to back cover, twice, without finding anything that could possibly help. The tax records were fine. The estate had financial troubles, but they weren't severe enough to push Lucazzone into selling. I had no idea what else to look for and was about to close the file when the tiny number printed at the bottom of each page caught my eye. The last page was numbered 147 of 148, meaning one page was missing.

Had it been filed with the others? I couldn't remember having seen it, but I searched the file twice nonetheless, then my desk and finally the kitchen, without much success.

In the end, I decided to ask Jett about it and commenced my administrative tasks. By the time I finished answering his principal business correspondence and postponed each and every meeting as per Jett's request, it was early evening, and the sound of crunching pebbles beneath tires told me it was time to call it a day.

***

Jett's business meeting hadn't gone well. I could tell by the way he slammed the door shut, sending a reverberating quake through the floor and walls. I had no idea what to make of it, so I stayed glued to the spot, inches away from the clothes hanging in my closet, wondering what to wear tonight. Until now it had always been one business suit after another, intermingled with the occasional jeans at night. Tonight I felt a need for a change, maybe something risky like a skirt or a dress. Something to entice the man who hadn't touched me since our outing to the beach. Why? Because I wanted to get it over and done with.

Anticipation or patience had never been my virtues. I didn't like this waiting game, spending hours a day in his presence with his sultry eyes on me. Every time he looked at me, it felt as though his heated gaze was undressing me while sending delicious trembles through my lower body. Ever since he touched me down there, I could think of nothing but his lips on my skin, teasing, sucking, sending me over the edge. I wanted to feel that electrifying cascade of emotions again, but I also intended to repay his efforts this time. The tell-tale tingling of arousal rushed through my belly, descending into a sensual pull just below my abdomen.

But now wasn't the time.

Pushing Jett to the back of my mind, I dressed in a pencil skirt that fell just below the knees and a soft Cashmere top with a plunging V neck line. I kept my makeup understated—a bit of mascara, blusher, and a touch of lipstick—and eased my ponytail. My hair cascaded down my shoulders in countless soft ringlets. Pleased, I inspected myself in the mirror.

Not too bad, Stewart.

Okay, I admit I was nowhere near model material, but I had a few things going for me—like my luminous, brown eyes, my round hips, and my thin waist. Besides, Jett had made no secret about wanting me, so for once the fact that my legs weren't long enough and my cup size could use the boost of a padded bra didn't bother me.

Biting my lip nervously, I shot the image in the mirror another look and ventured out in search of my boss.

I found Jett in the living room, standing near the open balcony door with his cell phone pressed to his ear, and the evening wind ruffling his hair. His back was turned to me, so I had a few short moments to regard him before he noticed my presence.

He was clad in jeans that hugged his strong thighs and a black tee that accentuated his biceps; the moisture in his hair shimmered in the light of the chandelier, making me want to run my fingers through it to test whether it was as soft and luscious as it seemed. He looked so yummy I could have died on the spot and gone straight to heaven. I groaned against the sudden need pooling between my legs.

Seriously? He didn't even need to say a word, and I was already considering begging him to take me. I couldn't be more obvious.

Easy lay.

Knocking lightly on the already open door, I stepped into the living room, my eyes fixed on anything but Jett. And then he turned and a panty-dropping smile jerked his lips upward. My gaze was drawn to him magnetically, and everything else was sucked out of my vision.

He was so hot it was unreal.

No, he was a sex god.

My breath hitched in my throat for the umpteenth time since I'd met him.

"Hey. Had a good day?" he asked in a low and throaty tone, sexy as hell.

I swallowed hard, forgetting my voice. He strolled toward me and bent down to place a soft kiss on my cheek as his hand moved to my lower back, barely touching the soft material of my shirt.

Too close for comfort, too electrifying.

I couldn't breathe. He was so confident it scared the living crap out of me.

Smiling bravely, I took two steps back, forcing myself not to dash for the nearest exit.

"It was good. What about you?" My voice barely found its way out of my throat.

"It's getting better now that I'm here with you." Jett's eyes descended into mine, sending my insides into upheaval. His thumb brushed my lower lip and a frown crossed his features, as though he couldn't decide whether to kiss it. I wanted to make that decision easy for him so I gently pressed my mouth against his thumb while my eyes remained connected with him. His breathing became shallow as I started to suck his finger into my mouth, pulling it in and out.

"You're playing with fire, Brooke," Jett said huskily. "I don't want you to get burned."

"You promised fire. I don't mind a little pain," I whispered against his hand. This was about the most obvious invitation I had ever spoken to a man. My heart began to beat wildly against my ribcage, reminding me of a fragile bird in desperate search for a way out of a cage. And in some way I was a bird, and my life was a cage. While I'd never let Jett or any other man inside, I figured I could safely venture outside for a change, in the hope that I might just forget my past. Be someone else for a while.

We stared at each other for a few moments during which I barely breathed…and then his cell phone rang, jerking him out of our moment.

Urgh.

Someone *had* to call at the most unfortunate time *again.*

Jett peered at the caller ID and pressed the response button, muttering something like, "Hold on." Covering the microphone with one hand, his lips crushed mine in a fleeting kiss. "Sorry, I have to take this."

I shrugged. His gaze darkened, and for a moment I couldn't tell whether with desire or annoyance.

"I hope you like barbecue," he said.

"Who doesn't?"

"Meet you in the kitchen in ten?"

I nodded, even though he couldn't see it because he had turned his back on me, his phone glued to his ear.

***

As I entered the kitchen, the grill was already set up and covered with a steel lid. Jett lifted it to reveal two servings of ribs the size of Alabama. The aroma of meat and grilled vegetables made my stomach rumble and mellowed out my annoyance. Maybe he didn't take me up on the offer because he didn't want to burn dinner?

His loss, right?

I shrugged and forced myself not to roll my eyes again like a petulant child.

"Your business meeting didn't go so well," I started, ready to steer the conversation onto known terrain. After all, he was my boss and we were supposed to discuss things that affected the company.

Jett smirked. "How could you tell?"

"By the way you slammed the door."

"Sorry about that."

"No worries."

I watched him as he piled up two plates in silence and headed out the balcony door into the backyard. I took the red wine bottle and two empty wine glasses, then followed him out.

The air was warm and thick with the aroma of wood and flowers in bloom. The garden table and chairs were situated just around the corner where the light from the kitchen barely penetrated the darkness. Jett had already lit up what looked like a huge golden lantern that shed a soft glow on the white porcelain and tablecloth. The lit tea candles arranged in a zigzag pattern flickered in the soft breeze and cast moving shadows across the whitewashed wall.

The whole atmosphere was chic yet relaxed, not too

romantic but not casual either. Where I came from, we never lit candles unless we celebrated a birthday, or someone had died.

Placing the wine bottle and glasses on the table next to a set of cutlery and the two plates, I sat down on the chair opposite from Jett. My gaze shifted around, looking at anything but him.

"Are you cold? If you are, I can bring you a sweater or we can eat inside." The concern in his voice made me peer up in surprise.

"I'm fine."

He regarded me for a moment, as though not quite believing me. The candlelight reflected in his eyes and made them shimmer like gemstones. In the soft light, his skin had a golden glow to it and his stubble was more pronounced, giving him a dark and menacing flair. I had never liked stubble on a man, but I found it sexy on him. It suited his character—rough but at the same time soft, strange but also familiar. He looks so yummy, I wanted to bury myself in his strong arms. I ignored the urge to lean over the table and draw his face to mine to feel the scratchy sensation on my skin.

"Wine?" His voice broke the silence, jerking me out of my thoughts.

I smiled hesitantly and reached for the half-full glass.

"To us," Jett said, chinking our glasses, his gaze never

leaving mine.

Swallowing hard, I nodded because something in his tone—maybe the slightest hint of a promise—ignited a raging fire in me.

I took a sip of the delicious wine, then another, to calm my suddenly racing heart. It didn't really help, so I focused on the contents of my plate, all the while keeping the conversation light and casual.

"Did you find anything in the Lucazzone file?" he asked me, handing me a basket of bread as I tucked into my spare ribs.

I shook my head and finished chewing before answering. "No, but there's something I meant to ask you. How many times have you and your lawyers looked through it?"

He shrugged, signaling that either he didn't care or he couldn't be bothered counting.

"Exactly," I mumbled under my breath.

He gave me a strange look. "I brought it so *you* could take a look at it. I thought getting a fresh opinion wouldn't hurt."

"Look, I—" I put my cutlery down and hesitated as I prepared my words carefully so he wouldn't think I was lecturing him. We might share sizzling sexual chemistry, but Jett was still my boss. As most of them come, they tend to have an oversized ego and an unwillingness to take 'no' or 'not possible' for an answer. "I can see the potential of this estate, but with the taxes and everything else in order, there's no way you'll get it unless the old man sells or you turn him in."

Jett's gaze darkened and his jaw set. "Your second option is a no go."

"Why?"

"Because." He drew a sharp breath and averted his gaze.

"Why?" I prompted, leaning forward.

"Who would want to buy a holiday home built on a murderer's estate?" His words made sense and yet...

"See, that's another point that's been bugging me. The offer price is way too high. Add it to the costs of lawyers, taxes, building, and decorating, and you'll end up with a ginormous asking price no buyer will want to pay."

"You'd be surprised to find out what rich people are willing to pay for a bit of privacy." He leaned back and smiled cockily. I bit my tongue so I wouldn't reply because he was the rich guy and probably knew better than I did. Still, his words didn't manage to convince me.

I raised my hands in mock surrender. "Fair enough. All I'm saying is that if you want that estate, you've got to go to the police."

He shook his head vehemently. "Not going to happen, Brooke. So find something else."

"You're killing me." I let out an exasperated sigh and

leaned against the back of my chair, my fingers tapping lightly against my almost-empty wine glass. The guy was as stubborn as a mule. Working for someone as determined as Jett wasn't going to be easy, but I had never backed down from a challenge. Even if it meant working my ass off knowing it was a dead end. "Right now I've no idea where else to look. Alessandro's on his deathbed. Why don't you just wait until he—" I had asked that same question only a day ago. However, I figured I had nothing to lose by starting one last persuasion attempt. "Once the estate is in the hands of charities, you'll be able to entice them with a much lower offer. You could save money, which would result in a higher profit for your company."

"It could take years. Besides, they might decide to sell to someone else."

"There is no one else," I said. Jett's silence made me look up in doubt. "Is there?" He remained tight-lipped, but the dark shadow clouding his features said more than a thousand words.

There was.

"I didn't want to tell you." His tone softened.

"Why not?"

"Because I didn't want to get you involved." He shrugged, as though it didn't matter, but I could tell from his dark expression whatever he wasn't telling me bothered him a great deal.

"You didn't want me to get involved in what? In my job?" I laughed, even though I felt like strangling him. "How am I supposed to do my job when you're detaining vital information from me?"

"You don't understand, Brooke. They're dangerous." His voice came so low for a moment I wasn't sure I heard him right. The meaning of his words slowly sank in, causing an involuntary shudder to run down my spine. I thought I had landed a relatively safe job: meet up with prospective clients, rent or sell their properties, cash the check, done. Okay, Mayfield Properties was playing on a higher scale, meaning they did a bit more than that, but still. I had no idea how or why the people I might meet could constitute any danger to me. It surely didn't say in my work contract.

"What kind of people are we talking about?" I asked carefully.

He winced. "Let's just say—not the kind you want to meet."

And then it dawned on me. In a twisted way he was trying to protect me, while letting me do my job. "Is that why you went to today's meeting alone?" His expression remained dark and impenetrable. Blank. But I didn't need his confirmation to *know*. "Oh."

Holy cow, no wonder they paid me so much. I was basically rubbing shoulders with the local thug, or worse.

Well, sort of.

Jett brushed his fingers through his hair and closed his eyes for a few seconds during which we remained silent. A strong tension hung in the air and mirrored in his face. He seemed torn, though I had no idea about what.

"You should tell me everything. As your employee, I have a right to know," I said eventually.

"No, Brooke." Short and to the point. Adamant. This was the Jett I had glimpsed through his business correspondence. This was the Jett I had feared I'd meet one day. The hard lines around his mouth deepened, just like the determination in his eyes. I was seeing a new side of him but, unfortunately, it didn't lessen my attraction to him. In fact, I found myself wanting to throw myself into his arms and let him take me places I had never frequented. Instead, I groaned and shot him the dirtiest look I could muster.

The corners of his lips jerked and his frown smoothed, but his tone remained hard as steel. "You're safe with me and I'll keep you that way. I won't get you involved in this crap, no matter how hard you push, beg, glare, or otherwise."

Whatever.

He had obviously never seen me in investigative mode.

My intuition told me there was more to this estate than Jett let on. How was I supposed to find a loophole with more mystery than an Agatha Christie murder mystery, particularly when the information he gave me barely scratched the surface?

I crossed my arms over my chest and regarded his beautiful face. "Is that why you tore out the last page? Because you didn't want me to see what's on it?"

For a second I thought I saw a spark of fear in his eyes, and then it disappeared just as quickly, leaving nothing but a blank expression behind. Damn him and his ability to bluff. I wished I could control my face like that. All other human beings would negate the claim vehemently, which in itself would be proof they were lying. Just not Jett. He simply remained silent while staring me down, unblinking, unmoving, unwavering, unwilling to put himself into any position, be it to his or my advantage.

I could definitely learn a thing or two from this guy.

"Fine. Don't answer." I grabbed my fork and began shifting my food around my plate.

"Let's finish up, baby," Jett said, his tone changing from cold marble to smooth velvet and sweet honey. "I think you're ready for your surprise."

18

WHAT SURPRISE COULD Jett possibly have in store for me? I mused over the question as I forced myself to finish my dinner, even though a hundred fluttering butterflies seemed to have taken shelter inside my stomach. He steered our conversation back to the house, local history and what not, but I couldn't force myself to pay attention to his effortless chatter. My sudden nervousness kept pushing my thoughts in one direction only. I didn't know what to expect and, being a planner all the way, I didn't like the feeling one bit. Surprises for me were like…opening Pandora's box. You never know what's inside until it hits you.

"Finished?" Jett stood and began to clear the plates, not waiting for my answer.

"Yeah, let me help you." I jumped to my feet and

reached out for the empty wine glasses. He placed a warm hand on my arm, stopping me.

"Wait for me in the living room." His tone left no room for discussion. I didn't want to be one of those women who follow a man's every command, and yet I found myself doing as he bid. Yet again. The thought that he was my boss consoled me for all of five seconds, and then doubts began to crawl back into my head.

Jett had entered my life a few days ago, and already I barely recognized myself. This wasn't the responsible woman who once swore she'd never again let a guy gain the upper hand over her—in body, mind, or otherwise. And yet here I was, wanting Jett to take control, waiting for him to decide which way to go. I scolded myself for being so weak, but I couldn't help it. Something had changed inside me, maybe because deep down I knew Jett was different and he wouldn't hurt me the way others had.

His footsteps thudded on the marble floor. A moment later he appeared in the doorway holding a huge crystal bowl with what looked like a strawberry sundae topped with chocolate sauce in one hand, and two dessert spoons in the other.

"Strawberry cake's my favorite. How did you know?" My dark thoughts instantly forgotten, I made room on the couch and watched him slump down next to me, the chocolate sauce missing the white leather by half an inch.

"Whoa, careful. The chocolate's running." I pointed at the thin rivulet of brown, sweet stuff trickling down the side of the bowl. Jett held the crystal up.

"Lick it."

Seriously?

I almost choked on my breath. "What?"

"I said, lick it."

Jett's eyes bore into mine with such intensity it made my insides quiver. I leaned forward and, dipping my head to the side, I touched my mouth against the cold glass, tasting the drop of sweet chocolate that slipped into my mouth. His gaze remained glued on me, his green eyes clouded by desire. I came up again and bit my lip hard, anticipating his reaction.

He dipped a dessert spoon into the chocolate-covered whipped cream and held it up to me. This time I didn't need his command to tell me what to do. I sucked it into my mouth and let out a soft moan. Partly because it really was the best sundae I ever had. And partly because I instinctively knew Jett would like it. He put the dessert bowl down and reached over to brush his thumb over my lips, scorching them with his touch.

"You have a talented little mouth. Want to go to bed, beautiful?" I shuddered at the need in Jett's voice. No man had ever made the word 'beautiful' sound sexier. The way he said it made me feel special...and wanted. Nodding slowly, I sat up and climbed on top of him. His lips found my earlobe, his tongue flicking over my neck as his exploring hands reached down to cup my breasts.

"I like to make you come. It's my new favorite hobby," he whispered in my ear, lifting me up in one quick motion and only put me down again when we reached his bedroom.

Sitting on his bed, I only now noticed the mirror on the ceiling, reflecting our every move as he shrugged out of his jeans and shirt, revealing a lean body with taut skin and strong muscles. My fingers itched to touch his flat muscles and the dark trail of hair stretching down his abdomen toward the waistband of his shorts. He towered over me like no other man had before, and that excited me and made me want to see whether I could force him into surrender.

Jett sat down, pulling me onto his lap.

"Let me get rid of this." I fumbled with the side zipper of my skirt but he pushed my hands away, a wicked grin playing on his lips.

"I'll do it. It'll be my pleasure."

He pushed me onto my back and removed my top, and then my skirt, his eyes never leaving my body as his hands caressed it in long and delicate strokes.

"Is this my surprise?" I whispered. "Please let it be."

"Maybe." His lazy grin showed me just how much my

question pleased him. "Are you sure about this? Because there's no backing out once we start."

Was I?

Hell, yes.

I wanted him now.

He was still staring at me, waiting for an answer. I nodded.

"Come here, pretty," Jett whispered a moment before our mouths connected in a hungry kiss that sent shivers of pleasure through me. His taste was indescribable—sweet and rich like wine, dripping with his intoxicating passion for me, and he wasn't afraid to show it. In some way, it turned me on more than his expert hands massaging every sensitive spot of my body. His tongue dipped into the inside of my mouth, twining and sucking as his hips rubbed against mine.

A warm sensation rushed through my abdomen. My muscles began to tighten in that electrifying kind of way that told me just how much I wanted this man. My body trembled in his arms and my breasts strained to be released from their confinement. As though feeling my sudden urgency, Jett reached around to unfasten my bra, releasing my breasts into his waiting hands. Stifling a moan, I tossed my head back, my body tensing beneath the pressure of his hot lips on my nipple.

"You're so hot I could do this forever." He began to

suck and flick his tongue in equal measures, sending jolts of fire down my spine, over and over again, until I lost all sense of reasoning.

"Jett."

My head jerked back against the pillow and my hips shot up, grinding against his crotch. He was hard beneath his shorts. I could feel his generous length sliding down my abdomen. My hands slid inside the waistband of his shorts and pulled down, revealing what I had been dying to see since the morning I woke up with him in my bed.

My gaze trailed down the muscles of his chest, past his abdomen, to his shaft. My senses reeled as my mouth went dry.

He was already hard for me, the tip slick with moisture.

I gazed up into his moss-green eyes now hooded with anticipation. He wedged his weight between my waiting thighs and entered me in one push, my soft flesh tightening around his thick shaft. I let out a deep moan and clutched at his shoulders, grinding my hips against his in the need for more. For a moment the pleasure consumed me, and I let out a deep moan, wondering whether a single thrust from him would be enough to send me over the edge. As though sensing my thoughts, Jett's lips jerked up and he stopped moving. I quivered against his chest, shuddering with the effort to hold back.

"Jett." My hungry eyes met his again as I chanted his

name, my cry for more burning on my lips, unspoken.

"You'll have to say what you want," he whispered. His eyes shimmered with fortitude, challenging me.

Two could play this game.

I slowly shook my head.

"No?" He grinned. "As you will, Ms. Stewart."

Cupping my buttocks, he forced his shaft deeper inside me, filling every inch. I threw my head back with a cry. A soft tremble rocked my body, signalling my need for release. But, damn, I wouldn't beg. In fact, I'd make him pay for his impudence and make *him* beg *me*.

"You'll have to do better than that," I whispered through gritted teeth.

His eyes darkened with need, taking me up on the challenge. Slowly, he pulled back and blasted into me, rotating his pelvis in the process so he'd stroke against my clit. A whip of passion rushed up my spine like fire and erupted in another strangled cry.

I was so damn near and yet so far away.

Something about his naughty smile told me he could keep this up all day. He might have the willpower, but I didn't.

I squirmed under him to better accommodate him inside me. The movement sent another jolt of pleasure through me, making me wince from the sheer torture. "Oh, for crying out loud just do me," I whispered, barely able to contain the need in my voice.

He laughed. "You forgot to say please." His gaze bore into me with such intensity I felt him inside my core. His hands reached to cup my buttock and then he began to move hard and fast.

I felt orgasms rippling through both of us. A moment later, hot moisture spilled deep inside me and his satisfied moan echoed within my own cry. The room seemed to spin as one wave of ecstasy after another washed over me. Eventually, Jett rolled us to the side and he wrapped his arm around me, pulling me closer. Still breathing hard, I snuggled against his broad chest, marvelling at how delicious his skin felt beneath my open palms. I touched the roughness of his stubble and gently rubbed my fingertips against it, the way I had been dreaming of doing ever since meeting him.

"Take tomorrow morning off," Jett said.

"Why?" I sat up to regard him, relishing the remnants of two orgasms in a day. The prospect of staying just a little bit longer in his arms delighted me.

As he placed a soft kiss on my forehead, I tried to come up with a witty line; something to make him smile and maybe even kick a tiny dent into that ginormous confidence of his, but as usual in his presence my mind remained surprisingly blank.

"Because I have other plans for us. Now go to sleep." A

wicked grin spread across his beautiful face. "You'll need all the energy you can muster."

19

I WOKE UP to an empty bed and a warm yet slightly sore sensation in my lower body. My arm stretched out to the imprint on Jett's pillow and touched the place where he had been sleeping a few hours ago. We had a written understanding, which included no clause on romance and intimacy. Hence, falling asleep in Jett's arms had been strange, if not to say scary, because deep down I knew this wasn't part of the deal. In the end, when his breathing had flattened and his muscles had become limp, I just rolled with it, thinking one night wouldn't hurt.

I had been wrong.

Bad move, Stewart.

Because, as I lay on my back, staring at my reflection in the oversized mirror above my head, I could see something in my eyes that hadn't been there before.

I was beginning to like him—everything about him. His body, his touch, his smile, his way of talking, and him as a person. Usually, when that happened in the past, I ran as fast as I could, leaving my feelings and the person behind. What I saw in my eyes was an unwillingness to run. For some reason I wanted to stay and see where it might take me.

"It's not going to take you anywhere because nothing's happening," I mumbled to myself, jumping out of bed annoyed. I had never fallen for anyone, and I wouldn't let it happen now. I had liked Sean, but I wasn't in love with him. I never was with anyone. Sure Jett was handsome, witty, and amazing in bed, but he was also the kind of guy you had fun with, not the one you brought home to meet the parents. When I signed the contract I knew what I was getting myself into.

I headed for my room to take a quick shower, brush my teeth, put on a clean pair of jeans and a shirt, and then joined him downstairs in the kitchen. He was leaning against the open balcony door, holding a cup of steaming coffee, his back turned to me. A warm morning breeze wafted in, carrying the sylvan scent of damp wood and blossoming flowers. He had slipped into a pair of blue jeans, but his back was naked—all flexed muscles under flawless, bronze skin. For a split second I just stood there watching him—mesmerized. I wondered how he would behave after our first night together. Would he bolt? Would he keep his distance? Pretend like nothing happened?

Lost in thought he didn't hear me, so I cleared my parched throat and took a step forward, watching him intently as he turned. For a brief second I caught a dark shadow in his eyes, and then it dissipated into appreciation, as though he liked what he saw, and a lazy grin spread across his beautiful lips.

"Good morning, gorgeous." His dark hair framed his face in a disheveled way that invited me to run my fingers through it. His voice was raw and sexy, rich with lust, just like his electrifying eyes. He reached me in two long strides and wrapped his arm around me, pulling me against his strong chest. My breasts rubbed against him, and the air charged between us.

He handed me his mug of coffee and watched me take a sip. It was black and unsweetened, just the way I preferred it. No one I knew had their morning coffee this way.

"Thanks." I handed the mug back to him. His arm remained wrapped around me as he took a sip and then handed it back to me. It was such a simple yet intimate gesture that it threw me off balance. I don't know why my mind made such a big deal out of it, but somehow, the way we shared this cup of coffee made my heart beat just a little bit faster and turned my smile just a little bit wider.

Post-coital bliss.

"I figured it's the way you'd drink it," Jett said.

"Why?"

"Because it's the way I drink it."

I peered up at the nonchalant expression on his face. Was he suggesting that we had lots of things in common? I wanted to ask, but decided against it. Did it really matter what he thought? In a few weeks, we'd be done shagging this insane attraction and lust out of each other, and then we'd move on as planned. No feelings whatsoever. Maybe we'd stay friends, and maybe not. It didn't matter either way. I intended to enjoy it as long as it lasted.

"Slept well?" Jett asked, changing the subject. I nodded. 'Good' was an understatement. Cradled in his arms, I hadn't slept this well in years. "You said something in your sleep." His tone changed slightly and I instantly froze.

"What?" I asked warily.

His eyes bore into me with such intensity I feared they could penetrate years of steel and rake through my soul. "You said, 'please don't hurt me'."

A cold shudder of dread rushed down my spine and turned my insides as cold as ice. The sudden urge to free myself from his embrace and get the hell away from him overwhelmed me. And yet, years of calculated planning kicked in, and I didn't move an inch. Jett wasn't the first man to come close to the truth, and he wouldn't be the last. No need to panic. I had enough experience to deal with this.

I drew a long, silent breath to steady my nerves and clutched at the coffee mug just a little bit tighter while hiding my hands from his view, so he wouldn't notice the white knuckles. "It was just a nightmare. I don't really remember it."

But I did. Vivid and cold in all its glory.

"Do you have those often?" His scrutinizing gaze brushed over my face, and his expression changed to brazen interest.

"Not really."

I did, almost every night for the past twelve years. Twelve years of blaming and self-hate, of wishing I could turn back the clock and do things differently.

Jett hesitated. He didn't believe a word I said.

Shit.

He was growing suspicious. I could see it in his intense gaze and worried frown.

"Did someone hurt you?"

"What?" I laughed, and almost choked on the sudden tears blurring my vision. "No, of course not. I told you it was just a dream. Just leave it at that."

His shoulders remained tense and he didn't look away. He didn't even blink.

Double shit.

I knew my words came out all defensive and

incriminating the moment he nodded slowly, as though I had just confirmed his suspicions. The vein in his right temple began to throb visibly beneath his skin. His jaw set and his eyes blazed with anger. I knew that look. It was the same look the police officer gave me the moment he told me they wished they could help, but it was probably too late.

I hated that look and everything it implied. You couldn't change the past, no matter how hard you tried to shake at the gates of your life. People kept saying time heals all wounds, but in my case the memories buried deep within my soul never stopped torturing me with their vivid pictures and hurtful words.

So all that remained was me pretending it never happened. I had been trying that for years and almost succeeded, until a card popped up in the mail a few weeks ago, and turned my carefully planned lie of a life upside down.

"Who was it?" Jett asked softly, his voice barely able to contain his anger.

I shook my head. "No one."

"Who was it?" he repeated more demanding. His index finger moved beneath my chin and forced my eyes to meet his. I searched his gaze, expecting anger and pity. The anger was there, but there was no hint of pity. Whatever he thought had happened to me, he also thought I was strong enough to deal with it.

Under his scrutinizing gaze the memories began to rush through my head, and a bolt of pain headed straight for my heart. I had pushed them deep inside the pits of my soul for so long, entombing them beneath layers of concrete and steel. But now the dam was about to erupt.

Shit and shit again.

"Please, don't do this." My whisper was so low I doubted Jett had heard it. Breaking free from his embrace, I dashed out into the backyard, eager to put as much physical and emotional distance between Jett and me as possible. I slumped down on the bench and pulled my legs to my chest. The warm breeze dried my moisture-stained cheeks, and I only now realized I was crying. I wiped at the tears hastily, angry with myself that I talked in my sleep, angry with Jett that he had to bring it up, angry with the world that shit happened and no one ever tried to stop it.

As I forced air into my lungs I began to rock back and forth, silently begging Jett to let it be, but I knew he wasn't the type to turn his back on a woman.

"Brooke?" His voice reached me a moment before he appeared around the corner, his eyes burning with worry and determination.

"Leave me alone." My demand was a feeble one; certainly not firm enough to fool anyone with a morsel of common sense. I had never talked to anyone. For some reason I wanted to talk to him; I just needed a few more minutes to gather my strength and exhume a past that had almost destroyed me once.

Jett's arms moved around my back and he pressed my head against his hard abdomen, rocking me like you'd rock a child. "It's okay." His words were meant to soothe me, but they only managed to stir up another wave of anger.

"It's not. It never will be."

"Tell me about it." He sat down beside me and pulled me in his arms. I cradled my head in the hollow of his shoulder and took deep breaths to steady myself for what was to come. Maybe it was the silence of the countryside and the serenity of the landscape. Maybe it was the fact that I was far away from home and the demons of my past. Or maybe it was his determined presence and the fortitude he seemed to exude from every pore. Whatever it was, it made both the words and my tears flow.

20

JENNA AND I weren't just sisters, we were best friends and as close as two people could get. Being two years older than me, she was my idol and everything I wasn't: skinny, blonde, and extremely popular. Everyone preferred her, even my parents, which was okay by me because I adored her, too, and looked up to her throughout my childhood. When she began dating Danny at age fifteen, I was jealous of the attention she lavished upon him and naturally disliked the guy, probably sensing deep down just how strange he was.

Danny was the kind of guy you didn't want around your squeaky clean daughter. He was older, and had just dropped out of school. Jenna told me that he used to hang out with his friends a lot and only met up with her when he felt like it; never when she needed him. The moment she began dating him, I could almost see her changing before my eyes. My once vivacious sister turned her back on most of her friends and transformed into someone who'd spend hours locked up in her room for no apparent reason, or become aggressive, smashing things. I often covered for her so she could meet Danny, and when she returned home from him in the early morning hours, she'd look beat-up and greasy, her eyes unnaturally big, and her hands trembling. I didn't know he gave her drugs. As a thirteen-year-old you were told of the dangers, but you didn't know the signs and couldn't put two and two together.

I don't know how long this went on. Maybe a few months, half a year tops. By the time my parents saw the puncture marks on her skin and sent her to a counselor, she was an emotional wreck and scared out of her mind. Jenna was hospitalized and remained in treatment for another half year, and when she returned I was naïve enough to believe everything would return to normal.

"It didn't," Jett whispered, jerking me back to reality. I shook my head and, realizing my nails were dug into the fragile skin of his arm, I peeled my hand off him. Five tiny red marks remained imbued where I had clutched at him for support. Jett showed no sign that it bothered him. He didn't even flinch as I brushed my fingers over the indentations, wondering whether it was my nature to hurt people without even realizing.

"Shortly after she returned, he invited us both over to a party. I didn't want to go because my parents had forbidden any contact with him, but Jenna wouldn't listen. She told me he was the love of her life, and I believed her."

I hesitated as I let the memories of the few hours that changed my family's fate scroll before my eyes like a motion picture. My hands were shaking. My unshed tears sat like a rock in my throat, almost choking me. Sensing my distress, Jett's grip on my hand tightened but he remained quiet, as though he knew all I needed from him was to listen to the story I had never shared with anyone.

"Jenna made me promise I wouldn't tell anyone. Jenna didn't come back that night. I didn't know what happened, so when she wasn't home the next morning I had to tell my parents, who called the police. We looked everywhere for her," I whispered, my tears finally finding release, spilling onto my cheeks in angry rivulets that soaked the material of my shirt. "They found her body in an apartment owned by one of Danny's friends. It turned out she had been plied with drugs, and her body had been sold to several men who gang-raped her. We were told she died of internal bleeding. When Danny was charged with murder, I was the one who had to testify against him. His friends kept threatening they'd hurt my family, and I had no one to talk to." I stopped, fighting for breath. How could I tell Jett I didn't have the courage to pull it through? My sister's murderer walked free because I feared for my and my parent's life.

"I'm sorry," Jett said softly.

I shook my head in response. No pity. I didn't deserve it. Not after the ordeal Jenna went through, and certainly not after the events her death brought upon my family. My tears slipped between my lips. I could feel the salty tang on my tongue, drying out the cave of my mouth. My heart beat so fast it seemed as though it wanted to tear my ribcage apart. The choking sensation around my neck tightened, and yet I wasn't going to back off from the panic attack gathering inside me.

Jett and I remained quiet for a few moments as I snuggled into his strong arms for support. His handgrip was so tight I feared he'd stop my blood circulation, but the sting was welcome. It kept my mind sane for a few more moments so I could finish what I had started. For once I was ready to share the pain and think about the consequences later.

"My mother never blamed me, but my father did," I began slowly. "He never got over Jenna's death."

"Are you still in touch?"

I hesitated as I considered my answer carefully. No, we weren't in touch. We couldn't be. "He killed himself a few weeks later."

"I'm sorry, Brooke," Jett whispered into my hair. His arms tightened around me, gathering me deeper into his arms, and I let myself fall into his embrace as I tore down the last shreds of defense I had built around myself in the last twelve years.

21

I DON'T KNOW how we ended up in his bed. It happened so quickly that my haunted mind didn't even register it. The sun was shining through the tall bay window, and my fingers were buried in Jett's hair, pulling him on top of me as my mouth tugged at his lips with an urgency I had never felt before.

My tongue thrust between his lips and my fingers began to unbutton his shirt to find the hot skin beneath. His muscles were hard and tense, just like the throbbing sensation between my legs.

"Brooke." His whisper was an unspoken question.

"It's fine." As though to prove my point, my right hand clasped around his neck and pulled him down harder, closing the space left between us.

"Wait." He pulled away slightly, his eyes burning with

need. "I don't want you to think I'm taking advantage of your state."

He wasn't a bad guy, I could feel it in my heart. Maybe it was the reason I had opened up to him about my past; why I wanted to give him everything I had, my body and mind.

"I told you, I'm fine," I said. "This is what I need right now. Will you give it to me?"

Our eyes collided and for a moment Jett was all I could see and feel. His fingers moved to trace the contours of my lips, leaving a tingling sensation behind.

"I wish I could ease your pain forever, Brooke," he whispered.

Yeah, I wished that, too.

My eyes swelled up with moisture. I tried to turn my head to hide my unshed tears but his hand clasped my chin, holding my gaze transfixed on his. Ever so gently he lowered his lips and kissed the corners of my eyes, then moved to my cheeks, then to my lips. Somehow his sensual and tender touch was more erotic than the passion-fuelled kiss we had just shared. His surprising gentleness stoked my arousal to a fevered pitch. I wanted him, and I wasn't afraid to take it.

My legs wrapped around his hips and I pulled him down until his weight crushed me, almost knocking the breath out of my lungs. His stubble grated my skin as I trailed my lips along his jawline.

"Fuck me, Jett."

I had never spoken this demand to anyone in my life. It made my cheeks blush with shame, and my nipples throb with anticipation. But I didn't care. The pain inside me had to be stilled somehow. If only for a short while.

"I've never wanted anything more," he groaned against my mouth. A moment later his lips found mine in a tortuously slow kiss. He sat up and lifted me onto his lap to remove my shirt followed by my bra. I shrugged out of my jeans and then helped him remove my panties. His fingers lingered between my thighs, rubbing gently between my folds.

"I like it when you're so wet." His electric eyes mirrored the desire in his voice.

He didn't just make me wet; he made me ache for his touch. But today, I wanted to touch him back and make him feel all the sweet things he did to me.

"Take off your jeans," I whispered, watching him as he followed my command.

Our eyes remained locked as my fingertips grazed the hard ridges of his abdomen and moved to the waistband of his shorts. Beneath them, he was already hard, the contours of his erection clearly visible under the thin material. I pulled them down his hips and watched his impressive erection jerk out. He looked even bigger in broad daylight, the slick crown engorged, ready to take me to pleasure heaven. I only needed to ask.

I ran my fingertips against his swollen shaft and soaked in his deep moan.

"Brooke." He moistened his luscious lips, and his eyes followed my every move, watching me with such intensity it sent jolts of fire through my sex.

I wanted to lick each droplet from his slick skin. Ever so slowly I held him with both hands and I lowered my mouth onto the thick head, sucking it deep between my lips. He quaked inside my mouth and a sexy rumble escaped his throat.

"Oh, fuck." His voice sounded just as choked between his ragged breaths, and for once I felt I was in control with no need to hide my desire.

"I want to know what you taste like," I whispered, repeating Jett's words when he went down and dirty at the lake.

Releasing him from between my lips, I licked the slit and sucked him back inside, my tongue darting over the broad head in a slow rhythm. He rasped my name once, then again. The sound of his voice turned me on to such an extent, I wanted to throw him onto his back and straddle him, drive his hard flesh into me and demand the climax I felt building within us both.

Not yet.

I wasn't nearly finished with him. Still gazing up at Jett, I ignored my own needs as I bathed in his lust. With a desperate groan, he pulled away, putting a few inches between us. His erection jerked in my hands. His eyes closed, as a deep shudder rocked his abdomen.

"What are you doing to me?" His voice stroked my senses like silk. He was close; I could see it in his clouded gaze and the way his ragged breath rocked his chest. My hands reached out for him, so I could finish what I had started. He groaned with desire but didn't protest as I put him back between my lips, sliding my tongue down his length.

"Do you want me to make you come, Jett?"

His breath hissed out between clenched teeth, and his eyes darkened with desire. "Only if you want to." No pressure, no demands. I liked that about him. It showed that he wasn't greedy; he liked to give as much as he liked to get.

"I want to," I whispered, wondering where this confident vixen had been hiding all her life.

Slow or quick?

I bit my lower lip wickedly, wondering whether to tease him mercilessly so he'd never forget me, or give him a hard but fulfilling release he'd never forget either.

In the end I knew what I had to do.

Smiling, I lowered my wet lips onto the swollen tip and sucked it into my mouth slow and deep.

"That's good, baby. Just like that."

His deep groans and words of encouragement spurred me on. His fingers tangled in my hair, but he didn't push. He let me do as I pleased.

"You're driving me crazy, Brooke." His whisper turned into a guttural rasp. Circling the base of his thickening shaft, my fingers worked up and down, slowly, then faster, until I felt the tell-tale tremble of his imminent release. I stopped and pressed my tongue against his slick slit, forcing him to a halt. His grip in my hair tightened and his hips rocked forward with their unspoken plead for more. I could feel his racing pulse beneath my fingers, could taste just how close he was in the salty tang of his moisture. The knowledge that I did this to him left me hot and flustered. The sounds and flavors of his arousal excited me so much, my own moisture began to slick my entrance, readying me for his touch.

In our moment of intimacy, I not only owned his lust and pleasure, he was mine.

Tightening my grip around him, I began to suck him deep into my mouth. He rewarded me with another groan, this one louder and more demanding.

Close. So close.

"Brooke." The muscles of Jett's rock hard torso tightened and he thrust forward. The big crown jerked and hot moisture surged within my mouth. I kept him perched between my lips until the waves of climax subsided and Jett slumped down next to me, pulling me to his damp chest, one leg resting between my thighs.

He was spent; he had to be because I had given it my all, exhausting every bit of energy. My body snuggled against his hard muscles as Jett trailed his fingers up and down my back. Silence spread around us like a blanket, and I was almost lulled into a morning nap when I felt his lips on my face.

My gaze flew up to take in the wicked smile on his gorgeous face, and I narrowed my eyes. "What are you doing?"

"I'm going to fuck you senseless," Jett said, "tease you the way you teased me, and make you come the way no one's ever made you come before."

My breath hitched in my throat, and I blushed hard and fast. "I see you've never heard of the magic of metaphors?" I pretended to slap his arm, mortified, but in secret I loved his dirty talk.

"Metaphors and flowery language are for those who don't know how to give their women a good ol' shagging." His shaft jerked to life against my thigh. He was up for it. Again.

Holy cow.

Where did he get all this energy from? I watched his hand move between our bodies to touch himself—once, twice, hardening, preparing—until he grew so big I doubted my small body could possibly accommodate him.

"Ready?" His eyes shimmered with humor and something else.

Hell no, I wasn't.

"Jett."

His erection rocked against the entrance of my body and in spite of my reservations, I moaned with anticipation. His fingers parted my private lips and spread the moisture pouring from within me.

"So wet and yet so tight," he murmured, pushing a long finger deep inside of me, followed by another. I panted as his fingers moved in and out in slow cadence, filling me enough to ignite a blaze, but not enough to prepare me for his huge erection. One more thrust and then he pulled out his fingers, replacing them with something much bigger, guiding himself inside my tunnel, impaling and stretching me, filling me up in a single hot movement.

I cried out in surprise as a rush of burning pleasure shot through me. My nerve-laden tissues parted around him as my sex struggled to accommodate the invasion. Burying my nails into the rippling muscles of his chest, I was unsure whether to pull him toward me or push him away. Hot waves of pleasure rolled over me, bringing the sweet promise of release…if only I could stand his sweet torture long enough.

Jett dipped his tongue into my mouth and began to

move, his tongue mirroring the fast movement of his hips. Pushing up on his elbows, his palms settled around my breasts. His thumbs began to pinch my hardening nipples, tugging and teasing, and his hard flesh plunged deep inside me. I arched my back to welcome his thrusts and bit my bottom lip hard, struggling to keep from moaning.

"Come for me, Brooke," Jett whispered. His thumb found the sensitive nub of my clitoris and began to massage it in slow, circular motions. I cried out at the quivering sensations meeting with the currents of fire his thrusts sent through my sex. My body quivered beneath him as my vision blocked out everything but his electrifying eyes transfixed on me, gazing into my soul.

"Jett." My lips released his name in a long whimper. With each thrust and caress, the pulsing sensation between my legs intensified until I thought I'd pass out from the sheer pleasure.

"That's it, baby," Jett whispered, cupping my buttocks and pushing himself inside me just a bit deeper. It couldn't be more than an inch but it was enough to push me over the edge. A strong tremor shot through my abdomen, bringing with it wave after wave of delicious release. Grinding my hips into his, I clenched my muscles around him, struggling to ride the roller coaster of lust just a little bit longer. Jett's groan joined my cry, and his hot seed spilled deep inside me, filling me with a new sensation.

Eventually, he pulled out of me and rolled to the side, drawing me into his arms like he had before, his lips whispering against my damp hair.

Wow. Just double wow. It was the most amazing sex I ever had.

"Are you okay?"

Cheeks burning, I nodded.

"This was insane. You're incredible," he whispered. "You've given me more than I ever envisioned anyone could."

I had to agree I felt the same way. Even though it was just sex, his words made me feel warm and woozy inside. My heart began to thump just a little bit harder as his lips found mine and engaged them in a slow and delicious kiss. As the tension of climax began to fade, we remained locked in our embrace, trembling from the faint ripples of subsiding pleasure. With the bright rays of sun warming our naked bodies, I fell asleep in Jett's arms, strangely laid-back about the array of emotions this man had started to evoke in me. For the first time, I had surrendered my whole self to a man.

22

JETT AND I spent another hour in bed, tangled in each other's embrace, while keeping our conversation light and mostly focused on his company. What drew me away from him eventually was my stomach's rumbling. Jett had made me burn through my energy supplies, and now my body demanded food.

"Why don't you get dressed while I check whether lunch is ready?" Jett's gaze burned down on me, and I could sense his hesitation at leaving the sanctuary of our bedroom.

I smiled and got out of bed, walking leisurely to pick my clothes off the floor. His heated gaze brushed my naked rear and sent shivers of pleasure down my spine.

"Damn." Jett shook his head as another smile lit up his face. If I had learned anything about my new boss it was that he was a man of monosyllabic expressions. However, one single non-descript word coming from him conveyed more flattery than I had heard in my entire life.

I rolled my eyes. "Stop the buttering up. You had me already." I held up two fingers. "Twice."

"I thought I might put in the legwork for tonight." His grin widened at my scowl. Truth be told, I didn't need his compliments. I was ready to drop my panties for him if he so much as smiled in my direction, meaning the panty-dropping smile wasn't a myth. I had finally found what Sylvie had been going on about ever since the day we met. Too bad I couldn't tell her about it.

Sylvie.

My brain briefly registered that I hadn't called or texted her last night, even though I had promised to. As much as I loved spending day and night in Jett's bed, there was a world outside those bedroom walls. And forgetting about my best friend was definitely a big, fat no-go.

I shrugged into my clothes and left Jett to take a shower, ignoring the invitation to join him. If I took him up on the unspoken offer of yet more fun, I knew we'd end up starved and, in my case, probably way behind my work schedule. While booting up my laptop, I checked my cell phone. There were five missed calls, two voice mails, and three text messages, all from one person. Even though it might sound like a lot, coming from Sylvie, who was addicted to her cell phone, anything under twenty calls and ten text messages wasn't urgent.

As much as I loved Sylvie, she could be a real pain.

Heaving an exasperated sigh, I texted to remind her I couldn't have private conservations during working hours and promised to write an uber long email, then went about checking Jett's business correspondence when my cell rang.

I knew it was Sylvie before I even glanced at the screen. Sitting on my bed, I pressed the response button.

"What the heck, Brooke," her voice greeted me. "Italy's only across the big pond, but the way you keep ignoring me, it might as well be situated on the moon and you have no reception." I could hear the sulk in her voice. Sylvie in a disgruntled state was never good. She could go on and on for hours.

"I'm so sorry. This job's been extremely demanding and—" I trailed off, letting her fill in the gaps. It was a harmless, white lie; Jett came with the job and he *had* been demanding a lot of my time and energy. Not that I complained.

"Mayfield has you working around the clock?" Her tone gave me a preview of the sarcasm about to erupt. "Seriously, Brooke, if I didn't know any better I'd bet my designer wardrobe on you shagging the boss."

I laughed nervously. "You're hilarious." My tone came out all wrong, because a moment later Sylvie gasped and the line went silent. I held my breath as my mind tried to come up with something—anything—to steer her away from her spot-on guess. Once she grew suspicious, she was like a hound dog that wouldn't back off from a hot trail. Come to think of it, she was worse.

"Okay, that was about the most laughable thing you've ever said." My tongue tripped over itself to assure Sylvie that nothing was going on. Unfortunately, Sylvie had an uncanny ability to read between the lines.

"What does he look like?"

"Who?" I knew playing dumb wouldn't be of much help.

"Mayfield."

"Old."

Sylvie clicked her tongue. The sound reverberated down the line right into my ear, making me cringe. "Please! Age never stopped anyone. Guys are like ripe wine: the older they grow, the more attention they get."

I forced a chuckle out of my throat, like I knew what she was talking about. Truth was, I didn't since I could count all the guys I ever slept with on the fingers of one hand, and they sure hadn't been the sugar daddy type.

"So," Sylvie continued. "You're doing the dirty with the boss, and I don't like it."

"What? No."

"Brooke. I know you better than you know the back of your hand."

She didn't, or so I liked to believe. I sighed into the line. If I couldn't convince her, the best way to get her off my back was to cut the call short. "I'm sorry about not calling or texting. I'm just tired." True. "And this job's been weird so far." Also true. "I'll make it up to you as soon as I get home next week." I had no doubt Sylvie would bully me into making that part true as well. "Please, can we just leave it at that?"

It was the second time I asked this question in twenty-four hours. Just like Jett, Sylvie had no idea when to back off.

"No."

"You told me to have fun."

"Yeah, but not thousands of miles away where I couldn't kick the guy's ass if he tried to hurt you."

I smiled at the picture Sylvie's words conjured before my eyes. As a Pilates goddess with muscles of steel, she sure as hell could do some major damage. Too bad she didn't use all that power on Ryan.

"Look," Sylvie continued, "I'm worried about you being all alone in a different country with some guy you don't know."

"Why?"

"Because—" she blew out her breath, pausing "—you're not like me. You have feelings and standards and you deserve more than that. Promise you'll stay safe and tell me everything when you get back?"

I nodded. "Uh-huh."

"One last word of advice, guys like him and Ryan are trouble. Good looks and successful careers are a dangerous combination."

Trouble—wasn't that the word I used upon meeting Jett for the first time? I frowned. "Thanks."

"Okay." She didn't sound too happy to drop the subject, but it was good enough for me. The air was clear. I had managed to dodge a bullet and buy myself a few more days before I'd be Sylvie-interrogated. "Have you found out who sent the Manila envelope still cluttering our expensive coffee table in the hall?" she asked, finally changing the subject. "I'm really scared to sleep with that thing inside the house. It looks like something from *Law & Order* that's ready to blow up."

I rolled my eyes, grateful she couldn't see it. "It's only a letter, for crying out loud. Just open it if it bothers you so much."

"Can't you send someone over to do it, like your mother? Or—" She paused and I could almost hear the wheels of her brain working away. The sad thing about Sylvie was that she actually meant every word. "I guess I could ask Ryan. Since he's dating some double DDs, he's as good as dead to me."

I didn't want to mention that guys like him, meaning

ridiculously rich and manipulative, always ended up going for plastic, be it bigger breasts or shiny new credit cards. But why state the obvious? Sylvie needed to heal, and expressing my disdain would only make her more obsessed with a jerk unworthy of her obsession.

"I'll be back next week," I said. "Until then, just leave it on my desk and forget about it. I bet it's not even important."

"It looks important."

Then open the darn thing, I felt like yelling. "Leave it in my room, and I'll take care of it when I get back home."

"And what about the foreign guy who keeps calling? He doesn't want to believe you're not around, and it gives me the creeps."

"I'll be back *next week*," I repeated slowly, emphasizing the last two words.

A sulky pause, then, "Fine. It really sucks without you. Promise me you'll never get hitched and have kids. Or if you do, we'll live next door from each other so I can visit any time."

"Sounds great." Living next door to each other was always our dream. However, if we ever ended up married, I doubted my husband would be so keen on the best friend's constant presence breathing down his neck.

"I'll think about it." We chatted for a few more minutes, mostly focusing on Sylvie's nightly escapades, before I hung up with the promise to call again as soon as I could.

Clutching my cell phone to my chest, it felt surreal to sit in a stranger's room thousands of miles away from home, keeping secrets from my best friend. Sylvie and I had always told each other the truth, even if said truth hurt the other's feelings. The contract clearly stated that I wasn't to tell anyone about the agreement, but Jett had assured me the rules could be changed. So why did I not ask him to change this particular one?

Because you're scared she'll tell it like it is, and you know it won't be pretty.

Had I fallen for my very own Ryan? Was I repeating Sylvie's mistake? It was just a thought that briefly crossed my mind, and yet I couldn't quite dismiss it. I long established that Jett wasn't a liar like Ryan. He never pretended to want more than a physical relationship, to which I had agreed. But somehow my mind didn't want to acknowledge that major difference between Jett and Ryan.

I sighed and forced my ugly thoughts to the back of my mind. Sylvie would find out about my agreement soon enough, upon which I'd deal with her candid opinion and metaphorical kick in the backside. Right now I enjoyed the present, doing whatever I felt like doing, without my best friend telling me how stupid I was for jumping into bed with my boss. Had she not been the one telling me to have fun in the first place? Would I have had the guts to do it if she didn't advise me to go wild and lose all inhibitions? Probably not, but for once I was happy to have listened. A week with Jett and I felt more alive than I had in ages. However, I wasn't so naïve to believe this trip would go on forever. It was just sex and a bit of fun. Sooner or later, one of us would grow bored and move on. No matter what happened, I knew I wouldn't go back to the old, dreary, safe me. I wouldn't go back to being *conventional*. At least not any time soon. And for that I was thankful to both Sylvie and Jett.

"Brooke, are you coming? I'm missing you already." Jett's sexy voice pulled me back to reality.

"Give me five minutes." I smiled at his choice of words. I loved the way he said my name because it made me feel special. Of course his words meant nothing because he couldn't possibly miss me after only twenty minutes. Shrugging out of my clothes, I jumped into the shower, my mind already filling with hundreds of thoughts of all the things I wanted to do to him before the week was over.

***

After a light lunch that consisted of grilled chicken fillets with salad, Jett headed for his private office to catch up on his workload, leaving me with the instructions not to bother him with any calls unless they were from his brother or father. His voice bore an urgency that didn't go unnoticed, and I wondered whether he had troubles I didn't know about, maybe a sick relative or family drama. In the end I didn't ask. I figured that even though I had spilled out most of my secrets, he had shown no disposition to want to do the same. Maybe he needed more time to confide in me.

My lips were still tingling from his heated goodbye kiss when I returned to my room to grab my laptop and then sat down at my desk. Even though Jett had cleared his schedule for the week, countless messages cluttered his email inbox and voicemail. I went through each one of them, registering names and queries. The urgent ones received an immediate answer with the assurance Jett would get back to them as soon as he could. Two hours later, the business correspondence had been dealt with, and I was free to accustom myself with the company's financial reports and major property accounts.

Mayfield Properties was a huge company with hundreds of millions in turnover and as such had a dozen board directors, all pocketing their fair share of profits. At the top of the ladder were Robert and Jonathan Mayfield, father and son respectively, followed by Jett, who at thirty-one was the youngest board member and probably the only one engaging in direct sales and property acquisition. Because of his young age, I had thought he was gifted his place in the company by his father, until I glimpsed the sales and profits

Jett had made in the last year alone.

Holy cow.

The guy knew how to make money, and a lot of it. I almost choked on my breath as I counted all the zeros on the spreadsheets: one hundred million worth of properties, most of them spread across the United States, with some sprinkled throughout Europe. There was a systematic approach to it. His clients were exclusively business moguls and celebrities who came to him based on recommendations. They either had a particular estate in mind or very specific ideas of what they wanted, and it was Jett's job to make it happen. He found the right estate, groomed the owner by paying for all-inclusive trips to the most luxurious places I only knew from tabloids and television documentaries about the lives of the rich and famous, and then somehow persuaded them to sell at a price convenient to his clients. Nothing new about that approach, only that Jett seemed extremely good at what he did, and with very little college education. I was impressed, not to mention a bit star-struck, at all the well-known names that seemed to pop up in his files.

The guy was famous in his own right. One day an equally famous or rich woman would adorn his side. Probably someone as tall and beautiful as Sylvie, with sky-high legs to match an exotic and luxurious name, which was okay since I didn't want to be with Jett.

Or did I?

I couldn't help the sudden pang of jealousy piercing through my heart. What would it be like to be part of his personal life, introduced as the girlfriend rather than the personal assistant slash secret lover, who had to sign a contract so the world wouldn't know about her? To travel the world and make plans for the future?

A future with Jett.

Sleeping with a rich man was one thing, wanting to date him was another. I rolled my eyes at the brief onset of fairy tale attitude and pushed the nasty thoughts to the back of my mind, hating myself for letting them cloud my perception of what our agreement was all about: no relationship, just no-strings fun as long as it lasted. I had been okay with it. Heck, I even stressed the importance of being able to get out if I so desired. When did it all change?

The moment you entrusted him with your past.

It was the look in his eyes—a tiny flicker of intimacy intermingled with a growing sense of trust—that broke through barriers and made me see him in a different light. I'd let him get under my skin, and now he had started to occupy my every thought. It was the way he touched me, as if what we had was special. It was also the way he made love to me, making me feel wanted like no one had done before. I wanted to know everything about him, which is what I was doing right now, investigating his life under the pretense of finding out more about his business, but in reality I was searching *Google* and the gossip pages of various online tabloids for glimpses into his private life and gossip on alleged dates and girlfriends. In my thoughts *I* had become *we*. My heart began to drum in my ears as sudden realization dawned on me.

I barely knew him, and yet I was falling in love with him.

23

FOR THE NEXT few days Jett and I established a routine: we spent most of the time inside the house, having sex in all possible places. Every afternoon, we'd half-heartedly return to work, and I enjoyed the break from him. While our physical relationship was taking me to new heights, so were my feelings for him, and I needed a bit of space to clear my head. It was the day before our flight back to New York, during one of those 'breaks from sex' that his father called. Not realizing I was talking to Robert Mayfield on the other end of the line, I tried to divert him with the excuse that Jett wasn't available to take any calls until he said, "Ms. Stewart, please be so kind as to get my son. I trust he'll be available when he hears what I have to tell him."

It wasn't like me to feel intimidated, and yet there was

something in the old man's voice that made me put him through right away, even if it weren't for Jett's prior instructions to do so. Focusing back on work, I managed to push Jett's father out of my system when Jett barged in, his face a mask of irritation and anger.

"Did he say anything to you?"

I bit my lip, confused. "What?"

"My father—Robert." Jett inched closer and sat down on the edge of my desk, regarding me intently. If I didn't know any better, I could swear I was having my very own private investigation.

"Did I do anything wrong? Because if I have then I'm really sorry and I—" Panic washed over me. I always thought of myself as a professional, but maybe Robert Mayfield was used to a different tone. Maybe he had perceived my cold politeness as a rude brushoff, and now he wanted to get rid of me. I couldn't lose another job. Not so soon after losing the last one.

Jett's hands cupped my face and his electrifying eyes bore into mine. "No, baby, you haven't. I just need to know what he said, that's all."

"He asked me to put him through."

"Nothing else?"

I shook my head. "No."

"Okay." The dark clouds of his bad mood lifted almost instantly, and he leaned over the desk, his mouth capturing mine in a lingering kiss.

"Jett?" I murmured against his hot lips. "Are you busy?"

He pulled back to regard me and cocked a brow in wry amusement. "Why?"

My sex twitched at the naughty spark in his eyes. He knew what I wanted; he just wanted me to beg for it. I walked around the desk and stopped inches from his towering body. Standing next to me, he was so tall and intimidating I had to toss my head back and peer all the way up to meet his challenging gaze. I might not be able to kiss him, but there was something I could reach just fine. Brushing my fingers down the front of his shirt, I pulled it out of his slacks and began to undo the buttons one by one.

"Because I thought you might be needing a break." Just in case he didn't catch on to my subtle hint, I rubbed my hand against the hard bulge beneath his slacks.

He groaned and closed his eyes for a brief second. When he opened them again, his face was a mask of desire sending my panties into ready-to-drop mode. "Sure, but we might need to meet after working hours to finish what you've started."

I barely had time to nod before I found myself flat on my back with Jett camped between my legs, doing incredible things to my panting body.

***

Later that night I sat on Jett's bed—our bed, because I had barely used mine—as he packed his luggage. I had finished mine earlier, and was now fascinated by how obsessively neat he seemed to be, folding and arranging the contents of his suitcase, as though his expensive shirts wouldn't get all crumpled up anyway.

His brows were drawn together in a frown, and for a few minutes I thought packing mattered a great deal to him, until he said, "We're leaving before sunrise. You might want to spend the night in here so at least one of us doesn't miss the alarm."

There was something in his tone, a strange undercurrent that made me look up, surprised. He was staring at me, his face an impenetrable mask that made reading his emotions impossible.

"Okay."

"There's something I need to tell you," Jett said, inching closer. His mouth pressed into a stubborn line as his eyes searched mine. In that moment I saw a hint of vulnerability in him that I hadn't glimpsed before.

"Okay," I repeated, unsure where this was heading. My heart began to thump just a little bit harder, and a sense of foreboding washed over me. He wanted to talk and that usually didn't bode for good news.

He sat down on the bed and clasped my hand in his,

caressing my palm with his thumb. "The night we met and you woke up with me in your bed—" He paused until I nodded. "I know I let you believe that we slept together, but we didn't. I would never take advantage of a clearly intoxicated woman who doesn't even remember her name."

Holy shit.

"But you said we did."

He shook his head slowly. "I never said we did. You assumed it, and I never corrected you."

I peered at him lost for words. He was right, of course, but wasn't hiding the truth almost the same thing as lying? I had fretted over that night, believing I had cheated on Sean, believing I had been easy enough to sleep with a stranger, only to find out nothing happened.

"Are you mad?" Jett asked.

I took a deep breath and blew it out slowly. Was I mad? No. But I wished he had been frank with me, in which case I might have discovered sooner just how great he was. Any other man would have used the situation to his advantage, or worse yet, raped me.

Even if I knew the answer, I still had to ask. "But why did you come home with me?"

"Because some drunken idiot hit on you, and I was worried. I helped you and Sylvie get home safely. You didn't want me to leave, so I stayed. But nothing happened."

I swallow down the lump in my throat. "You were naked."

His glorious lips quirked up in a cheeky smile. "You know I sleep naked."

Smiling faintly, I inclined my head, realizing it was a good thing he let me believe we had done the dirty before, otherwise I would never have had the courage to start a sexual relationship with him.

"For all it's worth, I'm sorry," Jett said. "I know I should have told you, but the opportunity never presented itself, and then I didn't really see the point."

I waved my hand. "It's fine. But never lie to me again."

"There's something else."

I glanced up at his face. His brows were still drawn but his eyes shimmered with something I couldn't quite pinpoint.

Seriously, what was this? Confession day? I eyed him warily. "What?" His lips twitched, and I realized he was having a hard time not to laugh.

"I'm not sure you remember, but the next day I helped you home from yet another bar. You were drunk out of your mind, again."

My memories flew back to the night I found out about my promotion, and Sylvie decided she wanted to celebrate by wearing a belt as a skirt. She had been adamant she saw Jett watching us, and I had been pretty sure I caught a glimpse of green eyes through my alcohol-induced haze.

I should have asked what the heck he had been doing at *Vixen's* and how he had found me in the first place. Instead, I found myself smiling like an idiot, thinking how cute he was for taking care of me...until I realized I most certainly hadn't been a pretty sight.

"Oh, gosh." I dropped my head onto my arms, mortified. "I don't scrub up so well drunk."

"You were very talkative, and definitely a lot nicer than when you're sober."

Was that a hint of humor in his voice? I straightened up to take in the amused curve of his stunning lips. He was making fun of me.

"What did I say?"

"That I had the most gorgeous eyes."

Oh god.

I loved his eyes, but he didn't need to know that. At least I didn't say anything about his lips.

"Tucked in your bed you said you wanted to feel my mouth on your whole body."

Earth, swallow me up whole!

I groaned. "You probably misunderstood."

Jett inclined his head in mock concentration, probably recalling every single shameful word of that fateful night. "I doubt that. You were pretty specific with the details." The fragile skin under his twinkling eyes creased, and his lips

238

twitched as though he was having a hard time not to laugh. "I could show you what exactly you wanted me to do."

I had made a fool of myself already, so why not make the best of it?

"Sure." My mouth found his in a heated kiss as I let him pull me into bed, stripping our clothes off, our luggage forgotten.

***

Our flight back to New York had a half-hour delay. Sitting in the waiting area at Malpesa airport with Jett holding my hand felt surreal. For some reason, I expected him to put some distance between us once we left the privacy of his mansion. To my surprise, he didn't seem in the least fazed by people seeing us together. It gave me hope that once we were back in New York, he wouldn't end whatever we had because I liked him more than I wanted to admit.

We stopped to buy newspapers for him and magazines for me, and then boarded the plane for the nine hour flight that would take us back home. In the harsh veracity of the real world, he was rich, successful, and one of the most desired bachelors in New York—and I was, well, me. A world I hoped wouldn't tear us apart by pointing out just how different our lives were.

"You're probably eager to get home," Jett whispered in my ear so the flight attendant serving coffee wouldn't hear us, "but will you stay with me one more night? I'm not quite ready to let this go."

"I'd love to." Smiling, I kissed him as my heat began to do one somersault after another, probably interpreting more into his words than I should have.

24

AFTER WAKING UP in Jett's stunning apartment sixteen hours later, we lingered in bed, fingers intertwined, bodies melting in a tight embrace. Jett smelled of cologne and sex, and for the first time in my life I found the scent intoxicating, just like the man beside me. And it dawned on me that Jett had brought many 'firsts' into my life.

"What are you smiling about?" he whispered, tracing the contours of my lips with the index finger he had so shamelessly driven into me only an hour ago.

"Nothing." I stretched out like a cat in front of a fireplace, enjoying the last few hours before routine would kick in.

We were about to step out of our shell and back into the real world, which worried me. The last two weeks had been interesting, with very little work and very much other stuff.

Back home, it was only a matter of time until reality would crawl back in, and I realized things would most certainly change. I wished I could hold on to *us* forever, lock us up in a protective cocoon, and let the world pass us by so nothing and no one could ever touch or separate us.

Was that what love felt like? Wanting at all costs to protect the frail shell of emotions coating our hearts?

It was so easy to get wrapped up in him and his body, to let him take control. My mother had always said that no man should lead the way and no woman should just follow but, even though I barely knew him, I wanted to let him into my circle of trust because I could feel he'd never betray me.

"Is there anything you want to share with me?" he asked.

His question took me by surprise. Why would he ask me that? I sat up on my elbow, fully facing him. "I don't think so."

"What exactly are you looking for, Brooke? Because, from what I gathered, you don't really do relationships."

Another surprising statement. My heart pounded hard against my chest. "What makes you think that?"

"The way you still don't talk much about you shows me you don't trust me fully."

I opened my mouth to tell him he was wrong, and closed it. Was it true? Did I shut him off in some way or another? I thought back to one morning when he'd asked about my past relationships, and I avoided giving a straight answer. Could Jett have interpreted the fact that I didn't like talking about my past as a sign I wasn't interested in a relationship?

"Trust doesn't come easily to me," I said, unsure of what Jett really wanted to hear from me.

His eyes turned a shade darker and his jaw set. "Why? Is it because of what happened to Jenna? Because if that's the reason, I can assure you most men aren't like that guy."

"I know that." I knew Danny had targeted and abused her to pay for his habit. My therapists had told me that over and over again.

His gaze bore into my soul, searching for the answer I didn't want to give. How could he understand when all he knew about my past were a few empty words that barely managed to express a fragment of the pain I had to go through?

"Why?" Jett persisted. "Please, help me understand. I need to know whether there's—" He hesitated, keeping to himself what he had been about to say.

I took a deep breath, feeling my resolve waning. I had told him about my sister, which was my biggest secret. Why not share my feelings with him as well?

"Why do you even want to know? Why can't you just

leave it the way it is?" I whispered.

He shook his head, hesitating. I held my breath as I regarded his dense lashes casting dark shadows beneath his eyes. He was so beautiful it broke my heart, and we weren't even done yet. What would happen once he tired of me? Would I survive the pain? I had let down my guard and now I was in too deep. I should have run—the way I always did, and yet I had made no move to leave, neither physically nor emotionally. And now I was facing an array of emotions I had never felt for anyone before. Fear, desire, hope, and yet more fear. Emotions I couldn't deal with. Emotions that would suffocate me the moment our arrangement ended.

"This isn't working, Brooke. Don't get me wrong, the sex is amazing. But it's turning into something else, and I need to know where I'm standing. I need to know whether we'll ever be together."

My heart skipped a beat. It tended to do that a lot ever since he entered my life. What exactly was 'more'? A relationship? Or a different contract? "You want more?" I whispered, daring not to hope.

"Yes, Brooke. I do. I want to see where this is heading." His voice was deep and low. Sultry.

I peered into his eyes to see if he was joking, but his expression remained serious. Half of me wanted to jump right into his arms and never let him go, the way you see in movies. And the other half, as strange as it sounded, wished she could wipe out each and every memory that included him. Because I wanted him too much and I couldn't handle it. Because I had never felt this way before, and it scared the hell out of me. If I gave it a try and it didn't work out, my heart would shatter and my world would crumble. If he lost interest and broke up with me, it would kill me.

"But...we signed a contract." I almost choked on the words. There were a hundred reasons why this wasn't a good idea, one being that we barely knew each other. You don't jump headfirst into a relationship when you met the person two weeks ago and haven't really dated. And then there was that one issue that made any reasoning turn into dust.

I was falling in love with him.

"You said you had done contracts before, and that this is the way you like it," I continued, hoping he would reveal more about his past and his feelings for me. Anything to justify the decision I had already made.

Jett shook his head slowly. "I never said I had done this before."

"But you had a contract drawn up by your lawyers."

He nodded slowly, his gaze darkening. "It was their idea after an ex-girlfriend tried to screw me over with some sordid sex stories that never happened." Hesitating, he ran his fingers through his dense hair, reminding me that I had done the same thing just a few hours ago. "You're different. I know you're not sleeping with me because of my money."

"How do you know that?"

He placed my hand onto his chest. Beneath his skin, his heart thumped fast and in unison with mine. "Because I feel it," Jett said softly. "I always have. I wanted you right from the beginning, but you pushed me away, so I had to convince you. Otherwise you would never have given me a chance."

I smiled at the memories of the last two weeks. So much had happened. Never in my life did I imagine the arrogant guy I met at a bar would interest me on more than a sexual level. Someone I might fall for.

"I want *us* but at the same time I'm scared because—" I took a deep breath and let it out slowly, gathering the courage to share with him my biggest fear.

"It's okay, baby." His fingers brushed my cheek gently, settling right beneath my chin, where my pulse pumped hard and fast, matching the erratic speed of my changing emotions.

My eyes met his warm gaze in which I found the courage I needed. "My parents were so deeply in love. They adored the ground beneath the other's feet. When my father killed himself, my mother's soul died with him." I laughed to mask the choking sensation in my throat. "She turned into someone else, someone I didn't recognize. I lost her the moment he died, and no matter what I tried, she never recovered. I don't do relationships because I don't want to love and lose myself."

"What happened to your family was a tragedy, but many people have loving relationships. You can't rob yourself of that experience just because you're scared of loss before you've even given it a try."

I could see his conviction in his eyes, hear it in his tone, and feel it in his gentle touch on my body. He believed the happily-ever-after story, and I couldn't blame him for it, when he'd never experienced the ugliness of having one's family torn apart, or seeing one's sister falling for the wrong man only to end up dead.

"You think I haven't seen my fair share of shit happening?" Jett said.

Clamping my mouth shut, I remained silent. No point in arguing with him. Of course he had. I never doubted that. It just wasn't the same thing.

Jett sat up and put a few inches between us, staring me down. Angry waves wafted from him, and I knew a revelation was imminent. "You know why I like to use my mother's name? Because it's one of the few things she gave me before she left us behind. You lost your dad, whereas I never really had a mother because she couldn't stay sober. She blamed her addictions on my father's work schedule and his unwillingness to lay off the secretaries, strippers, and every female who'd open her legs for him. In the end she finally had the guts to divorce him. She took half of his fortune and left me and my brother behind. I ended up doing some pretty bad shit, of which I'm not proud."

"I'm sorry, Jett. I didn't know," I whispered and reached to touch his shoulder. My fingers lingered on the Tribal tattoo I never asked about. Even in the bright light, it looked gloomy and mysterious. *Frightening and dark.* I wanted to know everything about his past and him as a person. And in that instant I understood that he had insisted learning about my past and previous relationships because he probably felt the same need to know.

"Tell me more," I whispered. "Please."

Jett's jaw set, and his eyes turned into layers of ice. "She barely made the effort to write a card or call. As a kid, I thought it was my fault for not being good enough. It took me a while to understand my mother wasn't just an alcoholic, she was a drug user. She loved us, but she loved her drugs more. She chose to be like that, which in some way is worse than tragedy. I tried to help her. We all did, but she pushed us away. I learned to live with it and made it my prerogative to turn into a different person. A person capable of love and trust and intimacy." His hands cupped my face, his gaze boring into me, shaking my core. We had similar experienes in life. Maybe we weren't so different after all. If my sister didn't die, she might have gone on the same destructive path, like his mother. "Tragedy may hit all of us in one way or another, but fate's not our enemy, Brooke. We are. By locking yourself away from the world, you choose your own mistakes and destroy any chance of ever finding happiness. You cannot control life, but you can choose who you are and what you make of it."

I could feel the truth in his words, and it spoke to me on an innermost level. Tears pricked the corner of my eyes, but I didn't hide them.

"I'm sorry for my outburst," Jett said softly. "I didn't mean to upset you."

He kissed my forehead. His eyes were no longer clouded, as though he could leave the past behind by just looking at me. He wanted to be with me. And I wanted to be with him. But was it too soon to let love happen?

"Why do you want me?" I asked, suppressing the trembling of my voice. "I'm strange, definitely not perfect, and fucked up. Actually, a lot of the latter."

"Perfect is boring and overrated." He smiled that lopsided grin of his that made my lower abdomen twist and curl with delicious desire. "I'm looking for sexy, fun, kind, and honest. And you tick all the right boxes, Brooke." Compliments weren't my thing, but for some inexplicable reason Jett's words made me return the smile. "And then there's the fact that we're kindred spirits. You're fucked up and I'm fucked up too, and that makes great dinner conversation." He winked, as though he didn't really mean that, but his expression remained serious.

Maybe he was right and we both were far from perfect, even though he seemed pretty perfect to me. What mattered was that he had all the qualities I wanted in a man. "I like honesty, and you're honest."

"Then let's always be honest with one another," Jett whispered. "I was disappointed so often in my life, I vowed to never trust anyone again...until you came along. You weren't available emotionally. You weren't talking relationships and building castles in the air. That's sexy as hell. Men don't like the emotional and the needy."

"I can be needy at times," I whispered.

"I don't mind that, Brooke. Whatever happens, *we'll* figure it out." His eyes shimmered with anxious hope, as though he feared I might push him away.

Us.

I liked the sound of that.

"Give me a chance to prove that I'm good for you," Jett said.

My fingertips brushed his chin and settled on his chest where I could feel his heart drumming to a frenzied beat, almost matching mine. This was it, the moment I decided to change my life around. Another first and, I hoped, one of many more to come.

"I'd love to give us a try," I said.

His glorious lips curled into the most stunning smile I had ever seen, melting my heart. "I thought nothing would change your mind."

"What can I say, you're a master of persuasion. In fact, you're a guy with many talents." Smiling, I pulled him on top of me and wrapped my legs around his waist, ready to demand that he put one of those talents to good use.

25

IT WAS EARLY afternoon when I finally managed to drag myself out of Jett's steamy bed to text Sylvie I'd be back home in an hour, in case she had forgotten. Because my car was still parked at the airport, costing me a fortune, Jett offered to drive me. Since I wasn't keen on Jett's speeding through New York's streets, I declined in favor of the subway, which didn't bode well with him. In the end we decided to call a company car that would drive me home. I left my car keys with him because he insisted on getting someone to pick it up for me, and I even let him carry my luggage downstairs from his apartment while his driver was waiting.

"You'll text?" Shivering in the damp chill of a rainy afternoon, I bit my lip nervously. Playing the clingy girlfriend wasn't like me, and yet I couldn't help it. This was different. *We* were different.

Jett touched my nose with the tip of his finger, his eyes shining with wry amusement. "Will it freak you out if I do so while you're still in the car?"

A warm, fuzzy explosion settled deep in my chest. "I'd love that." He placed a gentle yet lingering kiss on my lips, and then held the door open for me.

After spending two weeks together, it felt surreal to drive away from him. Jett was where I belonged. To my surprise, the sudden realization didn't weigh me down; it made my heart beat faster, and soft flutters like those of hundreds of butterfly wings gathered somewhere in the pit of my stomach.

It was the first time I'd ever ridden in a limo, and Jett's driver made the journey even more memorable by pointing to a tiny refrigerator with snacks and champagne, which I politely declined. I wasn't there to eat; I wanted to enjoy the view. And there was plenty to see.

Sitting in the back seat of the plush limousine, I stared out the tinted windows at buzzing New York. The city was coming to life, and in some way I felt I was too. We had defined the relationship, and today was our first day as a couple. I was dating a hot, successful guy who was very much into me. For the first time in my life, I felt I wasn't as plain as I always thought. We had decided to keep our relationship a secret for a few more days, until I settled into my job. We didn't want people thinking I got the job because I was sleeping with the boss. Theoretically I was, but it hadn't been my intention to sleep my way up the career ladder. I had sex with Jett because I was attracted to him. Jett hired me because he wanted me. It was lust at first sight.

We had cancelled our contract after our midday romp, and I was finally free to reveal our status to Sylvie. In fact, Jett insisted on it, not telling me why. In my logic, it was a sign he wanted to enter my circle of friends and be introduced as my boyfriend. And I couldn't wait for the whole world to know we were together.

I arrived at our apartment shortly after three p.m. and opened the door with apprehension, unsure what to expect. My best friend could be one of two things: so elated to see me that she'd forget I sort of hid the truth from her, or pissed because I kept a secret for two weeks. As I opened the door, I certainly didn't expect to see the whole neighborhood gathered in our living room, shouting 'Surprise' at the top of their lungs. How the hell did Sylvie manage to gather the whole clique, including people I didn't even know, in such a short time? She must have planned it for days. And that's when it dawned on me that Sylvie could be a third thing: in party mode.

"Thanks, guys." I put my suitcase down near the door and let a few of my friends envelop me in tight hugs, welcoming their congratulations on the new job. My gaze wandered across the room, sweeping over smiling, already intoxicated faces, and red drinking cups that littered our small living room. My attention fell on Sylvie who was squeezing her way toward me, her emotions clearly visible in her pouting lips and narrowed eyes.

She was mad but also curious. Our phone conversation hadn't been forgotten. Knowing her focus on being liked by everybody, I knew she wouldn't go for drama with so many people around. But there'd be plenty of hissed reproaches and venomous looks.

Taking a deep breath, I smiled.

I could deal with that. A crouching tigress was better than a pouncing one.

"Hey, you," I said, grabbing her in a tight hug. "I missed

you like crazy."

"Stewart, you're so screwed." Her blue eyes twinkled, but her pout remained in place.

I made a point of unbuttoning my jacket in slow motion as I regarded her from under my lashes, teasing her with a wicked smile. "From that I gather you don't want to hear the dirty?"

"You're killing me."

Laughing at her exaggerated eye roll, I grabbed a cup and took a sip of what tasted like Sylvie decided to empty an entire mini bar in there, and pulled her into a relatively quiet corner.

"Your plane landed yesterday. Where the heck have you been?" Her eyes spat fire. "Do you realize I had to keep this party up all night and day? You owe me a fortune for the booze."

"I slept with him and now we're together," I blurted out, unable to contain the excitement in my voice.

For some reason I expected her to ask who I was talking about, but Sylvie just inclined her head and kept silent for a few moments, the glint in her eyes not quite mirroring the excitement I felt.

"At least he called," was all she said.

"What?" I said slowly, shaking my head in confusion. "At least *who* called?" What was she talking about?

Waving her hand, she exhaled a long breath. "I told him I'd come after him with a pitchfork if he didn't."

"Who?" I crossed my arms over my chest, my gaze scanning her cryptic expression. I really had no idea what she was talking about.

"Who do you I think?" She rolled her eyes. "Jett, of course."

"You know his name?" Why did she know his name?

"Of course I do."

"How?" It was a stupid question. Her raised eyebrow said it all. They had exchanged numbers on that fateful night before I woke up with him in my bed. Or maybe during their morning talk while I was taking a shower and preparing myself for work. Later, she had offered to tell me his name, but I thought she was bluffing. I didn't like it. Not one bit. All heat drained from my cheeks as something else dawned on me.

"You stayed in touch?" My voice sounded like a bird's croak, all low and hoarse. The first wave of shock hit me hard. It wasn't because my best friend had his number. I wasn't *that* jealous and insecure. I just didn't like people talking about me behind my back.

"Did you talk while we were in Italy?" I asked, moistening my suddenly dry lips.

Her lips pressed into a thin line. So they did, and she knew something. Maybe everything.

As though sensing my annoyance, Sylvie opened her mouth to speak, and then closed it, only to open it a moment later. "Brooke, guys like him don't do relationships. I don't mind you dating him, but don't get too involved emotionally."

"You don't even know him," I hissed.

"Fair enough, I don't know him *that* well but—" She trailed off. As though she couldn't look at me, she buried her gaze in her cup, which gave me enough time to take in her demure dress reaching just below her knees, and the sweetheart neckline that barely revealed any skin. Maybe the fling with Ryan touched her more than I thought, and she couldn't share my enthusiasm because she had lost faith in all men. If I were lied to, sacked, and disappointed, maybe I'd also start thinking men don't do relationships. But I didn't experience her heartbreak, and Jett was nothing like Ryan.

I knew Sylvie meant me no harm; her emotional scars just hadn't healed yet. I wrapped my arm around her and rubbed her back gently. "Oh, sweetie. Thanks for being such a good friend."

As if my words broke the ice, a hesitant smile replaced the wary curve of her lips. "You're happy?"

I nodded. "Happier than I've been in a long time."

"Then I'm happy too."

Ignoring the sudden lump in my throat, I began to recall my trip to Bellagio, omitting the sex agreement and steamy bits, so I mostly focused on the landscape and beautiful Italian views, the mansion, and Jett.

"Shit, you're fawning," Sylvie said as I finally finished.

"Am not."

Was I?

"That's what falling in love does to one."

I had been thinking the same, but to hear the truth coming from her mouth, full of conviction, scared me. Falling in love wasn't meant to happen so fast...or so intensely.

"I'm not in love." My voice came out louder than intended. It was a lie. I could hear it, she could hear it. Heck, the whole world probably could.

A few heads turned in our direction. Sylvie waved them to turn away before she focused back on me. Her blue eyes sliced into me with an unnerving intensity, and she leaned closer so no one would hear her. "Listen, darling, I'm sure Jett is a nice guy and all, but he's also one of the richest men in New York. He might not want to hurt you, but others will. This is a whole different society. Even if you accompany him everywhere, wear and do what people expect of you, you won't be accepted into their circle because of your background."

She couldn't be serious. "What the heck are you talking about? You're making it sound like I'm getting involved with the Mafia."

"Worse," she mumbled.

"What?"

She raised her hands in defense. "Nothing. I just thought I'd warn you."

"About *what?*" The whole situation was so funny, I could barely contain my hysteria. Of course she knew everything about rich people and the high society. She had been born into it and spent eighteen years of her life trying to please her mother, before turning her back on it all. Apart from the regular check that came in the post and her fondness for expensive stuff, there were no reminders of her background. She never mentioned her past or family, and I didn't ask.

"Watch *The Real Housewives*, and multiply that by ten. And then you might get an idea," Sylvie said.

I didn't want to point out she was referencing a reality TV show, and they usually come scripted to their teeth. They don't film people doing normal stuff, like brushing their teeth and lounging around in their PJs because no one's interested in that stuff. "I'm so jet lagged I need to get some sleep." I stood and placed a soft peck on her cheek.

"What about the party?"

I shrugged. "Might be time to send them all home and call it a day." I loved my friends and appreciated the fact that they turned up to congratulate me on my job and making it back from Europe, alive. But let's face it, they were more interested in filling up their drinking cups than listening to my traveling stories. "But thanks for this. Did I ever tell you you're the best friend ever?"

Sylvie crossed her toned arms over her chest, still pouting, but for once she kept quiet. With an apologetic smile, I left for my room and locked the door behind me. I didn't even bother to change, just stripped off my clothes and snuggled into my cotton sheets, ready to catch up on all the sleep I missed out in the last two weeks. But, as tired as I was, Sylvie's words kept ringing inside my head. All I could think of was that I was in debt, with no savings left, and there were so many women richer than me, more beautiful, and more successful, who'd kill for a slice of Jett. If someone were to ask me what I could offer him on the long term, apart from my heart, the answer would be: I don't know.

***

The persistent tugging at my arm, followed by someone calling my name, jerked me out of my sleep. I blinked groggily against the glaring brightness and tried to pull the covers over my head.

"Brooke, wake up," Sylvie said, yanking my sheets off the bed.

Aware of my half-naked body, I sat up and pulled the sheets back over my breasts to cover my modesty. "What the hell do you want?" My eyes threw daggers at her sheepish expression.

"Sorry." She wasn't. "The guy I've been telling you

about is on the phone. He insisted that I wake you, so—"
She trailed off.

I checked my watch and groaned inwardly. I had slept for a mere three hours. "So you, being a good friend and all, risked giving a very tired me a heart attack because some sales shark told you so."

She shrugged and turned to leave, calling over her shoulder, "He has a nice accent. And he said you'd want to hear what he has to tell you."

Of course.

That certainly made sense.

Ignoring the urge to crawl back into my bed, I wrapped a bathrobe around my shivering body and walked into the hall to get this admittedly extremely pushy sales clerk out of my life.

"How can I help you?" My voice sounded a little hoarse from the lack of sleep, but you could still hear the frosty undertones.

"Miss Brooke Stewart? My name's Jake Clarkson from Clarkson & Miles. I've been trying to reach you for two weeks. Did you get my letter?"

Holy cow, he didn't beat around the bush. "I don't think I have," I said, slowly scanning the glossy magazines and newspapers stacked neatly next to the phone, when I remembered Sylvie had mentioned a mysterious envelope. I had asked her to leave it in my room so it wouldn't freak her out. "Actually, I haven't opened it yet since I only just arrived back home."

"No problem. We can discuss its contents. Would you be available to meet with me, preferably sooner rather than later?"

His questions struck me as odd. Why would he want to

meet with me, unless it was an emergency? "Did anything happen?"

He laughed briefly, and I knew it was fake. "No, of course not, Miss Stewart. Please understand that I'm not in the position to discuss such important business with you on the phone. I've come all the way from London, and I really need to talk with you in private."

Important business sounded grave enough without the serious undercurrent of his tone. And if a person came all the way from wherever he came from, I figured it was double serious business.

"What did you say your name was?" Regaining my wits, I grabbed a notepad and pen. As he repeated his details, I scribbled them down.

"Jake Clarkson. I'm an attorney with Clarkson & Miles. London headquarters."

An attorney. And he seemed even more no-nonsense than me. I didn't like lawyers. They had brought me nothing but bad news. My pulse sped up and my hands turned clammy. I wiped my palms on my bathrobe and cleared my throat to get rid of the sudden lump. The Britain part was pretty obvious from his accent.

What would someone like him want from me...unless I did something wrong and the offended tried to resolve the issue with the help of an attorney before the whole thing escalated into something ugly?

"Is everything okay?" I asked.

"Everything's fine. Are you available today?" he persisted. "Any time would work for me. Even evening. It wouldn't take long."

"Today? It's that urgent?" Given that the digital clock on our answering machine stated it was already ten past six, the guy sure seemed anxious to get a meeting. I briefly considered whether it was a bright idea to meet up at this time of day. It probably wasn't, so I decided against it.

"I could meet with you tomorrow after work. Maybe around six-ish?" I offered.

A pause, then, "Let's make it six."

I gave him the address of a café which was on my route home, about half an hour away. Good enough not to inconvenience me, but not close enough so he could follow me in case he had stalking tendencies.

"Thank you. Have a lovely evening." He hung up, leaving me no chance to ask him for his phone number in case I couldn't make it.

"Weird, huh?" Sylvie said from the doorway, not even hiding the fact she had been eavesdropping.

"Hm." I motioned her to follow me as I rushed into my room and found the envelope on my desk. With a quick flick of my wrist I tore it open, ignoring the look of dread on Sylvie's face. When nothing blew up, she inched closer to peer over my shoulder.

I pushed the white crisp paper into her hand. "It's just a formal letter inviting me to get in touch with them regarding *urgent matters*."

Skimming the contents of the letter, Sylvie nodded slowly and then placed it on my desk. "What do you think he wants?"

"No idea. I guess we'll find out soon enough." I couldn't quite hide the worry in my voice.

"Do you want me to accompany you?" She trailed off, leaving the 'in case' part hanging between us.

I shook my head. "Looks like he is who he says he is, so I'll be fine. It's probably not important. Maybe I won the lottery or something." In spite of my attempt at infusing humor to take off the heat, my voice didn't quite manage to hide my nervousness. Luckily, Sylvie always knew when to make me feel better.

She wrapped her arm around my shoulder and leaned in conspiratorially. "Tomorrow's your first day at the new office, huh?" I nodded, unsure where she was heading with this, and let her continue. "We never really got a chance to celebrate."

And that's when her intentions became clear. She wanted to party. Of course.

"Oh."

She nodded, and a huge smile lit up her big blue eyes. "Yeah."

I shook my head, laughing. "No, Sylvie. I can't. Not today."

"Just one drink. I'm not taking 'no' for an answer." She pursed her lips and scrunched up her face to give me a puppy look worthy of an Oscar. I knew her tricks. One drink never ever literally equaled one drink, but she was my friend, and I hadn't seen her in two weeks. Vowing to stick with soda and be back before nine, I grinned at her. "All right. But if you get drunk, I'm not helping you home."

"You won't have to. You know I'm not a lightweight. Unlike you. I should text Jett to join us, just in case you need a hot guy to tuck you into bed." She winked. "Like last time."

"You *texted* him?" My cheeks flamed up.

"Someone had to invite him to join our crew. After your hot night together, I thought I was doing you a favor," Sylvie said, sheepishly.

Oh, god.

"As my best friend, it's your duty to ask me before making such a huge decision." I pondered whether to be grateful, angry, or downright mortified. In the end, a mixture of all three won. "And you should have told me you got his number."

"Well, someone had to get it for you since you didn't have the guts to ask him about it. Thank me later."

I stared after her, open-mouthed, as she rushed out of my room sporting a self-satisfied smirk.

26

MANHATTAN WAS ABUZZ with life at any given time of the day, but this morning it seemed as though half of it had gathered in the elevators of Trump Tower, waiting to be beamed up into the corporate world. Waving my temporary security clearance card, I swooshed past security, and fought my way through the crowd of expensive haircuts, tailored suits, and high-fashion accessories. At eight *a.m.* sharp, I pushed through the heavy glass double-door to enter the Mayfield Realties lobby, holding my head high and my back straight, even though the throbbing pain in my temples was nearly strong enough to make me puke. Of course joining Sylvie in her quest to get hammered had been a mistake, and I shouldn't have trusted she'd stop after one drink, but as usual I had let her persuade me. And while I stayed true to my conviction to stay away from alcohol, the jet lag and subsequent lack of sleep had pretty much the same effect on me as an all-night bender. It had taken me an hour to shower, dress in one of my best suits, twist my hair up in a presentable knot, and apply makeup—enough to cover the dark circles around my eyes and the unnatural pallor of my skin, but not so much I would look like I was trying to woo the boss.

The brunette who had greeted me on my first visit was standing behind the reception desk, whispering into a sleek silver device I assumed was the newest and probably one of the most expensive phones on the market. Soft music intermingled with the sound of splashing raindrops echoed in the background, giving the impression I was entering my doctor's office. I swallowed hard and neared the brunette receptionist, not really expecting her to recognize me. To my delight, instant recognition sparked in her eyes, and she rewarded me with a pearl-white, warm smile.

"Miss Stewart—"

"Please call me Brooke," I said, figuring I could use a new friend at work.

Her smile widened. "Brooke. I'm Emma. Mr. Townsend hasn't arrived yet, but I'd be happy to show you to your office." Not waiting for my answer, she led the way down the corridor, and then turned the right corner at the huge plant I admired the last time. I followed a step behind her, through a broad corridor with see-through offices on both sides. The glass walls provided no privacy from prying eyes. It didn't bother me in the slightest. Since my desk at Sunrise Properties had been situated in the middle of a wide, open space within James's shouting range, I was used to having people around me at all times.

"Did you have a nice trip?" Resuming her small talk, Emma shot me a glance over her shoulder. My face caught fire as countless memories flooded through my mind. It had been a great trip, definitely one I'd never forget.

Grateful she couldn't see me, I nodded. "Yes, thank you. Italy's beautiful."

"That's true." Her brief chuckle and sudden bounce to her stride made me avert my attention from my surroundings to gawk at her. She was tall with slim legs, a well-defined waist, and glossy brunette hair that reached down her back. She was pretty, and I wondered whether she was Jett's type. The thought of Jett kissing her sparked an instant pang of jealousy.

"Have you been?" I asked, focusing hard to keep the bite out of my tone. Even if Jett took her with him to Italy, it was before we met. His past was none of my business, and I wouldn't concern myself with it, just like he wouldn't meddle in my affairs.

"Last summer."

I swallowed hard to get rid of the sudden choking sensation in my throat. I was over analyzing. A few friends of mine had been to Europe, so what? Her statement didn't have to mean anything.

"Lake Como was divine," Emma continued. "And even though it's just a lake and doesn't really have a proper beach, I liked the privacy of it."

Shit. She was there—at Jett's private place, which meant they most certainly spent the night in the same house rather than in a hotel. Bile rose in my throat, and the throb inside my head turned up a notch, as I imagined her in his bed.

"His place is heavenly, isn't it?" she gushed. "He showed me everything."

My stomach twisted into tiny knots as pangs of jealousy hit me with full force. Emma stopped in front of another glass office and turned to face me, unaware of the hurricane wracking havoc with my insides. Her smile was still in place, and a tiny glint played in her eyes as she continued down memory lane. "Did you get to visit the beach?"

"Once." I blushed again at the memory of Jett perched between my legs, lapping at my lady parts for the first time. He had such a gifted tongue, it couldn't possibly be an innate talent. He must have gained the experience from somewhere, which drew my attention back to Emma, and my initial fondness for her began to dissipate into thin air. Maybe being friends with her wasn't such a bright idea after all. I walked past her into the room, suddenly intimidated by her infectious smile and her perky ass.

"Is this my office?"

When she nodded, I tossed my handbag on the desk and slumped into my swivel chair. Booting up the desktop computer, I figured she'd get the hint and leave. Unfortunately, Emma seemed to have taken an instant liking to me and harbored no such plan. She popped into the leather guest chair opposite from me and crossed her sky-high legs, triggering another pang of jealousy. It wasn't her fault she was so gorgeous, and I sure couldn't blame Jett for being attracted to her. Heck, even I liked what I saw, when I had never been one to show bisexual tendencies.

Emma leaned forward and lowered her voice conspiratorially. "Between you and me, Mr. Mayfield has hinted he might be taking me again this summer."

My breath caught in my throat.

Over my dead body.

I smiled a saccharine smile so sweet I felt sick just imagining it. "Isn't he generous?"

"Yes." Sighing, she brushed her hair back. "The house belongs to his son though, and he's not so keen on Mr. Mayfield popping over." She trailed off, letting me fill in the blanks.

Son?

My eyes narrowed on her as my head put two and two together, and a flash of relief washed over me. She was talking about Jett's father.

"Isn't Robert Mayfield married?" I was vaguely aware of the idiotic grin on my face, but I couldn't help it. Jett wasn't a whore—his father was, which was perfectly acceptable as long as he hadn't passed that trait to Jett.

"He's been divorced for a few years. Told me he was heartbroken because his wife cheated on him, and this is the reason why he won't remarry so soon again," Emma said, probably believing every word that womanizer told her. She didn't even know he was the cheater and not his ex-wife.

I nodded, playing along, because having one Sylvie in my life was enough. I didn't need more friends who'd drag me to the local bar whenever yet another unfaithful guy broke up with them. But she was the only person I knew here and, most importantly, she wasn't sleeping with Jett, so I figured I wouldn't mind her tagging along. "Do you drink?"

"Not often."

An evening in Sylvie's company and that would change in a heartbeat.

"I'm meeting a few friends for after-dinner drinks on Friday night. You should come. You and my friend Sylvie will have lots in common."

Her smile beamed back into place. "Thanks. I'd love to."

We chatted for a few more minutes, during which Emma introduced me to my working schedule before she returned to the reception desk. At eight-thirty, the hall began to fill with people. Some walked past, ignoring me. Others peered in to introduce themselves, eyeing me up and down as though to determine whether I was fit for the job. These were the big players in real estate. While the prospect of meeting them had scared me two weeks ago, I found them no more intimidating than Sylvie's hair stylist, who kept pursing his lips in sheer horror every time he caught a glimpse of my unruly locks.

By nine *a.m.* the soothing background music was replaced with the shrill ringing of phones. I began to skim through Jett's meeting schedule for the day, officially starting my first day of work at Mayfield Realties as Jett's personal assistant, when a tall figure appeared at the periphery of my vision.

"Brooke, a word please."

My head snapped sharply in Jett's direction, and my heart jumped into my throat.

Holy cow.

He was steaming hot. With that disheveled bedhead, broad shoulders, strong chest, and moss-green gaze of his—he belonged on the front page of a fashion magazine. He was dressed in a black well-tailored business suit, white shirt, and a black silk tie. His trademark upper button was undone, allowing a glimpse of bronze, smooth skin. Skin I had licked and trailed with my fingertips all the way down his smooth torso to the narrow line of dark hair that—

"Brooke?" His tone was detached, but the flicker in his eyes betrayed his amusement.

He knew I found him attractive, and he made no secret of it. Damn him and his inflated ego. Somewhere in the back of my mind, it registered that I was still staring. But as much as I tried, I couldn't peel my eyes off him. The way his slacks rode low on his hips, emphasizing a bulge and strong quadriceps, reminded me I had rode on those thighs merely twelve hours ago. I could still taste his skin on my lips as we moved in perfect unison. Damn! Why couldn't I get the picture of him naked out of my head?

"You want me to come to your office?" Stupid question since he'd already said so.

He nodded slowly. "Only if you don't mind."

"Okay." I jumped to my feet and wiped my clammy hands on the front of my skirt nervously. Jett held the door open and motioned me to walk past, not moving an inch. I squeezed myself between his towering body and the hard doorframe, my ass brushing the front of his slacks, sending my dirty mind into a frenzy.

"This space is cramped. No wonder people can't wait to get the hell out of here for an early release," Jett whispered.

My gaze flew up to meet his. His poker face was still in place, but his eyes seemed to poke fun at me.

"I like cramped places," I muttered through gritted teeth, and headed down the corridor into what I hoped was the right direction.

"Shame," Jett whispered behind me.

Trying my hardest to ignore my acute awareness of him, I inhaled a sharp breath and held it as I slowly counted to five. It was my way to keep my calm in the face of a storm, only this storm was raging right inside my panties.

"Next door to your right," Jett said.

Even without his instructions, I would have been able to distinguish his office from his co-workers because it was the only one boasting blinds that were half-drawn.

Amazed by the design, I stepped into the large room and stopped to admire his workspace. His office resembled the one in his house in Bellagio, minus the mountain views, expensive art, and personal touch. A polished wood desk and swivel chair were set up in front of the window overlooking New York's skyscrapers. To my right was a huge sofa in chocolate brown leather and a glass table. To my left was a closed door that blended in seamlessly with the light gray wall. Two large palm trees and a minibar gave the impression of a laid-back attitude which, given Jett's reputation, couldn't be farther from the truth.

"You don't work here very often, do you?" I turned to face Jett and instantly regretted it. My statement sounded like he didn't work at all. The same thought probably crossed his mind, and his green eyes immediately darkened. An instant later, it was gone and his lips stretched into a hint of a smile.

"What gives me away?"

Swallowing past the sudden need in my throat, I pointed around me. "The barely used couch. The plants someone probably picked up at *Plantworks*. The fact that there's barely anything on your desk."

"Good observation skills, Ms. Stewart. I'm impressed."

His flattery shouldn't have had the effect it had on me, and yet I found myself grinning, pleased like punch that Jett Mayfield thought I had good observation skills. "You should see what other skills I have in store," I purred, not quite sure where I was heading with this.

His brow quirked up, and an amused glint appeared in his eyes. "I was planning to…right after discussing new developments in the Lucazzone case. Now that you're mentioning it, checking your skills is a priority indeed."

Ever so slowly, he closed the blinds and locked the door, sending my insides into a raging storm. A delicious shiver rocked my body. As our eyes connected, a heated ache began to throb between my legs.

Sweet mercy. He wouldn't do it here, would he?

With measured steps he inched closer, pushing me against the hard edge of his desk. I fought for breath, suddenly panting even though he hadn't even touched me yet.

"We're at work," was the lame excuse my mind came up with.

"So?"

My pulse spiked. I brushed my hair off my face, outraged. "People could hear us."

"I guess we'll have to be quiet." Jett's fingers trailed down my shirt to my skirt and he began to pull it up in slow motion, sending my imagination into overdrive. His hot lips moved to the soft patch of skin beneath my ear and he began to nibble gently. His deep moans resembled the soft moans suddenly escaping my mouth.

My breath hitched in my throat as his hands cupped my ass and lifted me onto the desk. His strong thighs wedged between my legs. As he started to kiss my shoulders, the bulge in his slacks began to rub deliciously against my sensitive lust bud.

"Jett," I whispered. My fingers clawed at his shoulders as I pondered whether to push him away or draw him closer so he could do all the unspeakable things his eager hands promised to do.

"You smell so good." His hand prodded my panties and in one swift motion, he pushed them aside before I could protest. I moaned when his talented fingers started to rub my clit gently until I felt my juices gathering between my legs. I wanted nothing but him and...his invasion. "So wet. I love it when you're like this, for me," he whispered in my ear. His deep voice quaked through me. His kiss sent another delicious pull in the deepest pits of my sex, taking my arousal to new heights. "I have a meeting in fifteen minutes. Think that's enough time to make you come?"

I loved it when he whispered.

"Seriously? You think it'd take you fifteen minutes?" I laughed briefly. If he kept talking in that sexy voice of his, he'd make me come in two.

"You're right. That's enough time to make you come twice." For a brief second he lingered over my clit, and then ever so slowly he pushed a finger into me.

Oh God.

He inserted another finger, increasing the speed as he thrust in and out of me, while his thumb circled my pleading clit, sending new sensations through my sensitive spot. No one had ever touched me with such a rugged intensity that made me want to scream for more. My sex clenched and burned from the almost painful pleasure. His finger moved faster and harder, pushing in and out until I thought I might just pass out from the unnatural torture.

"Please. I can't take it."

Throwing my head back, my mouth searched his in the hope of finding the mercy that comes with release. Jett's lips pulled back, unwilling to give me what I wanted. His heavy breathing matched mine as his eyes—two dark pools of devilish desire—bore into me, watching me like a hawk would watch a prey.

"Come for me, baby."

His hot breath burned my parted lips. The pressure on my clit intensified, making me gasp from the strong waves of lust that carried my body. A hiss escaped my mouth a moment before a mind-blowing orgasm sent me into a trembling frenzy. With the last wave, I slumped against his hard body.

"You're beautiful," he whispered. "I could watch you, and only you, for the rest of my life."

Was it the sex talking, or did he mean everything he said? I didn't ask because the moment was magical, and it just wasn't the right thing to say. But his words tugged at my heartstrings and overwhelmed me with a need to wrap my arms around him and keep him close forever.

Exhausted and content, I looked up into his gaze mirroring emotions I couldn't decipher. Warmth. Lust. Trust. Even before he unbuttoned his slacks, Jett's wicked grin declared he wasn't finished with me yet.

I wet my lips nervously as he pushed his slacks down his thighs. My hand moved down his flat torso and gripped the thick base of his manhood to return the favor, when his hand stopped me. In spite of the fact that I was depleted, my heart skipped a bit as his hard shaft throbbed against my opening, demanding to be let in.

"I don't think I'll be able to take more." My eyes begged him to understand my still clenched muscles couldn't possibly accommodate his generous size.

However, I would be more than willing to please him in a different way.

"You said that the last time. Yet, I still made you come," he whispered. A dimple appeared in his right cheek as he removed my panties, leaving me exposed to the air conditioning and his appreciative gaze. "Now, bend over."

He pushed me forward, bending me over his desk. His rough tone left me in both fear and anticipation, eager to find out what he'd do next. His shaft found its way deep inside of me and I winced from pleasure.

"Are you okay?" he asked, pulling out of me instantly and turning me around. "I won't hurt you. I never would." Deep in my heart I knew he meant every word of it.

"Don't stop. I want more," I said, grinding against his hard erection. My legs parted to invite him in. I wanted him and everything he could give. His body, for now, and maybe one day his heart.

"You were made for me, Brooke. I can't get enough of you." His voice was filled with rough, but his fingers were surprisingly gentle as he began to caress the nape of my neck. Once more, the slick tip parted my lips and then he was inside, filling me with inch after inch of pure gloriousness as the strong ridges heated up my core. His mouth stifled my delighted scream, his tongue imitating the thrusts of his hips. The intoxicating scent of our lovemaking hit my nostrils and blurred my vision as the telltale pull of another approaching orgasm gathered deep in my belly.

My nails raked the hard muscles of his chest, pleading with him to hurry his speed, to take me harder. As though he could sense the urgency building up inside me, Jett cupped my ass and lifted me off the desk, allowing him deeper access as he began to thrust with so much force I could feel him in the most secret recesses of my sex. A delicious jolt of pain shot through me, followed by a surge of hot pleasure, and a moan escaped my parted lips.

The room began to shift before me. My tongue flicked over my parched lips as my brain fought to stay focused. I couldn't be coming again, not when his fingers had just made me climax, and yet I knew I was close. So very close. And judging from the way his shaft twitched against my entrance so was he.

"You're perfect," Jett whispered.

Biting my lip, I whimpered and fought back my sharp cries of ecstasy. "Oh, god."

"This is where you belong, sweaty and panting in my arms." His green gaze misted and his plunges slowed down. I knew what was coming even before his hips undulated against mine, and he pulled out.

"Ready, baby?" His lips captured mine in a deep kiss. He brushed the engorged tip, now slick with our moisture, over my sensitive bud, before plunging back in, sending me off the edge into another mind-blowing climax. With my name on his lips, his shaft tore into me, prolonging the pleasure, as he released shot after shot of moisture deep inside of me.

Eventually, he pulled my shivering body into his arms and engaged my lips in a slow, lingering kiss.

Wow, best sex ever.

"You're so damn sexy, Brooke. I want to do this for the rest of my life."

There, he said it again. And this time *after* sex, meaning there had to be some truth to it. The earnestness in Jett's stunning eyes made me flush with pleasure. "I'd love that," I whispered, unable to contain my enthusiasm at the sheer prospect of having him in my bed forever and ever.

His damp skin felt hot under my fingertips and as my sense of reality returned, I wondered how the heck we could possibly hide the physical signs of our lovemaking from our coworkers.

With a sigh I peeled myself off his glorious body and pulled on my panties. I straightened my skirt as my gaze remained glued to his sturdy chest. He was stunning. In spite of the soreness between my legs, I knew I wouldn't be able to resist if he desired another round. "Oh god. You're probably late for your meeting."

He glanced at his watch with an amused glint in his eyes. "We're right on time."

"People will be able to tell."

"So?" His grin widened at my horrified expression.

"Are you kidding me?"

"Brooke." His long fingers clasped my chin and pushed up until I was forced to meet his electrifying gaze. "I don't intend to keep us a secret for much longer. But you're right. The boss shagging the personal assistant during working hours isn't going to boost work morale, so let's freshen up. Want a quick shower?" He winked toward the door I had spied earlier.

"You have your own bathroom?" Why wasn't I surprised?

"I'm the boss," he said sheepishly. "I can have whatever I want." His palm slapped my backside in case I failed to catch on to the not so subtle meaning of his words. Grinning, I rolled my eyes in mock annoyance.

"You wish."

His arms wrapped around my waist and pulled me against him, my back rubbing down the front of his slacks. "Such a shame we don't have time. I'd love to give this glorious ass of yours a good spanking." The dangerous undertones of his deep voice hit a note with me and I found my nipples straining against the silky fabric of my bra.

I groaned, irritated with myself.

Damn.

How the hell could he possibly have such an effect on me? It wasn't natural.

"You know who could really use a spanking? Your inflated ego."

"You didn't just say that, Brooke. I warned you, baby. I might need to cancel that meeting after all."

Laughing, I dodged his grip and shot for the bathroom, praying the sexy warning in his voice was nothing but a joke. Knowing Jett Mayfield's ego and his fondness of keeping a to-do list, he wouldn't forget. Secretly, I hoped I'd soon get what he thought I deserved.

Say tonight.

I was screwed.

Literally.

And the sad thing about it was that I couldn't wait. For him. For what he had to offer. For the way he made me feel. I loved every minute we spent together.

27

I SPENT MY first official day at Mayfield Realties following Jett in and out of meetings, redirecting countless phone calls, and spurning at least twice that many, while familiarizing myself with Jett's important accounts. Everyone's eyes had been on the boss's new personal assistant, so naturally he kept his hands off me. By the end of the day, I had barely had time to look at the newest developments in the Lucazzone case. I wanted to tackle the case because the sooner I was finished, the more I could prove that I deserved this position, and that Jett had made the right decision by hiring me.

Although I loved spending time with him, I was thankful when Jett announced he'd be caught in an early business dinner, and would have to leave now to make it on time across town in the late afternoon traffic.

After kissing me goodbye, he promised to text as soon as dinner was finished. I grabbed another cup of coffee, spent a few minutes chatting with Emma, and then returned to my office and the file waiting on my desk. I took a sip of my coffee, ready to get engrossed in my first multi-million dollar project, when a red stamp caught my attention. I almost spit out my coffee as I read the two words in capital letters: UNDER OFFER.

The old man had finally decided to sell. My gaze fell on the price.

Forty million.

Holy shit.

Twenty million more than planned.

Luxury estates weren't my specialty field, but even I could see the estate wasn't worth it. The company would make a loss so big it could swallow up Alaska. Why would Jett take such a risk? I took a deep breath to steady the nervous flutter in my stomach.

It might not be my job to advise him on how to conduct business, but I sure wouldn't shut up and let him make such a brainless move. The contracts weren't signed yet, so we could still get out of it. Ignoring the incoming call, I picked up my cell and speed-dialed Jett's number. He picked up on the first ring.

"Hey, pretty. What's up?"

Taking a deep breath, I mentally prepared my words. He was a successful business mogul who'd take crap from no one. After pondering for two seconds, I decided being direct and to the point was the best way to go. "I just had a look at the Lucazzone file and while I see the estate's potential, I feel it's my duty to tell you that the price is too high."

Silence, then, "Brooke, the decision has been made. Leave it at that." His tone was sharp, leaving no room for discussion.

"But—" I brushed my hair off my face. This was the real Jett Mayfield. The one that did as he pleased. But hadn't he said he hired me for my attitude? And did he not tell me he believed in me and in my talents? Wasn't that the reason why he entrusted me with the case in the first place? "It's too much, Jett. You'll be in the red. Trust me on this one."

He let out an annoyed sigh. "We need to get this deal, no matter what."

"But...you're risking losing millions and I don't understand why. The place is not worth that much money."

"You don't need to. I'm giving the all clear and it's happening. That's my final word. Anything else I can do for you, Brooke?" He was brushing me off like an annoying fly. My temper flared, and I threw my hands up in exasperation. Jett Mayfield was stubborn, I got that, but unless he had a pretty good motive for moving forward with the acquisition, his obstinacy was unfounded, and I was hell bent on making him aware of it.

"I was a realtor before you hired me. And a pretty good one, you said so yourself." I paused, waiting for his reaction—any reaction—but it didn't come. So I continued. "The airport is only an hour away, meaning there's bound to be some noise. The view is stunning but it's just *one* lake. You'd have to divide the waterfront land into ten, which doesn't leave much space for spreading out your beach towel, let alone go water skiing and sailing, and what else rich people do. It's a mistake. It's far too—"

He cut me off. "Brooke." He wasn't listening. How the hell could I make him pay attention? I began to type furiously on my computer, opening accounts to quote examples of asking prices so I could finally drive my point home. I wasn't willing to give up. Not in this matter. I wasn't going to lose the company forty million and risk sending them into a large black hole.

"I'm paying out of my pocket," Jett said so low, I wasn't sure I heard him right.

My hand froze over my keyboard as my brain fought to grasp the meaning of his words. He had that much money in his back account? And he could part with it just like that, in the blink of an eye? I knew he was rich, but I never realized to what extent.

I shook my head in disbelief at how easily he could throw money out the window. It was his money, and he had a right to do with it as he pleased, but still. There was no guarantee he'd make a profit. There wasn't even a fifty-fifty chance he'd earn his investment back. He was more likely to make a loss than if he tried his hand at gambling.

"But why?" I tried to control my voice as I tried to rack my brain for the best reason. "You're acquiring a potential murderer's estate."

"My father wants it. Thinks he can make a fortune in Europe. I have no choice."

"Does he know you're spending this much money?" I don't know what made me ask that question. Probably my desperate subconscious clinging to any possible argument that could change his mind. The longer we talked this over, the more he might be inclined to change his decision. Regardless of whether our relationship lasted, I cared about him enough to try to stop him from making stupid mistakes. And buying this place was a mistake, whether he wanted to acknowledge it, or not.

"Does he know, Jett?" I asked again.

He still continued to hesitate, and in that instant I had

my answer.

"Oh. My. God," I said, burying my head in my hands. "You haven't told him."

"My father wants this estate and I'm getting it for him. Apart from you and my lawyers, no one knows how much I'm paying and I'd like to keep the actual price undisclosed," Jett said. "Look, I wish I could explain but can we do this another time? I'll take you to dinner tomorrow and then we can talk some more."

"But—"

He cut me off again. "No, Brooke. I'm in a meeting and the clients are waiting. I'll call you later."

"Okay," I whispered, but the line was already dead. I closed the file and locked it away in my cabinet, my mind circling around the grave edge in Jett's tone.

The strain in his voice didn't go unnoticed. Maybe he was stressed, or maybe worried. Either way, he was being stubborn about the whole situation. For the first time I wondered whether there was more to that estate that Jett didn't tell me.

***

I arrived at the café with ten minutes to spare and parked near the entrance where I could both keep an eye on my car and make a fast exit if need be. It didn't surprise me that the place was empty. Most people were either still at work or stuck in rush hour traffic. Signaling the barista to take my order in a few minutes, I slumped into my usual spot at a four-seat table and fished out my cell to place it on the table so I wouldn't miss an important call or text message.

Heart Strings Café opened in my first year of college. I discovered it when Sylvie tried to hook me up with a blind date and the guy invited me to meet him here. The place hadn't changed one bit: it was small but flamboyant, carrying the colored furniture and checkerboard tile floor trademark of the retro sixties. I loved this place, not just the food but the whole Night Fever atmosphere, and tried to come here often. Taking in the vintage records on the vintage harvest gold colored wall, I realized this might not be the right place to meet a lawyer from London.

Too late for that.

I spent the next few minutes in edgy silence, alternating between watching my car through the window, and watching the door. At six sharp, a tall guy carrying a briefcase walked in and stopped in the doorway to scan the café. Given the fact that there was no one in here but me and an elderly couple, my chances of being overlooked were pretty slim, and yet for some reason I found myself standing and waving him over.

Jake Clarkson was a tall man in his forties with sandy hair, a strong jaw, and sharp, gray-blue eyes. His tailored suit fit him to perfection as he stretched out a manicured hand to greet me.

"Miss Stewart. It's lovely to meet you."

"Brooke," I offered, returning his confident smile, and pointed at the seat opposite from mine. "Please."

"Thank you. Please call me Jake." He lowered himself into the plush chair and undid the first button of his suit jacket, as though he wanted to infuse a sense of ease into this meeting but not too much. My gaze followed him as he pulled a few sheets out of his leather briefcase and placed them neatly in front of him, resting an expensive-looking pen on top of them.

"Good," he said by means of starting the actual conversation.

The air was charged with foreboding, which I attributed to the fact that lawyers scared the crap out of me. I knew my fear was unfounded, and yet I couldn't help the slight tremble of my hands.

The waiter appeared, and we ordered—a tall latte for me, espresso for Jake—and then we waited in silence until our beverages were served. I watched him take a sip of his coffee, indifferent to the heat that would have burned my tongue. My people knowledge was pretty basic, but it was good enough to help me draw the conclusion that Jake Clarkson was a tough guy, and not just when it came to sipping hot beverages.

"My firm has been trying to get in touch with you for two weeks, Brooke." The thin skin beneath his eyes crinkled, but I didn't quite feel his amusement.

"I was away on business. Europe."

"Ah." He nodded sympathetically, as though he knew exactly what I was talking about.

"I gather you had a nice trip?"

"I did, thank you." My cheeks flamed up at the sudden memory of lazy days in Jett's arms. You said you flew over from London?"

He nodded. "Yesterday morning. Your roommate told me when you'd be back, and I decided it might be the best way to share the news." His gray-blue gaze flickered to life as he pulled out a sheet of paper. My curiosity killing me already, I peered over the rim of my cup.

"Did I win the lottery? Because if I did, I can tell you it must be a mistake. I don't do lotteries." I laughed to mask the nervousness in my voice.

"No, Brooke." He pushed the sheet of paper toward me so I could read it. "It's a testament."

"A what?" I frowned, grabbing the paper. My eyes almost jumped out of their sockets as I read the title, and all of a sudden, my vision blurred and I almost fainted. It couldn't be. But there in front of me, it said: The last will and testament of Alessandro Lucazzone.

28

LAST WILL AND TESTAMENT
OF
ALESSANDRO LUCAZZONE

I, Alessandro Lucazzone, of Bellagio, being of sound and disposing mind, do hereby make, publish and declare the following to be my last Will and Testament, revoking all previous wills and codicils made by me. This Will may at any time be revoked by me at my sole discretion.

ARTICLE 1
IDENTIFICATION OF FAMILY

I declare that I was married to Maria Agrusa, to which I have referred herein as my 'spouse'. We had no children, living or deceased.

All of the properties of my estate (the "residue"), after payment of any taxes or other expenses of my estate as provided below, including the property subject to a power of appointment hereby shall be distributed to BROOKE MARY STEWART.

I sucked in a sharp breath at seeing my name. My mind was spinning. Somewhere in the back of my mind, I knew I was in shock because I couldn't think clearly. My brain was numb.

"Do you understand what this is, Brooke?" Jake asked, forcing me to look up.

"Yes, it's Mr. Lucazzone's last will. But…why are you showing it to me? I don't know him personally." My voice sounded choked as I fought to grasp the meaning of what looked like the photocopy of an original will written in legal English. In theory, I had read about the old man's life in Jett's files. But the whole situation was too huge to grasp. I was supposed to handle the case, not meet with a lawyer and talk about the next of kin. If there was proof of alien life on another planet, I would have been a lot less surprised.

I shook my head. A will, my name, and Alessandro's— three things, and all on one paper? That was impossible. Insane.

"This must come as a bit of a shock but," Jake tapped the end of his pen on the paper, right where Alessandro had signed his name, "you are the heir."

"It can't be." I shook my head in denial. "It must be a mistake."

The will declared Maria Lucazzone's relatives as the beneficiary, even though according to Jett's file there was none.

"Initially Mr. Lucazzone decided to pass the estate on to various charities," Jake said. "However, a few weeks ago it came to his attention that his deceased spouse had relatives in the United States. It took us a while to ascertain your father's identity, but since he's no longer with us and he has no siblings, you're the next of kin. In a gesture of goodwill, Mr. Lucazzone changed the testament in your favor upon one condition." He paused for effect and smiled. I stared at him, open-mouthed, still not getting his drift. "My client is a very ill man, who could pass away any minute. He wants to meet his heir before he dies."

I knew the answer, but I still had to ask. "How can I possibly help you?"

He pushed an envelope across the table, toward me. "Brooke, we've wasted enough time searching for your father, and when we discovered he had passed away, it took us a while to get hold of you. We'd like you to come with us straight away, so you can meet with your great-great-uncle and sign the necessary paperwork. I took the liberty to purchase two tickets for you, in case you want to bring a person of your trust along."

I peered inside the envelope at two first class flight tickets, and all blood drained from my face. He wasn't joking. I shook my head, forcing huge gulps of air in and out of my lungs.

"I'm—" My speech eluded me. I felt stupid thinking that I was the heir to an estate, let alone utter the words that burned a hole in my head.

An estate worth millions—millions Jett offered Alessandro Lucazzone.

A thought entered my mind that maybe it was all a con. Maybe Jett tricked Alessandro into thinking I was the heir, when I wasn't. The old man might not want to sell his property for the original, more than generous offer, but the heir was more than likely to. And Jett always told me he trusted me. Maybe he'd go this far to get the estate. It was a possibility I couldn't discard. Countless questions and theories flashed through my head, but there was little time to think them all through.

"Are you interested?" Jake asked.

Hell yeah, I was. Who wouldn't be?

"Yes," I said slowly.

"Very well. I'm glad to have made your acquaintance." Jake smiled and reached out his hand to shake mine, then pushed yet more sheets across the table. I caught a glimpse of financial reports, plot measurements, and contracts. "Congratulations, Brooke. You're the future heir of the Lucazzone Estate. Clarkson & Miles couldn't be more delighted to represent your interests and, I hope, build a thriving and long-lasting relationship for the future."

29

HALF AN HOUR later, I maneuvered my old Volvo through the slow traffic. I was still hyperventilating from the shock. The more I thought about it, the more everything felt surreal. Almost like a dream. Maybe it was nothing but an error, a case of mistaken identity, a scam. Maybe Clarkson had the wrong Brooke Stewart, because inheriting a large European estate sure didn't sound like something that would happen to me. To my surprise, the first person I wanted to share my news with was Jett. I tried to reach him on my cell, and when he didn't pick up I left a voicemail to call me as soon as he got my message. The second person in line was Sylvie.

My head was giddy with excitement as I parked my car across the street and dashed through the lobby of our apartment complex, then up the stairs because the elevator was busy. When I entered—half-breathing, half-choking—Sylvie didn't even look up from her comfortable seat on the couch. My heart was beating so fast, I figured it was only a matter of time until it burst. But Sylvie noticed none of it. Only when I bent over, trying to catch my breath, did she look up surprised.

"Hey. Did you run a marathon?" She sounded rough and looked the part, dressed in sweatpants and a washed out, oversized tee. Under normal circumstances I would have paid attention, but her face looked okay and her hair was its glossy self, so I figured it was nothing but post binge drinking depression or something. Whatever was going on, it couldn't possibly beat my news.

"Guess what." I kicked my high heels off and slumped onto the couch, minding her outstretched legs. She pushed them onto my lap and leaned back against the pillows with a bored sigh.

"You got sacked."

"No." Frowning, I shook my head. "Why would I be happy about that?"

Sylvie shrugged and let out another bored sigh. I made a mental note to help her find a job so she finally had some meaning in her life.

"I met with that lawyer today." Of course that barely managed to spark a glint of recollection, as though it hadn't been the subject of our obsessive compulsive speculation the night before. I stared at her, realizing even though she was sitting inches away from me, she wasn't here mentally.

"Yeah?" She sounded about as interested as a five-year-old listening to a long and drawn out PhD thesis.

"Want me to switch on the TV instead?" I tickled her feet in mock annoyance, knowing she hated it.

She pulled her legs up to her chest and sat up. Her blue eyes glowered at me. "Sorry. I'm so tired and bored. This day's been dragging on forever." She had reached the unemployment slump. I nodded sympathetically. "I need something to do. Like—"

"Find a job?" I suggested. She returned my smile and I continued, "Or you could come with me to Italy. I know this magical place with mountains and lakes and the most amazing Tiramisu you've ever tasted."

She eyed me carefully, not quite sharing my enthusiasm. "Another business trip?"

"Nope. I'm the sole heir of the Lucazzone estate."

Her jaw dropped. She opened her mouth, and then closed it again, and a frown creased her forehead. I could almost read her thoughts in her fast changing expressions, as she tried to make sense of my statement. Eventually, she said, "The Luzzone what? You don't mean that place across the lake?"

Of course she was stunned. And in disbelief. I had been too, but speaking out the unspeakable helped me wrap my mind around the sheer incredulity of it.

"It's Lucazzone," I corrected her. "The attorney kept calling to arrange a meeting and discuss the will's content. The old man, Alessandro Lucazzone, wants to meet me. Jake's secretary's booked two flight tickets for tomorrow night." I jumped up and grabbed Sylvie in a hug. "We're going to Bellagio. How about that?"

Her expression didn't quite catch on to my enthusiasm. "Are you sure you're not being scammed? You know, like getting an email telling you you've won or inherited a million, and then you're supposed to enter your bank details."

I shook my head, ignoring the urge to groan. "It's a legitimate law firm. Jake never asked for my bank details. And may I remind you he knew my name, address and so forth prior to contacting me?"

From the glint in her eyes, I could she was having a hard time believing it. To be honest, so was I.

"You're right," Sylvie said. "But just to be on the safe side, let's ask Doctor Google."

She booted up her laptop, and I entered Clarkson & Miles in the search engine. After less than a second, a picture of Jake popped up along with his company's details. A few minutes later, I found some mention of the Lucazzone Estate and that Clarkson & Miles had been the appointed law firm for the last five years. Everything looked legitimate.

"That's him and that's the estate," I pointed at the screen and inched forward to regard the tiny picture of Alessandro Lucazzone and his deceased wife. Even though it was blurred, and probably old, I could make out a few details about her, like her stubborn jaw and the way her brows arched in a slight V shape, just like my father's.

Maybe I was beginning to see similarities where there were none. Or maybe half of my family descended from Italy and no one ever bothered to tell me.

Sylvie leaned over me and sucked in a sharp breath. "Jesus, Brooke. You're rich!"

***

"Didn't Jett take you to that place?" Sylvie asked.

"Bellagio?"

She nodded. Motioning her to wait, I poured two cups of café latte, grabbed the cookie box, and returned to the sofa, where Sylvie sat cross-legged, eagerly awaiting my full account. I placed the cups on the couch table and passed her a cookie dipped in milk chocolate—my absolute favorite.

"There better be lots of hiking opportunities, because I'll need lots of it after this." She held up a cookie before biting off half, and moaned with ecstasy. I laughed because it was our inside joke. Sylvie could eat like a horse and wouldn't gain a pound.

"So, did he take you to the same place?" Sylvie asked. The cold undertone in her voice surprised me and I remembered what she said about him moving in a different society.

"Well, sort of. We stayed on the other side of the lake."

"But it's still the same place, isn't it?" she insisted.

Where the hell was she going with it? I scanned her face for any clues. Her expression was impassive, all except for the strange glint in her eyes. I swallowed the half-chewed cookie inside my mouth, suddenly oblivious to the buttery taste of the dough dipped in the creamiest chocolate twenty dollars could buy. She took my lack of response as an affirmative.

"Yes," I said. As though I was confirming her suspicions, she nodded. "Why are you asking?"

"That's quite the coincidence."

"I've no idea what you're talking about."

She brushed her long hair back and moistened her lips as her blue gaze bore into me. "I know you're still under the influence of his big dick and the dreamy stuff it did to you, but you need to switch on your brain. And pronto." She raised her hand to stop the angry protest on my lips. "I'm not suggesting anything. But you've got to admit it's a big world and he took you to the one place you'd inherit. Do you *really* think that's a coincidence?"

A cold shudder ran down my spine. She didn't even know half of it. How could I possibly tell her the rest and not feel completely stupid? "Actually, it's the same estate he's been trying to buy." And the same estate I, as the heir, probably would have given to him, just to see him happy—had he just asked. But he didn't. Which led me to my next concern. Did he use me? Was I naïve to believe what we had was real?

We stared at each other for a few moments. The magnitude of our words hung heavy in the air.

"Maybe it's a coincidence," Sylvie said, breaking the silence. "Maybe he didn't even know there were relatives."

According to Jett's file, the company had watched Alessandro Lucazzone for ten years. Was it really possible the private detective never found out about a possible heir? Possible. And then he hired me? Unlikely. Coincidence?

"I don't know. This is fucked up."

"When was the will signed?" Sylvie asked.

I grabbed the copy of the will Jake left me and scanned it once more until I found the date.

Shit.

"About six weeks ago." Jett and I hadn't met yet. The way I saw it, it must have taken Jake at least four weeks to prepare the necessary paperwork, double check my identity and heritage, and then contact me. Only I wasn't around to receive the news because Jett had whisked me off to Italy. But why hire me to acquire the estate in the knowledge I was the heir? Unless he wanted me to fall for him in the hope I'd do anything to please him.

"I think he tried to set me up," I said slowly as the realization dawned on me. A pang of pain shot through my chest, threatening to kill me. I snorted and shook my head.

Coincidence, my butt. You're not usually hired on the spot without even applying for the job, get jetted off to a luxurious mansion, enter a relationship with the hot boss, and inherit an estate worth millions, which happens to be the one estate your boss can't seem able to buy.

"He tried to set me up," I repeated. "I can't believe I didn't see it before."

"Why would you say that?" There was no surprise on Sylvie's face, no sign of disagreement, just caginess, as though she knew it was the truth but needed me to acknowledge it first so I wouldn't blame her.

Don't shoot the messenger.

I smiled bitterly. How very true. "Jett gets whatever he wants. He simply makes it happen. His tactic is to sweet-talk the owners with expensive trips and meals, and then get them to sign." I wondered if he slept with all his female targets, or just me.

"Maybe it wasn't his intention. It could still be coincidence."

"Don't bullshit me, Sylvie." My voice raised a notch. "He made me believe he cared for me, and I fell for it. I fell for his whole love, attraction, sex stuff."

"Are you going to let him explain?" Sylvie asked.

I shook my head, wiping away the tears gathering in the corner of my eyes. What would be the point? Now that I had the entire picture, I *knew* I was nothing but a pawn in his game, and I had stupidly fallen for it. The guy was like poison. Getting near him was the last thing I wanted. I had fallen for the wrong person, even opened my heart to him. The realization of my stupidity hurt me more than anything.

Sylvie hugged me as more tears streamed down my face. "Are you going to expose him for the rat he is?"

Smiling bitterly, I shook my head. "And how would I do that? No, I'll do something else. I'll break up with him in a way he'll never forget."

Jett might have broken my trust in him, and probably in all other men in this world, but he didn't yet get what he wanted, which was Alessandro's estate. He might usually win, but not this time. Alessandro Lucazzone wouldn't sell; I'd make sure of that.

"Just be careful," Sylvie said, hugging me tight. "Guys like him always get far, but not without gathering a few skeletons in their closets."

"Thank you." I placed a soft kiss on Sylvie's cheek.

"For what?"

"For being honest. If you didn't tell me, if you didn't make me aware of it, who knows whether I would have seen through his lies." I shook my head as I remembered how much I had wanted this man. I winced at the pang of pain rocking my chest, right where my heart was. It shouldn't have hit me so hard, but it did. Maybe because he was the first person I trusted after what happened to Jenna. Maybe because I thought if we shared our life stories, the good and the ugly, we might indeed be kindred spirits. Maybe because I thought he knew me and liked me for who I was, rather than for who I pretended to be.

I needed to get away from here. Leave him and the pain behind. Forget everything that happened.

Forget him.

I jumped up from the couch, pulling Sylvie with me. "Come on. We need to pack."

30

NOW THAT IT was over, I wished I had seen all the things I didn't see: Jett's enthusiasm to be with me, to listen to my life stories, and deal with my commitment phobia. He had been trying to get me to fall in love with him, which I had foolishly let happen when I should have listened to my gut feeling instead. After years of putting up defenses I let my guard down, trusting the one guy who'd go on to conquer me with beautiful words and attention, only to betray me.

He always acted so composed, so perfect. Was it because he never really cared about me? Irrespective of how I tried to see it, what excuses I gave him, he had broken my heart in a million pieces. And to think of all the times I trusted him. All the hours I prayed we'd last forever. How I thought he might be 'the one'. The way glass shatters—so did my trust.

How stupid of me. Why did I always end up loving the person who hurt me the most? Why was love so cruel?

I wanted to banish and forget the moments we spent together, I needed to erase him from my mind and heart. But the harder I tried, the more I thought about him. His image had been engraved into my mind, invading every fiber of my being like poison. I couldn't tell Sylvie how much his actions had hurt me, so I kept my head high in the hope she wouldn't guess how broken I felt inside. I smiled at my best friend, telling her that I'd find a way to hurt him; that the world didn't end with him...but the truth was, I wasn't okay.

I couldn't see him without feeling the magnitude of his betrayal.

I couldn't speak to him without thinking of the way he kissed me. And how little it meant now.

Our past together was nothing more than a bottle tossed out into the ocean, its message never reaching the owner.

Although Sylvie had put things into perspective, I had recognized the kind of man he was the moment I met him. I should have trusted my instincts rather than listen to his sweet words. It had all been too good to be true. I should have known the moment he lavished me with attention, the way he cooked for me, and swept me off my feet. I should have known deep in my heart it wasn't real.

He was nothing but a lie.

A terrible, hurtful lie.

But the heart is foolish, and I had been a fool to let it lead the way. It had made me blind, leaving me with no option to get out before I got too involved. Surrendering to love was a mistake, just like letting Jenna visit Danny, even though I knew it wasn't right.

"Brooke? Are you okay?" Sylvie's hushed voice carried through the quiet room a moment before she peered through the door, hesitating. "Can I come in?"

I barely managed a choked "Yeah".

"Oh, sweetie," Sylvie said, grabbing me in a tight hug. "I'm so sorry."

I melted into her motherly embrace, my face turned away from her, hiding the tears I had thought depleted.

***

Nearly twelve hours later, I stepped into the elevator riding up to the Mayfield Properties head office, knowing it'd be a brief visit. I had risen at four *a.m.*, unable to sleep, and spring-cleaned the apartment to keep my mind from venturing onto dangerous terrain. By six I had finished and drove through the pre-rush hour traffic to reach the office as early as possible. My back pressed against the smooth metal wall, I forced conditioned air into my lungs to calm my racing heart. Less than three weeks into the job, and I was already searching the classified ads for another position. But this time it wasn't the prospect of unemployment that sent hot and cold shivers down my spine.

I tilted my chin up to inspect myself in the narrow mirror strip on the left side of the elevator. My navy skirt and the white ruffle top that emphasized my narrow waist looked presentable enough, and certainly didn't reflect the way I felt inside. Soft ringlets of dark hair cascaded down my shoulders. My lips were painted a sheer red tint, and my cheeks were dusted with just a hint of bronzing powder to highlight my new tan, courtesy of the lovely Italian weather. Come to think of it, I had paid way more attention to my outfit and hair than I should have. I didn't want to be pretty for him. I *wanted* him to look at me and acknowledge what he couldn't have anymore, what he was losing out on. That was how I want him to remember me...composed and poised, as though his actions never hurt me.

Deep down I knew I had to get him out of my system as fast as I could, but the thing with love is, you cannot choose who you fall for. Falling in love often happens at the wrong time, in the wrong place, with the wrong person. Just as much as you cannot stop growing feelings for a certain man, there's no switch to turn off your heart. And even though my mind knew better, it was powerless against the weak, sappy fool I called my heart. To me, love was a drug. Jett was my drug. It kept me addicted to him, making my thoughts circle back to him and him alone. The best way to escape was to get away, which was the plan, right after breaking up with Jett.

The elevator doors opened, spitting me out into the chic reception area. Emma was nowhere in sight, and I used the opportunity to dash for my office. Not that I didn't like Emma, but in my twisted logic she belonged to Jett's world, and if I was to push him out of my life for good, I had to ensure I was getting rid of all accessories in the process. If I could erase all traces and memories of ever being here, then I would. As much as I liked this building and some of the people working here, I didn't like that everything belonged to *him*. Forgetting the past involved leaving everything behind—everything I'd ever associate with him.

I squeezed all my belongings into my oversized bag and searched the drawers for the rest of my stuff. It wasn't much, just a bunch of pens and notepads, a diary and address book, a digital voice recorder for taking notes on the go, and the cactus I brought over from Sunrise Properties. It wasn't much, and from all the belongings I probably would have only missed my plant, but I didn't want to forget anything.

At ten past seven the hallway was quiet, with only a handful of people sipping their morning coffee in the company's own kitchen cum bar area. I used the opportunity to leave my office and sneak behind their backs into Jett's office with no one noticing, and closed the door behind me. Luckily, Jett didn't lock the door. I closed the drapes, and then moved over to his desk. I knew he hadn't arrived yet because he never started work before eight, and I would have seen him pass by my office. I figured doing what I was about to do would scare me.

It didn't.

My heartbeat remained surprisingly calm as I sat down in his chair and began to open one drawer after another, skimming through his files. People say the truth can set you free. I hoped that by finding evidence in a written form I could finally force my heart to let go of its foolish hopes. By knowing the truth, I could maybe free myself from Jett's magic and expose him for the bastard he was. A few minutes later I found three files, all marked as Lucazzone's estate. My heart hammered in my chest, as I picked up the largest one.

I sat down in his chair and opened it with trembling as ice cold dread settled in the pit of my stomach. The first page provided a summary of everything he needed to know about the estate, from its value to its size, to the current owner.

My name was right at the bottom, marked as the heir. A small sob escaped my throat. There was my answer and all the proof I needed. I had no more excuses left for him.

Instead of immediate relief, more pain shot through me because I knew some part of me had still hoped, prayed, wished that I was wrong, even though I had known all along I wasn't.

Unshed tears pricked the corners of my eyes as I closed the file and returned it to its drawer, and then I resumed my seat in his chair, mentally preparing my words. I knew I couldn't possibly mean anything to him; it was just a ploy to get what he wanted. His feelings for me weren't his weakest point, but his ego was. I wanted to hurt him as much as he had hurt me.

31

EYES CLOSED, MY forehead pressed against the cold glass window to cool my feverish skin, I didn't know how much time passed or how long I just sat there, lost in the dark void of my emotions. When reason finally pushed through, urging me to leave this place, I re-arranged the files in his cabinet and grabbed my bag to leave. The door clicked open and Jett entered. As usual, he looked divine dressed in one of his business suits with his hair all messed up, his green eyes twinkling at my sight, leaving me weak and exposed. A sharp pang of pain cut off my air supply, and I turned my gaze onto the soft rug beneath my feet so he wouldn't see the damage he had inflicted upon me. I didn't want him to see all the uproar he had caused. He didn't deserve the knowledge.

"Brooke?" His voice came gently, as he inched closer. "Are you okay?" He wrapped his arms around me and tried to pull me to his chest. I took a step back, putting some distance between us.

"Don't touch me." I tried to keep my voice as nonchalant as possible "And it's over."

He didn't say anything. Several moments passed by and I looked up to see his reaction. Our eyes connected, and for one minute I could feel the spark. It was still there. Along with my feelings—my stupid, cursed feelings. But much stronger was the pain that I cared so much about him while he couldn't give a crap about me.

"You found out," he whispered, his beautiful eyes slicing into me, begging me to understand a truth that was a lie. "I can explain."

"You're not even denying it?" I raised my voice as anger consumed me. The dam was breaking. I couldn't hold it inside any longer. "You're an asshole, a liar. You're worse than the lowest scumbag. I trusted you, while you were planning to use me. I don't need your fucking explanations, not now and not forever."

"Brooke, please calm down. I wasn't planning to use you. Just listen to me." He grabbed my arm to pull me to him. I pushed him away and took a step toward the door, as tears gathered in my eyes, clouding my vision.

"Don't touch me."

"Brooke, please listen." He inched closer but didn't attempt to touch me, probably knowing I'd run out the door the moment he so much as laid a finger on me.

"You've destroyed everything I thought we had. You've broken my trust. There's no way I'll ever listen to any more of your lies. And there I was thinking you cared about me, when it was all about money."

"I care about you, Brooke. It wasn't a lie. I didn't mean to hurt you. You have to believe me."

"I can't, I don't trust you. You lied about everything," I

spat, unable to contain my voice.

He shook his head and for the first time I could see pain reflected in his features. A stubborn glint appeared in his eyes. "Not everything."

"No, you're right. You didn't lie about everything. You just chose to keep the truth to yourself. That's not better than lying. It's worse."

"Okay, I admit I didn't tell you everything. But I had a very good reason. I didn't tell you that I'm in love with you, and I didn't tell you the whole story, but I was afraid, for you, for us. You don't understand."

For a moment, the fact he said he was in love with me almost made my heart flutter with renewed hope, until I realized it was a lie. He was trying to wriggle his way out of the situation. I had made myself too available, let him sense my growing feelings for him, and he used that as an advantage. He wasn't going to manipulate me again.

"How can you say you love me when you lied to me?" I moistened my lips to gather my thoughts. "How can you say you care for me when you only care about yourself and money?"

"Because it's the truth," he whispered. I searched his gaze and found no traces of lying, but then again wasn't he a master of persuasion? We had even joked about it.

"Let me explain, please? Just not here. It's too dangerous." His gaze implored me to come with him. He reached out his hand, waiting for me to grab it.

"No. We're not going anywhere." I turned my back on him, unable to look at him, unable to take the pain his sight caused me. I couldn't bear him telling another lie.

"Tell me the truth. Just say yes or no," I said in a tone that could have frozen over a desert. "Did you plan to meet me because of the estate?"

"It wasn't like that."

"No," I cut him short. "Just say yes or no."

"Yes." A defeated sigh escaped his throat.

Swallowing down the choking knot inside my throat, I reached the door in two long strides, but he was faster. His arm pushed past me to block the door.

"Brooke, please...stop. We need to talk. You have to trust me," he whispered.

"No." My voice, my whole being, trembled. I drew a shaky breath to steady myself for what I was about to say. "I'm sorry, I can't do this anymore. There's nothing more to be said, nothing that would ever make me trust you again. You did what you had to do. But it's time to let me go because you'll never get the estate. I'll make sure of it. And if you ever cared about me, even if only for a bit, then you'll let me go."

Tension emanated from him in strong waves. His gaze brushed my cheek and lips, sending my heart into a deep plunge. Before I could move away, he inched so close his hot breath caressed my skin, making me tingle all over.

"I care enough for you to let you go," Jett whispered. "But I'll never stop protecting you."

I pushed him aside, opened the door, and walked out, ignoring the curious glances in the hall. He didn't follow me. With each step I took putting distance between us, the pain in my chest increased, but I had no choice. This one time, I had to listen to my mind and ignore the feeble attempts of my heart telling me to at least listen to him, to give him a chance to explain because, maybe, just maybe, he meant what he said.

But I didn't want to know, so I forced myself to keep on

walking.

Leaving the building, stepping outside, I took a deep breath of the exhaust fume infused New York air.

Morning's rays of light warmed my skin, and people hurried past me. New York was abuzz with life. Even though my pain overwhelmed me, I was still alive, and that was what really mattered.

I took another steadying breath and let it out slowly, thinking I'd be okay...in time. My heart would heal. Maybe someday, I'd find someone who'd prove he really loved me. Someone who'd hold me rather than let me fall. Someone who'd never lie to me.

But that someone wasn't Jett.

Even though moving on was hard, I knew I'd do it eventually, so I could look back one day in the knowledge that I had learned from my mistakes.

JETT'S PERSPECTIVE

Fuck! Fuck! Fuck!

Why did I have to tell Brooke I love her? It was the wrong time and wrong place. She didn't believe me and I couldn't blame her. Why would she believe when she has no reason to?

Even to me my words sounded like I was trying to win over her heart, to make her forget what happened, to force peace into the turmoil my actions caused. But standing in front of me, telling me it's over, with her beautiful face a mask of pain and tears shimmering in her eyes, something inside me broke, and the words slipped out of my mouth. In that moment I realized how important she is to me. That what we had is the kind of relationship I want to keep. When she entered my life, I wasn't ready for the array of feelings she'd arouse in me. It just happened: I fell in love with her and it's fucking stupid, because it happened too fast, and she doesn't feel the same way for me. Seeing her vulnerable and upset—with all that pain mirrored in her face—was more than I could bear. Her pain hurt me a thousand times more than I ever imagined. And even though I wish she'd return my feelings—or calls—I have to keep in mind that it's not about me. It's about her.

The truth is: I declared my love because she was shaken, and I didn't want to lose her trust. I knew the tension between us would harm our relationship and I wanted to redeem myself. I hoped for forgiveness for the things I didn't tell her...for her own safety. Because that's what I've been trying to do—protect her at all costs. I wish I could turn back the time and explain the situation right then and there, but we were at work and I feared someone might overhear us. I should have told her in Italy, when I had the chance. But would she have listened to my theories of conspiracy and evil? She's a realist and only believes the things she sees.

It's the third day and I cannot reach her. Her phone continues to remain switched off and her friend won't answer. The apartment has remained bathed in darkness. Have they moved out? Gone to visit relatives? Has something happened already? Am I too late?

My private detective is investigating her whereabouts and my driver's on standby, ready to take me to the nearest airport. I have to protect Brooke from people she doesn't know. She has no idea what she's getting herself into by taking over that estate. She has no idea what that estate represents to some people and how dangerous they are. So it's true: I love her and I am a fuck up. I fucked up big time and now I don't know what to do. I can't blame her for thinking I'm a jerk. I'd think the same if the roles were reversed. But at least I'm a jerk who'll give up his life and existence so she can live hers. She might not love me yet, but maybe one day she will—once she understands it was never my intention to hurt or use her.

Jett Mayfield

Jett and Brooke's story continues in the powerfully sensual sequel in the Surrender Your Love series,

Conquer

your

LOVE

COMING SOON!

A THANK YOU LETTER

Surrender Your Love was an emotional journey for me. Writing it represented a challenging time for me and my children, but I needed to share this story with the world. It took me several months to complete my first romance novel, and now that it's finished, I can say with good conscience, I poured my heart and soul into it. It was my greatest wish to entertain you, and I truly hope I have achieved that.

I want to thank each and every reader out there for giving this book a chance.

I want to thank those who have given a shout out on Facebook, on Twitter and on their blogs, and who have supported me by spreading the word to friends and family.

I want to thank those who have taken the time to leave a review, no matter how short. Reviews are hard to come.

Particularly indie authors, who don't have the means and support of a big publishing house, struggle. To every reader and blogger out there: thank you for your time and effort. I appreciate it.

There are so many more things I'm grateful for: the wonderful bloggers who took a chance on a new contemporary romance author, my beta readers' encouraging words and enthusiasm at hearing what's next in store for Jett and Brooke, my amazing editors and cover artist who went above and beyond the call of duty, and lastly my kids accepting that mommy's busy writing a book at night.

To everyone who's supported me: I will never forget you. Without you, this work would not exist. If I could hug you all and send flowers to everyone, I would. You have been amazing. You have been wonderful.

And I thank God every day for meeting amazing people like you.

Thank you.

Jessica C. Reed

Connect with me online:
http://www.jcreedauthor.blogspot.com

Made in the USA
Lexington, KY
18 March 2014

Meeting Jett was like lightning. Dangerous. Better left untouched. And better forgotten. But lightning always strikes twice.

Brooke Stewart, a realtor in New York, doesn't do relationships. When she's sent to a remote estate to finalize a real estate deal, she discovers her new boss is no other than the guy she left naked in bed.

Sexy, dangerously handsome, and arrogant Jett Mayfield attracts trouble, and women, like a lightning rod.
But the night he meets Brooke he gets more than he bargained for. The green-eyed millionaire playboy isn't used to taking no for an answer, and he isn't about to start now.

When he proposes two months of no strings sex, Brooke is intrigued and accepts his proposal. Little does she know Jett's determined to claim the one woman he can't have, pulling her deeper into his dangerous world.

A man who doesn't take 'no' for an answer.
A woman afraid to surrender to love.
Two lives that are about to cross...and secrets laid bare.

ISBN 9781482747638

9000

9 781482 747638